LAST CHANCE CHRISTMAS

A LAST CHANCE FIRE AND RESCUE ANTHOLOGY

LISA PHILLIPS   **MICHELLE SASS ALECKSON**

LAURA CONAWAY

Last Chance Christmas
Last Chance Fire and Rescue Anthology
Published by Sunrise Media Group LLC
Copyright © 2025 Sunrise Media Group LLC
Ebook ISBN: 978-1-966463-24-5
Paperback ISBN: 978-1-966463-22-1

This book is a work of fiction. Names, characters, places, and incidents are either products of the author's imagination or used fictitiously. Any similarity to actual people, organizations, and/or events is purely coincidental.

Scriptures taken from the Holy Bible, New International Version®, NIV®. Copyright © 1973, 1978, 1984, 2011 by Biblica, Inc.™ Used by permission of Zondervan. All rights reserved worldwide. www.zondervan.com The "NIV" and "New International Version" are trademarks registered in the United States Patent and Trademark Office by Biblica, Inc.™

Scripture quotations are from The ESV® Bible (The Holy Bible, English Standard Version®), © 2001 by Crossway, a publishing ministry of Good News Publishers. Used by permission. All rights reserved.

For more information about Lisa Phillips, Michelle Sass Aleckson, or Laura Conaway please access the authors' websites at the following addresses: authorlisaphillips.com, lauraconawayauthor.com and michellealeckson.com.

Published in the United States of America.
Cover Design: Sunrise Media Group LLC

PRAISE FOR LAST CHANCE CHRISTMAS

Last Chance Christmas is a high-stakes, high-octane holiday anthology that will pull you in right from the beginning. Lisa Phillips' story is first and sets the scene for all three stories, and I love the way that this plot arcs over the entire book. If you like holiday stories that are heavy on the action but will put you in the Christmas spirit, grab a copy now.

AMY, GOODREADS

I loved and devoured *Last Chance Christmas* as quickly as I could. If you are a fan of Chicago Fire and PD, you'll enjoy this fast-paced, edge-of-your-seat anthology as the Last Chance County police and fire and rescue work together with four convicts on the loose at Christmas time.

ALLYSON, GOODREADS

RESCUED JUSTICE

LISA PHILLIPS

She's built walls to protect her heart. He's the one man who might tear them down...

Officer Olivia Tazwell became a cop for one reason—to protect others the way no one ever protected her. She's perfected the art of keeping people at arm's length, especially devastatingly handsome firefighter Izan Collins, who's been trying to ask her out for months.

Izan Collins knows what it's like to be unwanted. Abandoned as a baby with ties to a violent cartel family, he was saved by the Collins clan—and now he saves others. When Olivia finally agrees to one date, he dares to believe his Christmas wish might actually come true.

Then four deadly convicts escape prison, and their fragile new beginning explodes into chaos.

Among the escapees is Alonzo Sosa—a ruthless cartel killer with a personal vendetta against Izan. As the manhunt intensifies and bodies pile up, Olivia faces an impossible choice: maintain her safe distance or risk everything to keep the man she's falling for alive.

When Sosa takes Izan's family hostage at a church event, both their worlds shatter.

Olivia must tear down every wall she's built around her heart and trust a man with the power to destroy her. But Izan faces an even more devastating choice—walk away from the woman he loves to keep her safe from his dangerous past, or fight for their future knowing his cartel connections could cost everyone he cares about their lives.

Will one night of courage overcome a lifetime of fear—for both of them?

ONE

Officer Olivia Tazwell gripped the steering wheel and swung the squad car around a turn onto Rutland Boulevard. She'd broken her wrist a couple of months back, but it had healed since. The memories? Not so faded.

Her partner, Officer Junior Ramble, sat in the seat beside her. "Are we in a hurry for some reason?"

"Just keeping my skills sharp." Truth was, she was restless in a way that she hadn't been since college. That had caused her all kinds of trouble, getting in with the wrong crowd. Hooking up with the wrong kind of guy. Getting her heart broken and the downward spiral that followed.

She didn't want to go back to that dark place.

Not just because she was a cop now and had been for four years. She lived on the right side of the law rather than skirting the dividing line and hoping she didn't get caught. Thankfully she never had been. Otherwise a career as a cop would have been out of the question.

The last thing she wanted now was to get fired and have the

people of Last Chance County think she had never deserved their respect.

"How's your mama?"

Olivia blew out a breath, rolling her eyes. The usual reaction anytime he brought up her mom. "Ornery as usual. Complaining that the night manager hates her. She wants to get switched back to the day shift so she can get back on a cash register."

"We should swing by. Say hi." He checked his watch.

"Too early for lunch break."

"It's after midnight."

"Exactly. We should wait at least another hour, or you'll start complaining at four, and you'll be miserable until we get off at seven."

Junior liked to grumble under his breath.

Mostly she ignored it since he was a solid partner and he'd never tried to hit on her. They were more like brother and sister and had settled into a friendship that had developed over the last few years working together. Since they'd both graduated from the same academy class.

He'd been born and raised in Last Chance County. She'd grown up in Benson, Washington, and the minute she'd been able to leave, she'd gone. Olivia had persuaded her mom to come with her, and they'd left that town in the rearview—with Olivia eighteen and driving because her mom had been wasted at the time. These days she had periods of being sober and on the right track, then rocky weeks where she needed some help.

The fact both of them loved Christmas in a way that bordered on obsession was about the only thing they agreed on.

Their radios came to life at the same time, the sound by her left shoulder, where the unit was clipped to her uniform shirt.

"All units, robbery in progress. Bridgewater Café."

"Finally." Junior grabbed his radio. "This is unit twelve, responding."

Olivia flipped on their lights and hit the gas. "Finally?"

"Not that hanging out with you, driving around doing nothing but shooting the breeze isn't fun and all…"

"You're a man of action?" Olivia chuckled. She took the next corner at speed, fast enough Junior grabbed the handle at the top of the door, which made her grin.

He muttered, and she thought she heard the name "Meg" in the middle of it.

Olivia turned another corner, passed a truck that had pulled over to the side of the street, and hit the gas again. "How are things going with Meg?"

"They aren't." Junior shifted in his seat.

"What?"

"I'm working on something else."

"Since when?"

Junior shrugged. "Saw a woman at church. Introduced myself. I'm making progress." Sounded like he was talking through gritted teeth. "Meg is history."

But he still cared about her, and if she was in the café, she might be in danger.

They'd learned the hard way not to process what might be happening at a scene before they even arrived. Right now they had no idea who might be in the café and what the situation was. There was never any point speculating about whether someone was hurt.

Olivia saw his knee start to jog up and down and drove faster, pulling up outside the café. Junior was out of the car, the gun in his hand down at a low angle, before she'd even rounded the hood with her own weapon drawn.

He went in the front door of the café first. "Doesn't look like the lock is busted. Maybe someone left it open."

"Her security system should have called it in, but this seems more like someone reported an intruder." She frowned. "Let's clear the place quick, then call in and find out." After all, someone could be hurt.

Inside the café was dark, but she knew the layout. Junior and Olivia both clicked on the flashlights that attached to the barrels of their guns. Junior worked his way through the tables, calling out as he went. "Police department! Is anyone here?"

Olivia listened and heard a rustle followed by a crash in the back. "Police department!"

Junior picked up his pace and went first down the hall. He looked through the circular window before he pushed open the swinging door into the kitchen. And then stopped to laugh.

A low, throaty chuckle.

"What? What is it?"

"A trash panda." He holstered his weapon and bent forward to laugh some more.

Olivia slid her gun into its holster but had to pause. "A what?"

The back door to the café was open.

"A raccoon."

"A trash panda?" She shook her head.

"You've never heard that?"

Olivia went to the back door and looked around outside. She saw a car pull up, a little blue compact. Meg climbed out of it. Probably also alerted by her security company that there had been a break-in. Olivia waved so Meg would know everything was all right. "I'll get dispatch to send animal control."

Junior sized up the animal, currently over by a set of wire rack shelves, reaching for dry goods just above its head. "I can take it."

She grabbed his shoulders and steered him to the back door. "You speak with the owner. I'll take care of your trash panda."

He made a noise in his throat but didn't get the chance to say anything before Meg stepped in the back door from outside. "Meg, hey. Everything's okay in here."

"Junior." Meg cleared her throat. "Good to see you."

Olivia heard him start explaining what it was and stepped into the kitchen. The raccoon had a package of cookies open and was enjoying his treat. She grabbed her radio and called in the need for animal control.

"Understood, unit twelve. Hang tight and I'll get you an ETA."

"Thanks. Twelve out." She stepped out of the kitchen, back into the hall.

Meg let out an adorable sound, like a giggle but more mature. It had a light quality to it.

When Olivia laughed it sounded like a choking snort, so she tried not to laugh aloud if she could help it. Most times she settled for a grin. But when was there all that much to laugh about?

It wasn't like her life had been fun and games, with her mom working all hours to take care of her and trying to manage being a somewhat-functional alcoholic at the same time. The community in Benson had treated them like white trash, and the churches her mom sent her to—so she could get free childcare—hadn't exactly been welcoming. The other kids hadn't played with her. Not even when their moms weren't around.

Olivia found a chair and wedged the kitchen door shut so the raccoon couldn't escape. Animal control needed to remove the thing and release it somewhere it could thrive. With Junior and Meg still making awkward small talk, she went to the front window and looked out.

From here she could see a few streets over, where the roof of Eastside Firehouse stretched above the new gas station roof. Her own kind of addiction, proving she wasn't so different from her mother. She had things she wanted that weren't good for her.

Olivia's life was about keeping things tight. Maintaining control at all times so that no one could look at her or treat her like people had when she was growing up. The less people knew about who she was and where she'd come from, the better.

Her radio crackled. "Unit twelve, this is dispatch. Animal control will be to your location in ten minutes. Advise the owner to clear out and secure the structure."

Olivia wanted to ask why but wasn't going to interrupt.

The dispatcher continued, "Reports of shots fired and a traffic collision on highway, mile marker six."

And they were closest.

She spun around. "Junior!"

"I heard it."

Olivia grabbed her radio. "Unit twelve responding."

"Confirmed, twelve. Dispatch out."

She heard him giving Meg instructions, and then he appeared in the main café room. "She's going to wait in her car."

"Good." Olivia caught the door and held it open for Junior. She made sure it was shut, and they raced to the squad car.

Junior got to the driver's side first and climbed in.

They peeled out, lights and sirens going. Olivia said, "Shots fired and a traffic collision?" That would mean more than just them responding. Probably the fire department, though it would be up to Olivia and Junior to contain the situation.

Not that she knew if Izan was even on duty tonight.

She might not see him at all.

But there was a big difference between what Olivia Tazwell wanted and what she usually got.

TWO

Izan Collins stepped back and admired his handiwork. "It's perfect."

The three-foot-tall Christmas tree stood in the corner of the men's bunk room, between the end of Izan's bunkbed—he had the lower bed, Zack took the upper—and the wall. In addition, he'd strung up Christmas lights around the room, tacking them on the wall with about a hundred pieces of tape.

Decorating the firehouse didn't happen all in one day, and he liked to draw the season out as long as he could. Wring out every ounce of Christmas cheer. Bask in the music, the fun, all the parties and extra events. Go to the church services and kids' concerts.

All of it.

If it was about Christmas, Izan wanted to be there.

Eddie Rice, his fellow firefighter, leaned over his shoulder. "It looks like Christmas threw up on your tree."

"I know." Izan grinned at his friend. "Isn't it great?"

Eddie slapped him on the back, laughing. "Sure, bro. Whatever you say."

From his bunk, where he'd been reading a parenting book,

Zack Stephens said, "It's like you forget every year how he acts around Christmas."

"I don't want any Grinches," Izan told them. "Got it?"

"I'll leave a sternly worded note for B shift *not* to mess with it."

Izan winced. Eddie had the right idea, but…"Doesn't that usually make them mess with it more?"

"Hmm. Good point."

Zack said, "We can tell them it's Amelia's tree. They'll never mess with it then."

"Or the chief's wife and kids put it up. Spent hours decorating it," Izan suggested. Not that he wanted to be a liar, but desperate Christmas times called for desperate Christmas measures. "I'll figure it out. Coffee?"

Eddie frowned. "It's nearly one in the morning."

"Any time is coffee time." Especially with the life they lived. No one wanted to be dragging or slow on the uptake in the wee hours when someone's life was on the line.

Izan trailed through the hallway to the day room, which was a long rectangular room with a kitchen area at the far end, a dining table to the left, and the living area to the right. Zoe was curled up in the recliner, reading a book, while Della watched the local news report from earlier in the evening.

"…storms rolling in. You can expect heavy rain the next few days and dropping temperatures, bringing the possibility of snow in the forecast. So take care out there on those roads. More in the next segment. Back to you, Wilma."

Izan headed for the coffeepot to fill his and Eddie's cups. "Anyone else want coffee?"

"Yes!"

Izan glanced back and saw Della's attention on him from over the top of the couch. He lifted his chin. "Had enough tea?"

She smiled. "Never. But coffee is fine once in a while. I took my grandma to the doctor, so I had to get up early." She stretched her arms above her head.

"Everything okay?"

Della rolled her eyes, smiling. "She wouldn't let me go in with her. Said it was *old lady things* and apparently none of my business."

He brought her a full mug of creamy coffee with sugar. "Here. This is strong enough to put hair on your chest."

"And that's something I want?" She took a sip and sighed. "Good stuff."

He chuckled. "As good as Christmas."

"You're like the Christmas evangelist."

"You know you love it."

Della just snorted.

He'd worked with Zoe, Della, and their lieutenant, Amelia, long enough to know the three women pretty well. Zoe had two boys, her husband was deployed, and her mom looked after the kids while she was on shift. Della lived with her grandma and read books a lot.

Izan knew Della well enough to have run up against the things she didn't want to tell anyone, the dark parts of something that'd happened to her. She wore a bracelet sometimes, when she wasn't on shift, with the name *Lily* on it. Amelia, their lieutenant, was in a category all her own. A force of nature.

Izan could've easily fallen for Della or Amelia, but the moment he'd seen a certain police officer, he'd been a goner. It was better that way, because he could keep things at work professional and friendly. It had never gotten weird between him and any of the female firefighters due to attraction.

Too bad they'd noticed his crush on Olivia just enough to give him a hard time whenever that certain police officer came around. Junior Ramble, who happened to be *her* partner, was one of Izan's best friends. They frequently commiserated about their pathetic attempts to get the women they liked to even notice them.

He pulled out his phone to text Junior about going to the shooting range in a couple of days, but the dispatch intercom sounded through the firehouse. First an alarm, then the call, "Truck 14, Ambulance 21, vehicle collision. Multiple victims."

Della set her drink on the coffee table and left it. Zoe turned down the corner of the page she'd been reading. They followed Izan out the door.

The alarm overhead sounded again. "Rescue 5, person trapped."

Everyone converged in the engine bay. Amelia met Izan on their side of the truck. "Guess Rescue has their own job."

Izan shrugged on his turnout coat. "Good thing we don't need them."

Amelia grinned and climbed in. Della had the engine on already. Zoe settled into the back beside Izan, and they pulled out.

"Where's this vehicle collision?" Izan leaned back and braced his boot against the back of the seat in front.

Amelia tapped keys on the dash laptop, one of those indestructible things you could drop off a building. "Mile marker six on the highway."

"Shouldn't take us too long to get there," Della said.

Izan wanted to move up to the driver spot one day, but it hadn't happened yet. He also wanted to be a lieutenant at some point. However, that would probably involve moving crews. Not something he would be okay with. This group of firefighters and the EMTs they worked with had become a family over the last few years.

Considering his history, he needed family who were good people. Not the kind who'd brought him into their savage world of drugs and guns and murder, but who made sure a child was raised by kind parents like the Collins family, who'd adopted him. In the same way, this crew of firefighters had invited him to be part of their family.

Knowing his life would always be intertwined with the Crawfords made him feel like this firehouse where Bryce worked—where Andi and Logan had both worked at one time—was where he belonged.

Della stopped so hard he nearly slid off the seat. Izan snapped his attention back on the scene in front of him just as Della loudly exclaimed a series of nonsensical words.

"Exactly," Zoe said.

"I've never seen…" Amelia shoved her door open. "Let's go."

Izan jumped out onto the asphalt. Two cars had collided up ahead, and between the fire truck and that was a minivan that had plowed into them and was now lying on its side.

A cop car had pulled over behind the wreck, but he didn't see the officers.

One of the cars was on fire, the flames licking out from under the hood. He spotted the sheen of something spilled across the road. Most likely gasoline or another fluid from the car, which meant there was a risk that it would catch and send the whole thing up in flames.

They ran to the closest car, and he pulled the door open. No one in the back. One passenger on the driver's side that Della reached in to help.

Trace and Kianna, their EMTs, pushed over a gurney.

Izan turned to Amelia. "We need—"

"Help, and more ambulances."

He nodded.

"Get these people out, Collins."

He ran to the next car, searching inside. The kid in the back was crying, probably four years old. About the same age as his cousin's kid. "Hey," Izan crooned. "You're having a rough day." He did a cursory assessment.

Mom in the front seat turned to him, gasping aloud at the pain. "Is he okay?"

"Car seat did its job, didn't it, buddy?"

The kid hiccupped and quieted down.

"Mom's gonna be fine, and you're A-okay. All right, kiddo?" He turned to her. "Can you move?"

"It's just my elbow. I smacked it when we hit that corrections van."

"Say what?" Izan shook his head and said, "Actually, I'll come around and you can get out. Tell me all about it then." He scooped out the kid and carried him gently around to where the mom turned to put her feet on the ground. "Don't get up if it hurts, okay? Move *slowly*." He dragged the word out.

She nodded. "I can walk."

That would help them, considering there were others here with more serious injuries.

"What's your name?"

"Kathy, and that's Elliot."

"Hi, Elliot." He shifted the child against him. "I'm Izan." He held out one hand and helped Kathy stand, holding her steady while they walked toward the EMTs.

The cars on the opposite side had slowed to watch the chaos. Firefighters and EMTs all helping people get out. Treating the injured. This stretch of highway was surrounded by townhouses and apartments on both sides.

"What did you say about corrections?"

Amelia watched them approach.

Kathy said, "The van that flipped on its side at the front. It says *Department of Corrections* on the side. A bunch of guys in orange and a woman in black uniform jumped out and ran off the road, over the concrete divider. The two cops that showed up chased after them."

Amelia's eyes widened. "We have a prison break?"

THREE

Olivia pumped her arms and legs, regulating her breathing. Pushing her normal workout run pace almost to her limit. If these criminals insisted on running more than six miles, she was going to have a problem. Junior, on the other hand, seemed to be just fine. Of course. Her partner chased the bad guys up ahead, running like he could go forever. Like he wasn't even sweating.

She rolled her eyes and grabbed for her radio, calling in their location in the neighborhood—a complex of townhomes—requesting backup to their location.

Units were on the way, but she needed them here *now* if they wanted any chance of ending this without anyone getting hurt.

The four convicts and one corrections officer had fled the scene of the crash almost as soon as she and Junior had shown up.

Tires squealed.

She raced around the corner of the next street, and between two rows of garages that faced each other, a pickup truck raced away from them with at least two people inside. A prisoner and the guard? She wasn't close enough to see. Two more men in orange jumpsuits continued to race down the street.

"Stop! Police!"

One of them, a gray-haired man, hesitated, turning slightly. As if he wanted to be caught. Did that make any sense? These were hardened criminals, by the look of them, but she really didn't know if they were serving long or short sentences. They could've been sent to prison for any number of things.

Olivia lifted her gun slightly, holding it with both of her hands. "Stop, or I shoot!"

She wasn't about to shoot anyone in the back, even if they were a convicted criminal. Especially not when they were unarmed. She just needed them to believe she might.

Junior closed in on the other man, who had focused back on his attempt to flee.

At the end of the street, a patrol car pulled in with lights flashing. Their K-9 unit. She relaxed a fraction.

The man Junior was chasing made a hard left and ran between two garages. A nondescript man except for the jumpsuit. Dark hair. Pale.

Her older guy did the same but took a right. She followed him down someone's back walk. He stopped at the door to the house and kicked hard, beside the handle, but it didn't open.

She closed in. "Hands up! Stay where you are!"

He turned to her.

Recognition flashed through her. She'd been part of the operation that had brought this guy in over a year ago. "Damien Wallace."

His eyes narrowed. "You want me, come and get me."

"That's not how this works, Wallace. Turn around and put your hands on your head. We do this my way."

He started to chuckle and took a step toward her.

"Sir!" Cole, their K-9 officer, was here. "If you do not comply, if you resist in any way, I will release my K-9, and you will be subdued."

Wallace's attention flicked over Olivia's shoulder, and he didn't like what he saw.

Olivia couldn't see behind her, but Cole was no doubt there, holding the collar of his K-9 German shepherd, Titan. She took a slight step to the right, just so she didn't get in the way of their tag-team training.

She'd had a bad experience with a big dog a long time ago. As a rule, she didn't hate dogs, but she would never be comfortable around them.

"Turn around. Hands on your head." Olivia didn't allow for any argument in her tone.

Behind her, shots rang out across the street. *Junior.*

Cole said, "You want me to get this?"

She backed up until she was level with Cole, keeping her attention—and her weapon—focused on Wallace.

"Go." He knew she wanted to get to her partner.

"Copy." She turned and ran, reassured at leaving Cole to bring in Wallace. He had the man pinned with nowhere to go— and he had his partner with him.

She needed to go help hers.

Olivia raced between the two rows of garages, the backs of the townhouses facing each other. Most were three-story and thin, stacked side by side. Painted with fall tones in different sections so that they were interesting.

One door was open.

She listened first, then entered. "Ramble!"

A distant "In here!" was the only reply.

She raced through the house, which had minimal furniture all in the style of that Swedish store. Light pinewood and low, clean lines.

Toward the front door, in the entryway, Junior sat up against the wall. "He got my gun."

Olivia hissed. "Looks like he shot you with it."

"Shoulder." He gritted his teeth. "Help me up. We need to go after him."

"Did he take a hostage?"

Junior shook his head. "House was empty."

"Can you ID him?"

"Never seen him before."

But he could confirm the man's identity when they got the prisoner transport list. "Did he say anything?"

"I had him cornered. I closed in and he tackled me. Got the gun." Junior hissed out another breath. "But before he did…he said, 'Not looking a gift horse in the mouth.'"

"I've never understood that expression."

Olivia's teachers had told her that she, uh, wasn't the smartest person. Which didn't help her desire to study hard if she was only going to fail anyway, but she'd managed to pass at least. "What is he going to do?"

"Get revenge. He was babbling about 'little mouses'—that's what he said—and all the ways to kill them and how fun it's going to be. Who knows? That guy wasn't right in the head."

"That your diagnosis, Doctor Ramble. Clinically insane?"

"My shoulder hurts."

She got hers under his good arm. "Up we go." Olivia lifted him to his feet, and they walked out the back door together. Across the road, Cole led a cuffed Wallace out from between two garages, his K-9 walking beside them.

She stiffened. Couldn't the dog be on a leash?

"Careful, he'll realize you're afraid." Junior seemed to think it was at least a little amusing.

"Ambulance?" Cole called over. "I called in for another car so he can be taken to holding at the station."

Cole's K-9 vehicle held him and another cop, and the dog in the back. It wasn't designed to hold prisoners or suspects, as it had no back seat.

"I don't need an ambulance."

Olivia said, "Yes, you do. You were shot."

"I'll bet it missed anything vital."

"Doesn't matter. You faced down a criminal and got hurt. That makes you a hero."

Junior said, "Heroes don't let their duty weapon get stolen."

Cole's expression shifted. He knew how bad that was—and not just that it meant a lot of paperwork. They needed to find the criminal who'd run off and get Junior's gun back, or he would feel responsible for any crime committed using it. Whether he was guilty or not.

Cole said, "Come on," and led Wallace to his car.

Olivia got on her radio and requested an ambulance for an injured officer. The dispatcher told her that all ambulances were occupied on other calls and asked for more details.

Junior grunted. "I can make it to the car."

She looked at him out of the corner of her eye, but he was too close for her to really focus on his face. "Sure?"

"Nothing wrong with my legs."

Another patrol car pulled onto the street. Officer Anthony Thomas got out. "You guys see a Hispanic guy, kind of pale?"

"Orange jumpsuit?" Cole walked Wallace over to load him in the back of Anthony's car.

Anthony shot him a look. "That's the one. I spotted him a couple of streets away. Wasn't sure if he'd come this way."

"That's not the guy who shot me. He was white."

"I lost him. I think it was Alonzo Sosa." A tendon in Anthony's square jaw flexed. "I circled a couple of times, but he got away." His eyes flared. "I should've triple-checked the streets around here and found him."

Olivia said, "He could be hiding in a hundred places around this complex. It would take hours to go from room to room and search all of them."

"He got away."

She said nothing because there was a lot of responsibility to go around, and it wouldn't lessen Anthony's feelings to tell him not to have them. "I'm taking Junior back to our car so he can get checked out."

Anthony nodded. "I'll get Wallace to the station and touch base with the lieutenant."

"Keep us updated."

Cole came back over. "Titan and I are going hunting."

"Catch something good." Olivia steered Junior toward the end of the street so they could head to the car. He really didn't need her help to walk, but she wasn't interested in letting him go right now. When they were out of earshot of anyone else, she said, "I'm glad you're okay."

Junior could've been killed.

That guy probably thought he *had* killed her partner.

"Guess you feel like…maybe you should get me an awesome Christmas present right now. Since I might've died."

Olivia would've shoved him away if he wasn't injured. "Who says I didn't *already* get you an awesome Christmas present?"

"Sweet." He moved his arm and groaned. "Ouch."

"Come on, hero."

She knew as soon as he was patched up, he'd want to get back to work.

They had escaped criminals to find.

FOUR

Izan watched the Life Flight helicopter take off, lifting from the highway into the sky, where raindrops started to fall. A thick bank of clouds obscured any stars that would've been visible. His helmet started to slip back on his head, so he quit watching the chopper and turned back to the scene.

Two cops climbed over the concrete barrier that separated the highway from the street beside it and all those townhomes.

Olivia.

She had Junior with her—and he was injured.

Izan jogged over. "You guys okay?" He pulled back the shirt on Junior's shoulder. "Through and through?"

The cop nodded, his lips pressed together tight.

"Let's get you to the hospital."

Olivia had a pinched expression on her face. Worry for her partner. "Got a seat on an ambulance?"

"Trace and Kianna are just about to leave again. Life Flight took the officer from the van and a civilian caught up in all this who was the driver of one of the other cars. Both are critical." Izan wasn't sure if either would make it, but they had to try.

"We'll get Officer Ramble here on a bus so he can get patched up."

Junior leaned against the back of their squad car, looking tired and uncomfortable. He'd lost blood, but not so much that the situation was dangerous.

Izan called out across the first responders and vehicles. "Medic!"

When Trace glanced over out the back of his ambulance, Izan waved an arm and pointed at Junior. Izan had been an EMT for years and still held the qualification. But with Junior being his best friend, he technically couldn't treat him. Thankfully his friend was getting top-quality care.

"I can walk." Junior pushed off the car and headed that direction. Amelia caught him as he passed her and helped him stay steady the rest of the way.

Izan turned from watching Junior to check on Olivia. "Are you okay?"

She might not have been injured, but she could still be hurt.

"The people. The situation. Then me."

Her order of priority? He could agree with that, as a first responder. But as a guy who cared about her and didn't like that worried expression on her face? He wanted to tell her to flip her order. "Rescuer safety first."

She frowned at him. "What?"

"If you aren't okay, you're no help to anyone." He knew he was standing close, talking low so she had to lean in to hear him. He took her hand, strategically holding her wrist in a way that he could feel her pulse.

But maybe she needed to hear it from the top once again so she could get her head on straight. "We got all the victims out, treated, and off to the hospital if that's what they needed. Two were critical: the driver of one of the cars and the corrections officer, Richard Brighten. The guy looked like he'd been pistol-whipped, because Brighten didn't get those injuries from the crash."

He waited a beat, aware he was repeating himself and wondering if she was in shock, then said, "What happened to you guys?"

She blew out a long breath. "When we realized it was a prison van, we called for backup. But we couldn't let them out of our sight or allow them to hurt anyone else. So we began a foot pursuit. At least one got away in a pickup truck with the other prison guard. We arrested one, Damien Wallace. Another shot Junior. Anthony let one go."

He could tell she was rattled, buzzing on the adrenaline still coursing through her system. She would crash hard when it dissipated, but the police department wasn't a one-woman show. There were other cops who would tag in when she tagged out to get some rest.

"Even if the hunt for these convicts takes days, you'll have a chance to get some rest. You need to take it." He counted the beats of her pulse.

"I know how to do my job, Izan." She stopped short. "Are you checking my pulse?"

"I was an EMT for years before I became a firefighter. And I'm not telling you how to do your job, I'm telling you to be careful. Do it smart."

"Oh, so you think I'm a dumb blonde. Is that it?"

Here we go. No matter how they met or what the circumstances were, it always ended like this. He tried to help her. She got defensive about it, like she was determined not to need help, and around and around they went.

"We don't need to talk about this." She tugged her wrist from his hand and stomped out some of the jitters in her legs. Or cold from the rain that had increased to a drizzle now. Dampening everything. She had a fitted long-sleeve shirt that looked like a base layer under her uniform shirt, but she could probably use a coat. "I have to get to the station so I can find out what the plan is next."

"Collins!"

He heard that yell in his dreams. Or was it his nightmares? He glanced over at Amelia, who had her hands on her hips. "Yes, Lieutenant?"

He might've heard Olivia chuckle under her breath but wasn't sure.

Amelia said, "Let's clean up this scene and get the road open! If you're done with your chitchat."

That time Olivia did laugh.

Izan groaned.

"I'm going to look at the van before you guys have my evidence towed away." Olivia wandered off.

It was on the tip of his tongue to tell her to be careful. Or ask her if she had a coat. Instead, he went to the fire truck and got a heavy broom so he could sweep glass off the road. A tow truck with flashing yellow lights made its way up the highway, headed for the scene. Everyone else backed up by the crash had been directed to turn around over the center island and head back to the previous cross street.

When he turned back with the broom, Olivia was pulling on a heavy coat from the trunk of her car and tugging a beanie over her blonde hair.

Izan let out a long and drawn-out sigh. The deep sigh of unrequited, incredibly frustrated love.

Della nudged his shoulder. "Amelia is watching."

Izan started sweeping.

"One day you'll figure it out."

"In the meantime, I have a job to do. Is that it?"

Della shrugged, pushing a brush of her own beside him. "You tell me."

Rain got in the back of his collar, below the edge of his

helmet. Cold, wet drips that chilled his skin. Kind of like the cold shoulder Olivia was giving him.

Okay, fine. He was being overly dramatic about it.

The ambulance, now with three patients inside, pulled away, lights and sirens going. More cop cars showed up. One had the emblem for the police chief on the side, and a dark-haired, suited man climbed out. A woman got out of the passenger side, her dark hair pulled back into a ponytail. She wore a coat, open because she was considerably pregnant. Chief Barnes's wife had been an ATF agent and currently worked as a liaison between city hall and the police department, often coordinating between federal law enforcement and state police as well.

Izan had heard they were having another baby, due early next year. They went to the same church he did, as well as a lot of the other first responders in town, and Grandma Collins worked in the nursery. She'd told him that another of the officers, Lieutenant Basuto, had children who were menaces, though she always said it with a smile on her face.

He knew more about them than he did about Olivia Tazwell. The woman was a mystery. He'd never seen her outside of work. She didn't go to the same church. Grandma Collins didn't even know who she was, but after he'd mentioned her a while back, she always asked how Olivia was doing. Every Sunday. Like she was waiting for the week when everything changed—when he brought her to family dinner.

Izan was pretty sure it was never going to happen.

"Earth to Collins."

He glanced over at Della, who grinned at him.

"It's gonna be a busy week now that there are escaped prisoners on the loose."

He nodded. "Once the story breaks, everyone in town will be on edge until they're caught."

Della worried her lip between her teeth. "It's just that..."

She shook her head. "Never mind. I'm probably worried over nothing."

"It's a worrying situation." But still, it seemed like there was more to her concern than just the danger to the general public until those men were brought in. "We can pray though. Maybe that's about all we can do outside of our jobs. Good thing is it's also the most effective thing for us to do. Prayer can change a whole situation."

"Thanks. That's a good reminder." Della went back to sweeping.

Izan looked over at the police van, where the chief had climbed in the open door. His wife hung back to the side, but he could see her talking. Olivia climbed out, and the chief's wife made a phone call, both of their movements betraying a tension he had no doubt they were feeling, given the situation.

The question was, how could he help Olivia personally while she took care of business professionally?

Something about tonight had changed things, making him want to show her his intentions in a way she couldn't ignore. Or argue away. Izan didn't know what it was, but he had an odd feeling things had shifted in a way there was no going back from.

He was going to prove to her that if she chose him, she'd be making the best decision ever.

FIVE

Olivia filled both mugs with coffee, Jessica Cartwright —one of their detectives—beside her. "He said they're stitching him up. He'll get some meds and orders to stay home and take it easy for a few days."

Jessica snorted. She accepted the coffee Olivia handed her. "Thanks." She took a sip. "He'll probably be back here tomorrow, helping with the manhunt."

"Probably," Olivia echoed. "There's plenty he can do from his desk that doesn't involve using his off hand. But he's gonna be mad until we find his gun."

They took their drinks to the main bullpen area of the police station, where everyone not currently out on patrol had gathered. Looked like every cop with a badge was here, whether they were supposed to be on shift or not. It was all hands on deck right now.

Chief Conroy Barnes stood over by the door to his office. Through the window behind him, Olivia spotted his wife at his desk, typing on his computer. She had his phone between her shoulder and ear, talking animatedly. Looked like she was giving orders to whoever she was on the call with.

"Okay, I'm gonna make this quick because every minute we stand here is another minute one of our escapees could hurt someone." He picked up a stack of files and handed them to Donaldson. "The sergeant is handing out the passenger manifest. We have three escaped convicts. Thanks to the quick actions of Officer Tazwell, and Officer Stuart and Titan, Damien Wallace is in custody, currently being interviewed by Detective Wilcox."

The chief nodded in Olivia's direction. "Well done."

Someone clapped her on the back. But she didn't want congratulations right now. She wanted orders to get out there and keep looking for the other three.

She accepted the file from Sergeant Donaldson. "Thanks."

He nodded and moved on.

Chief Barnes said, "Take a look at the files you have, talk to your CIs. We need to know where these guys have gone and who they might contact."

Olivia frowned. "Sir? Won't they just run? Leave town and get as much distance as they can between them and us?"

"Maybe. Maybe not," Chief Barnes said. "We don't know what agendas they have. Scores they need to settle. So figure out where they would go first and bring them in."

She nodded.

"We're setting up a command center in the parking lot of the grocery store on Allerton Street."

That made sense, considering it was close to the crash site. Hopefully at least one of the convicts was dumb enough to stay in the townhouse complex. She could hope this was easy, anyway.

"Everyone checks in for assignments. As soon as you come on duty, got it?" The chief lifted his chin. "Let's find these guys."

Olivia turned to the collection of officers around her. Anthony Thomas opened his file and flipped through the pages.

He flinched. "I was right. It was Alonzo Sosa." A tendon in his jaw flexed. "And I let him get away."

"I don't have time to argue with that," Olivia said. "It's not my job to persuade you to feel differently about it. But I will say that tracking him down is going to make you feel better." She wanted the guy who'd shot her partner and taken his gun.

"Thomas!" Donaldson called out over the bullpen.

Anthony turned. "Sarge?"

"Officer Stuart needs backup."

Anthony hustled away, eager to get back out there. Olivia looked over her file. Jessica came over, and they compared.

Olivia said, "Blair Mackey. Sentenced to sixteen years for the murder of two foster kids he had stealing for him. He's got the smarts to plan something like this."

"Jason Vaynes." Jessica whistled. "Nasty guy with some nasty habits. He's a serial killer, convicted of kidnapping and homicide. We need to lock him down quick before he gets any ideas."

Olivia found the page with his information. "That might be the guy who shot Junior. Told him he had things to do. Something about catching a mouse." She didn't want to know what horrible ideas a serial kidnapper and murderer might have. "And Alonzo Sosa makes four."

"I'm getting on Vaynes. It's not worth the risk focusing on anyone else."

"They're all dangerous."

Jessica nodded. "True, but I won't be able to sleep until Vaynes is behind bars. Guys like him?" She shivered. "I'm going to touch base with Savannah and find out what Wallace is saying."

"I'll go with you." She followed the detective to the viewing room where Savannah and Lieutenant Basuto were questioning Wallace. They'd turn him over to the Department of Corrections soon enough so he could get back to his cell, but right now he was a source of valuable intel.

"Any updates on Officer Brighten?"

Jessica winced. "Still critical. His wife told Chief Barnes that the doctor said it doesn't look good."

She looked at the file for each prisoner who had escaped while she half listened to Wallace talking about what had happened in the van. Mostly looking for a place to start with one of the three they still needed to catch.

Jessica turned up the volume dial on the wall as Wallace was saying, "No idea he was gonna do that. I thought Mackey was joking about getting loose."

"How'd he crash the vehicle?" Basuto asked.

"Someone shot at us from outside. It sounded like a hunting rifle. Shot the tire out, and we flipped."

Olivia glanced at Jessica. "We weren't looking at the outside of the van. We figured they overpowered the vehicle somehow and caused it to flip. Or the driver was in on it."

"Officer Athers is the one on the run with them, isn't she?"

"Probably dating one of them, or fell for him and he used it to coerce her to go with them." She shrugged because all she had was supposition and no evidence.

Basuto said, "What happened after the van flipped?"

"Other cars hit us." Wallace sniffed. "Mackey got through the grate to the front, since it was all mangled, and got the keys. We were free. But Brighten tried to stop him, and Vaynes grabbed his gun. Killed him with it."

"He shot him?" Basuto asked.

Izan had told her the guy had been pistol-whipped, which meant Basuto was testing Wallace to see if he was telling the truth. She and Junior hadn't been able to check on Brighten in the seconds before they'd realized the occupants of the van were running away and dragging a corrections officer with them.

Wallace shook his head. "Beat him to death with the gun."

Apparently Wallace didn't know that Brighten wasn't dead. Though, he also had a slim chance of recovering since he was in critical condition.

"Did they say where they were going?"

"Mackey knew there was a vehicle waiting. He'd arranged it."

"And Officer Athers? What did she do while Vaynes beat her partner?"

"Nothing she could've done," Wallace said. "She didn't try and stop Mackey. No one does. You don't mess with that one. He poisoned this guy in lockup a few months back just because he didn't like his mustache." Wallace shifted in his chair. "Put something in his food. The guy keeled over, and his face went in the mashed potato. He was just dead."

"We need to know who they're going after or what their plans are for escaping." Basuto folded his arms. "All of them."

"Or what? I'm already going back to jail, and I ain't never getting out. What do I care?" He sat back in his chair. "Unless you wanna talk deals. With my *lawyer*."

Olivia went back to looking at her file. She scanned the page for Alonzo Sosa since Anthony wasn't going to rest until he found the guy and redeemed himself.

Jessica said, "Sosa?"

"I was around when his girlfriend was killed and they brought him in finally. He went after the Crawfords pretty hard. Maybe he wants revenge." She found a note in the file under family members. "Izan?"

"What about him?"

"This says that Alonzo is related to him." Olivia frowned. "Alonzo is Diego Sosa's nephew."

"He inherited control of the cartel, right?"

"But Diego's second-in-command had a baby with his side-piece. Camilo Rojas had an affair with Renata Perez, who was Diego's girlfriend. All this was, like, thirty years ago. But Camilo worked with Elizabeth Crawford to place the child with a family. The Collins family. Izan was that child."

"Does Alonzo have a reason to target him?"

Olivia shook her head. "I guess we need to find out. He could be the one Alonzo wants to meet up with, for any reason. We have no idea."

"You don't actually think Izan is in league with a cartel guy, do you?"

"No way. But he also doesn't need to get caught in the cross-fire because he wasn't warned he's in danger."

Jessica nodded. "Good idea. Maybe he has intel about where Sosa might hide. Could be he knows all those guys, the cartel henchmen, and what they're up to now. You know we didn't catch all of them."

"Doesn't matter how many we catch. There are always more."

But there was no way Izan was one of them. She would never believe that.

Which meant he could be in serious danger.

SIX

I zan glanced at the clock, checking when their shift ended.

"Eighty-seven minutes to go." Eddie took a bite of his pancakes.

When Izan made them, he either did blueberry or chocolate chips, but when Bryce made pancakes, he put ground breakfast sausage in the batter. It was always good.

Zoe and Della wandered in to get themselves plates. Amelia and Ridge sat at the other end of the table, their heads together. Smiling at each other, discussing something that was probably *not* lieutenant business.

The dark blue of a police uniform caught his eye. He looked over and lifted his chin to Olivia in the doorway, glancing around. He offered, "Pancakes?"

Olivia didn't look like she was here for a social visit. "I'm starving. But I also need to talk to you." She wandered to the dish on the stove and grabbed a pancake, holding it with a paper towel before she came back over to the table.

"Can I talk to you?" She glanced over at Bryce but said nothing, addressing Izan when she said, "Somewhere else?"

Izan grabbed his coffee and left his plate. He wanted to think this was about them dating, or going somewhere for breakfast when they both were off duty. However, given what had happened last night, he couldn't help but think this wasn't personal. "Are you here on official business?"

She finished her bite of pancake, stopping in the entryway, where they had a few chairs. The receptionist wasn't in until nine each workday morning, so it was a quiet alcove right now. "I need to ask you a few questions."

"About last night?" He settled by her and took a sip of coffee.

She finished the pancake, wiping her mouth with the paper towel. "That was really good." She sighed. "Okay, you know we had a prisoner escape."

He nodded.

"We caught one, but there are three still out there. One of them is Alonzo Sosa."

Izan didn't like the sound of this. "You should probably talk to Penny and Bryce, then. They're the ones who brought him in a few months ago, after he nearly killed them. They're the reason he's in jail, right?"

"His girlfriend was killed, and Alonzo was sent to prison." She held his gaze. "Have you ever visited him while he was in prison, or had other contact?"

"Why would I do that?"

Olivia said, "I'm just curious if you've ever had personal contact of any kind with Alonzo Sosa."

The straight answer was no. But that didn't satisfy the questions that collided in his mind. "You don't actually think we're friends, right?"

"It's not my job to draw conclusions. Just to ask questions." She paused. "Your family and his are intimately connected. He's Diego's nephew."

"My mother was Diego's girlfriend. Until she had an affair with my father." His father had ended up in prison, arrested shortly after Diego caught up to them and murdered Izan's mother. Later, he'd died there. A sad end to a dangerous life. "I have nothing to do with the Sosas. I was adopted by the Collins family after my father made Elizabeth Crawford promise to take care of me. The Crawfords are more my family than the Sosas will ever be."

Izan got up to pace the entryway, trying to bleed off the antsy feeling of being pent up and exhausted. They'd gone hard this shift, and he was ready for some sleep.

"No one is accusing you of being in cahoots with a criminal. I just need to check a box so the police department can say we're 'exploring all avenues' and I'm not wondering if I made an assumption that might turn out to be wrong later."

She couldn't let her personal feelings affect her judgment when it came to her job. The same way Izan couldn't presume what a fire might do. Situations turned a corner in seconds and were always a hair from becoming volatile.

But that didn't mean he had to like the accusation.

"They've both been dead for a long time, and the Sosas are the people who killed them. I'm not going to help Alonzo if he shows up." He turned to face her, sliding his hands into his pockets so he could try and contain some of the frustration. "Who do you think told the ATF that the Sosas were working in Last Chance County in the first place?"

"The person who has nothing to do with them?" She lifted her chin, as if she'd caught him in an inconsistency.

"That was years ago. Jude is here now, and the Sosas came after the Crawfords."

"Because of you?"

Izan shrugged off any guilt he should've felt. "They were stopped. But people got hurt. That's what happens when you tangle with a cartel."

"And the money your parents stole from the Sosas?"

Izan wanted to shrug again, but that would be redundant. "If I had all that money they siphoned from the cartel, you think I'd be living here?" He could be a firefighter...in Miami. Or San Diego. Drive a flashy car. Take expensive vacations.

But if it was just him, it would seem kind of empty.

"Has anyone from the cartel ever threatened you, or tried to contact you?"

Izan shook his head. "I have no idea if Alonzo even knows who I am." Still, he should probably confess at least some of the truth. "I went looking for the Sosas a few years back. It's how I knew they were here in Last Chance County. I guess maybe I did have designs on finding the money or finding out who I was, but I got my hand slapped pretty quickly. It's a dangerous world."

Maybe at one time he'd had a wild idea to bring down drug dealers. To go on a one-man crusade to dismantle the criminal element destroying lives in Last Chance County. But he wasn't a cop—she was. Izan could make a difference in his job here at the firehouse. Olivia's job was to uphold the law and protect innocent people in the way that cops did.

He'd matured a lot in the last few years and left that wild bent behind.

Her phone buzzed, so he went over and sat down, resting his head back against the wall. "Everything okay?"

"Junior needs a ride home from the hospital."

Izan said, "I'll go get him. I'm just about to get off shift."

"What are you going to do the rest of the day?"

"Take a nap." He glanced over. "Are you going to be working?"

"I have no idea." She stood up, stretching her arms above her head and rolling her shoulders. "But I doubt anyone at the department is going to rest until these three guys are back in custody. One of the corrections officers is still missing, and the other is in no condition to tell us anything. We're relying on what Damien Wallace has told us happened."

He wanted to ask her out for coffee, but it would have to

wait until she was done with this case. Maybe she'd want to come with him to the firehouse Christmas party.

Izan watched her leave and saw how exhausted she was in her movements as she walked to her squad car.

He clocked out and, instead of going home, drove to the hospital. Junior stood in the waiting area, his arm in a sling. Talking to a shorter woman with red hair, wearing scrubs. She laughed at something he said, shifting on her white canvas shoes.

Izan knew that look on Junior's face.

The problem was the woman he was speaking with.

"And here I was gonna buy you a cup of coffee on the way home." Izan nearly turned around and walked back out. She could take him home if she was that eager to spend time with him.

She spun around. "Izan." All red hair, freckles, and wide eyes. Totally innocent.

Yeah, right. "Ainsley." He looked at Junior. "You've met my sister. Ready to go?"

Junior looked between Ainsley and Izan. "Your sister?"

He'd kind of thought everyone knew he was adopted. "Let's go." He turned away and heard her tell Junior she was glad he was all right.

Junior followed after Izan. He caught up as the doors slid open. "Bro, I had no idea she was your sister."

"It isn't like you did anything wrong." Izan glanced over. "Or did you?"

Junior was the kind of guy who'd laugh and say *Not yet.* So Izan braced for it. But instead, the guy shrugged one shoulder. "It's been a long night. Coffee sounds good."

Izan drove his buddy back home so he could rest after getting stitched up, hitting the pharmacy on the way to fill Junior's prescriptions. When he finally got home to his little rental house, tucked at the back of a cul-de-sac and hidden from the road between two houses, he sat in the drive for a second. Exhausted didn't quite cover it. He was dragging, but if he wanted to maintain some semblance of a sleep schedule, he had to push through and not take a nap until after lunch.

He grabbed his duffel bag and headed for the side door that led into his kitchen.

Two steps into the house, the door closed behind him of its own accord. Izan spun around and faced a man wearing his clothes. A man who could've been his brother.

"Alonzo."

The escaped convict lifted a gun and pointed it at Izan. "Hello, cousin."

SEVEN

Olivia pulled onto Izan's street but parked close to the turn-in because there was a fence where she wouldn't block anyone's drive or mailbox. She'd clocked out, changed clothes, and come in her personal car, but in a situation like this, she wasn't about to go unarmed. There were dangerous criminals roaming the streets, and all the cops in Last Chance County were out looking for them.

She'd been ordered to clock out for six hours minimum and get some rest, but that didn't mean letting her guard down.

One quick chat, and she was going to get some sleep. There was no way she could leave their conversation the way it had ended at the firehouse. On duty, she had to be a cop. Now that she was off shift, she could be Olivia Tazwell, a woman with a mega crush.

Not that she was going to act on it.

She didn't feel like she needed to apologize for asking those questions. She'd been doing her job, after all. She hadn't done anything wrong. But she did feel like it was worth at least clearing the air between her and Izan.

Olivia headed for the kitchen door without thinking much of

it, since the last time she'd been here—months ago now, for a summer barbecue—Izan had everyone come in the side or go right to the cute little backyard he had.

She was kind of jealous of it, even though the place could use some TLC. Weeds needed to be pulled and maybe some flowers planted. But the whole area was so peaceful. The kind of spot where you could sit and pretend the rest of the world didn't exist.

Raised voices interrupted her thoughts.

Olivia's footsteps stalled. She instinctively reached to her gun, but didn't pull it. As a cop, resting her hand on her weapon meant something far different than drawing it. She unsnapped the catch that held it secure in the holster.

Ready.

For what, she didn't know. Olivia crept closer.

"That's my gun, Sosa." Izan didn't sound happy. Or cooperative.

"Not anymore," the convicted criminal responded. "Where's the money?"

"What money?"

"As if you don't know. They were your parents. They took Diego's money."

She eased up to the door and lifted onto the balls of her feet so she could peer in the tiny window at the top of the door. She was barely tall enough to see inside, but she spotted the back of Alonzo's head.

Izan faced her, the gun pointed at him. "I never met them. I don't have your money."

Olivia backed up from the door and pulled out her phone, going to the front of the house. She called dispatch and informed them that the escaped convict Alonzo Sosa was at this address, Izan's house. Armed and dangerous.

"Copy that. Units are being dispatched to your location. Be advised: Do not approach the suspect, but wait for backup."

It was almost as if the dispatcher knew that Last Chance County cops had a tendency to go into a situation solo and try to take down the bad guy. Especially when the life of someone they cared about was at risk.

"Understood." But...she could just go inside and check. An innocent was in danger, after all.

That was the problem with regret. Something could happen to Izan, and she would never have the chance to say what she wanted to say to him.

She would have to live with the knowledge that she could've saved him but hadn't done everything she could, regardless of the consequences.

Olivia hung up, exchanging the phone in her hand for her metal credit card. She jimmied it between the front door and the frame, bumping the lock and opening the door. She caught it before it opened all the way, just in case it creaked and alerted Sosa to the fact someone else was here.

She crept down the hall, safety off on her weapon. Gun first. Right to the entry of the kitchen. Ignoring this first look at the inside of Izan's house. She'd been here at that barbecue but hadn't roamed the house like this. Or seen what he had on his walls. How he decorated the living room. She wanted to linger and study the place he'd claimed as his own and see what it said about him.

She stopped at the entry to the kitchen and listened.

"Just go, Sosa. Get out of here before I call the police."

The other man chuckled, the sound low and dark. "I'll kill you now. Save myself the trouble of being followed."

"No, you won't." Olivia stepped into the room.

Izan had his back to her from this vantage point, much closer to Sosa than he was to her. She spotted his shoulders stiffen but didn't take her attention from Sosa.

"Drop the gun and put your hands on your head."

His eyes were dark brown, almost black. His tanned skin

slightly lighter than Izan's. This man had spent months in prison, awaiting his trial. He didn't have much access to vitamin D.

"You aren't getting out of this, and killing someone will only make things worse for you. So put the gun down." She held hers steady, not wanting to use it if she didn't have to. "Do it, Sosa."

Alonzo did nothing for several seconds, then launched forward and grabbed Izan.

"No!"

He didn't heed her shout. Alonzo spun Izan and pointed the gun at the side of his neck, while Izan fought to get away from him. The moment the gun touched the skin of his neck, Izan froze. Wide-eyed. Aware that with one squeeze of that trigger, his life would be over.

"Let him go." The guy was racking up charges upon charges right now, and it wasn't going to make his eventual sentence any smaller. "Sosa, let him go!"

Both of them would realize she didn't have much control when it came to a gun pointed at Izan. But there was nothing she could do except her job, regardless of the pure fear rolling through her, turning her thoughts into sparks like lightning she couldn't tame and chilling every muscle in her body into something like cement. She couldn't look at Izan again or she would lose it.

"Let him go!"

Sosa's lips curled up slightly. He shoved Izan at her, and she just about got her gun out of the way before he slammed into her. His arms went around her, and they kind of caught each other, both of them breathing hard.

The door slammed open like it had bounced back on its hinges.

She stepped around Izan, both of them still holding each other, and looked at the empty doorway. Sosa had made a run for it—with a gun. Armed and dangerous, and now on the loose.

"I need to go after him. Are you okay?"

He nodded. "Go."

"Meet the officers who show up. Tell them what happened." She ran out of the kitchen door and looked both ways, seeing Sosa jump the fence by Izan's oak tree.

She raced after him, tearing across the yard as fast as she could while a clap of thunder rumbled across the gray early-morning sky. The clouds were thick enough they threatened to dim the whole day, not just breakfast. But she'd much rather chase a suspect in the cool than the heat of summer—so hot it seemed like everything was about to catch fire. She didn't know how those firefighters withstood running into a burning building every shift.

Olivia holstered her gun, grabbed a tree branch, and hoisted herself up so she could swing her legs over the fence. Thankfully the top edge was flat, not jagged, and she rested there a second just to make sure she wasn't about to get shot.

Sosa was halfway down the street behind Izan's cul-de-sac.

She pushed off the tree and made it over the fence. Not entirely graceful, but she landed on two feet and drew her gun again. "Stop! Police!"

Sosa kept running.

She chased after him, her intention focused on this one man. A guy who could have ended Izan's life just moments ago. Thank God he hadn't.

It felt like she'd been about to lose everything.

She wanted to ugly cry with relief now that Izan was fine. Even though Alonzo was loose still. He could hurt someone else. Take somebody's loved one, the person who was their whole world. She shouldn't be so relieved Izan was all right.

Olivia turned the next corner so fast she didn't realize what she'd done before it was too late.

Alonzo waited by the fence, and he was on her quicker than

she knew what was happening. He grabbed her shoulders and spun her, slamming her against the fence.

He grabbed her head and slammed that against the fence as well.

The double hit brought the ground up way too fast.

Everything went black.

EIGHT

I zan rushed out his front door just as a patrol car pulled in. Two officers climbed out, guys he didn't work with much. He strode toward them. "Alonzo Sosa was here. Olivia chased after him."

Izan put a hand on his chest, trying to still his racing heart. Should he have said *Officer Tazwell*? Maybe she didn't want everyone in the department to know they were friends. He'd been so surprised at finding Sosa in his house that now everything was upside down and he needed a second.

She'd gone after Sosa.

He turned back to the house. One of the officers said, "Which way did they go?"

"Through the back. They climbed the fence. It'll dump you out on the street behind." And he didn't want to be here when she was out there, running down a dangerous man with Izan's gun.

Yeah, he was gonna have to explain that.

Izan started walking down the sidewalk. He could go around, get to the street behind.

"Hold up, buddy."

Izan said, "It's Collins."

"Eastside Firehouse, right?"

He nodded. "Olivia is a friend of mine."

"I know, but you're not chasing down Sosa. That's the cops' job."

"I'm not trying to interfere, but she went after him alone." He glanced back. The partner had probably climbed the fence. He would get there quicker.

"Tell me what happened."

"I came home and Sosa was in my house. He took my gun, and when Olivia came in, he ran off. She can fill you in on all the rest." He didn't feel like rehashing it. What he wanted to do was contend with this urgency in his chest making his heart pound. The way he'd rather run after her than anything else right now.

Kind of like the way she'd run after Sosa.

But it wasn't that.

It was the look on her face.

The second Sosa had dragged Izan in front of him, she'd flipped out. He'd seen it in her eyes, blazing with fire. She'd kept a lid on it and maintained control. But seeing him with a gun to his head? She'd been about out of her mind in those few seconds. He was so sure he would've put money on it. She'd freaked out—and it wasn't about an innocent being in the line of fire in a dangerous situation. Or her being a cop.

It was *him*.

She cared about him. She'd recognized the moment he'd been about to die, and she'd had a visceral reaction. Which let him know that there was a distinct possibility she felt the same way about him as he did about her.

Something he hadn't dared to hope before, but he could now. He'd seen it on her face.

They reached the next intersection, and he spotted the other officer, crouching. "Over here!"

Izan and the cop ran to where he knelt by Olivia, who lay on the ground. "Make some room. I'm an EMT." He crouched. "Olivia?" He glanced at the officer. "Was she unconscious when you found her?"

The guy nodded. "No response." He turned to his partner. "No sign of Sosa."

"So go find him," Izan said. "But call for an ambulance to this location." He turned back to Olivia, whose eyes hadn't opened. "Can you hear me, Tazwell?" He pressed two fingers to the pulse in her neck and bent to listen to the air escaping her nose, turned to see the rise and fall of her breathing.

He vaguely heard the cop asking for an ambulance for an injured officer.

She had a steady pulse, but she wasn't awake. He lifted her lids and saw her pupils react equally. So no spinal injury.

"Tazwell, can you hear me?" He did a sternal rub, putting as much authority as he could into his voice. If she thought he was a disappointed superior, she might wake up faster.

A moan escaped her lips and she shifted.

"There you are." He couldn't assess her further unless she was awake. "Wake up for me, Olivia. Tell me what happened."

She groaned again. "Sosa."

The officers shifted closer. One said, "Ask her what happened. Where did he go?"

Izan wasn't going to press her when she was barely conscious. "I'm not asking her anything. She's going to the hospital. If you want Sosa, then go find him."

He didn't bother to see their reactions to that. He focused on her.

Soon enough, the ambulance pulled in. Trace and Kianna were still on shift right now.

When they raced over, Izan said, "Good, it's you guys."

"You okay, buddy?" Trace knelt, shifting immediately to assess Olivia.

"Don't worry about me."

Kianna touched his throat with gloved hands. "Nice bruise."

He gently nudged her hands away. "I'm fine. Olivia was found unconscious." And for some reason, he was still terrified. She would be fine. She was going to get taken care of.

He got up and paced away a few feet, probably feeling the same thing she'd felt seeing him with a gun to his head. *You protected both of us, Lord. Help us still.* He prayed for the three missing convicts and the officer who'd gone with them—presumably an accomplice—to be located and brought in by the cops.

Izan didn't want to face down Alonzo Sosa again.

But he was going to have to explain one thing to Olivia. Or the cops, at least.

Kianna and Trace got Olivia onto a backboard, and her head lolled to the side. She was only partially conscious. Izan helped them lift her onto the stretcher and into the ambulance.

"Coming with?" Trace asked.

Izan said, "I'll meet you there." He closed the doors and hit his palm twice on the back window, then turned and went back to his house. He didn't really want to go inside after what had just happened, but he grabbed his wallet and keys and locked up.

He drove to the hospital, his stomach rumbling. If Sosa hadn't been there, Izan would have eaten by now. Olivia probably would have as well. He swung through a takeout place with breakfast burritos and grabbed an extra one for Olivia, just in case.

Right as he entered the hospital's emergency department, he ran into his sister Ainsley again. She stood by the nurses' station in the center of the ring of side-by-side emergency bays. Most had a clear slider door to cut down the noise. Some only had a curtain separating the patient from the rest of the room.

"Peace offering?" She indicated his bag of food.

"Uh, sorry. No. It's for Olivia."

"Another one of your friends got hurt?" A worried expression shifted across her face. "What happened?"

Izan didn't know what to say. He hadn't told the rest of his family anything about looking into the Sosa crime family. Months ago, he'd shared a little with Ainsley about the firefighters getting involved with Bryce going missing, and all that stuff with the governor and the plane crash, but he didn't want to talk about it right now.

He wanted to see Olivia.

"What is going on with you?" Ainsley shook her head. "Seems like everyone's having an off day since that van accident. It's scary to think criminals are on the loose."

"One of them was in my house."

She gasped.

"It's fine." *He just held me at gunpoint and called me "cousin."* "Don't worry about it, Ains."

"Not worry! Are you serious?" She slapped his shoulder. "I'm telling Mom."

Izan rolled his eyes, because a man with two sisters in addition to the three brothers he had was an expert at doing that. "Don't tell them. I was on shift, and we worked the van crash scene, that's all. The cops in this town are friends of mine."

Her expression shifted.

"They're friends of yours too? Or is it just Junior?"

She rolled her eyes right back at him. "We've only gone out a couple of times. I can't believe he got shot." She covered her mouth with her hand. "His job is so dangerous."

"So is mine, but you deal."

Her eyes filled with tears.

Okay, maybe she *didn't* deal as well as he thought she did. "We're all highly trained. Yes, we take risks, that's part of the job. But we do it as safely as we can."

He wanted to point out that they always had someone to

watch their backs, but Junior had been alone. The same as Olivia when she'd faced down Alonzo Sosa.

Izan dragged his sister over and gave her a hug, kissing her forehead. "Junior is gonna be fine. Hopefully, my friend will be too."

"Is this Olivia a friend or a *friend*."

"None of your business."

She giggled and shoved him away. "You're serious about her. You like this woman."

"Shush your face."

She erupted into laughter. "I'll go find out if she's okay."

"Thanks."

"I'm fine!"

Izan flinched, turning to the side where he could see into a bay with the curtain drawn back. Olivia lay in the bed, resting on one elbow. A slightly dazed expression on her face—but he wasn't sure what that meant. "Olivia!"

"Don't you 'Olivia' me, Izan Collins." Her elbow gave out, and she collapsed back on the bed. "Ouch."

He rushed over and took her hand. "What is it?"

NINE

Olivia watched Izan walk toward her, a sheepish expression on his face that she'd never seen before. She was familiar with a few of his facial expressions—focused at work, laughing during one of those backyard cookouts.

"You're mad at me." He stopped at the end of the bed. "Or mad that you got hurt?"

"My head aches too much for me to be angry." She also wasn't sure she should be, given he'd essentially admitted that he liked her. Sure, he hadn't been aware she could hear the entire conversation.

You're serious about her. You like this woman.

Olivia smoothed down the blanket. "Are you just going to stare at me?"

He squeezed her foot gently through the blanket and deposited a fast-food bag on the rolling table. "I'm glad you're well enough to give me a hard time."

She chuckled. Was she supposed to just straight up ask him if he liked her? Or was he going to ask her out? He'd done that a couple of times, and she had shut him down. Now she wondered what might've happened if she hadn't worried how things would go down when everyone found out who her mom was.

"Happy to oblige." Olivia lifted her gaze, smiling.

Caught the soft look on his face.

Yeah, definitely wondering what might've happened.

He cleared his throat. "So, you heard me talking to my sister."

She nodded. No backing down or backing out of this.

"I've liked you for a while. You probably know that."

"I wondered if you still did."

He said, "The feeling hasn't gone anywhere. But you never gave me an opening to ask you out again."

Because she'd been too afraid of what might happen. "There are things you don't know about me."

"You have family who are cartel members as well?"

She wanted to laugh, but it wasn't really a joke.

Before she could say anything, he shifted to sit on the edge of the bed by her feet. "I didn't entirely tell you the truth about Sosa. About me not knowing him. Kind of."

Olivia frowned. Her head pounded where Alonzo had shoved her at the fence and knocked her out. She didn't like powerful narcotics, so she'd only let the doctor give her something over-the-counter. It was sort of working, but she wasn't willing to take anything else.

"So what is the truth?"

Izan let out a long sigh. "I used to come home from a twenty-four-hour shift and find someone had been there while I was working. Looked like they'd thrown a party and left the cups and debris all over the living room and kitchen. I called the cops a couple of times, but with no suspects and no evidence, there wasn't much they could do about it unless I got cameras."

"You never told me about that."

He shrugged. "I wasn't going to ask for a favor."

"Any sign of a break-in?"

"Nope. And I never knew for sure who it was coming in the house, but it stopped when Sosa was arrested."

"Did they take anything?"

His lips curled up.

"I'm just asking. I am a cop."

"I know you're asking because you care. That's not in question."

He thought it was because she cared about any citizen of Last Chance County, people she had sworn to protect. That she treated him no differently than anyone else in town. But that only meant she had successfully hidden her feelings from him. Maybe too well.

"I'm asking because it's *you,* because I care."

Izan held her gaze with that steady stare of his.

"You're an interesting guy, Izan Collins." A dichotomy. A Hispanic man raised by Protestant Anglo-Saxon parents, who still felt a connection to his roots. Only, he couldn't go there, because those roots were poison. He probably yearned to know more about his family, but with both of his parents dead and the people who'd known them either criminals or deceased, there wasn't much chance of finding out about them.

It likely colored how he saw the world. Not quite feeling like he fit. Knowing there had been something else out there for him, but having to come to terms with the fact he'd never know.

"I don't mean that in a bad way," she said. "I am a cop. I need a good mystery to solve."

"Still not sure that's a good thing."

She smiled. "It's a good thing."

"So if I ask you out again, you're gonna say yes?"

Her smile faltered. "There are things you don't know."

Now she was repeating herself. He would probably get frustrated and walk away, like all the others. Not that she had dated this long list of men who didn't try hard enough to break through the barriers she put up. But Olivia wanted someone to believe she was worth the effort to try. To put in the work to convince her that her fears were unfounded.

Instead of acting like everyone else in her life—bosses, teachers, friends—and dismissing her because of where she'd come from.

"I'd love to hear them," he said softly, laying his hand on hers.

She intertwined her fingers with his, enjoying the feel of his warm hand against hers. "I just...I don't let people in. I do my job, and I go home. I've never brought anyone home. Not even in school. I used to go to my friends' houses."

"The way we are is often about where we've been or the things that have happened to us. You protect yourself from being vulnerable." Izan paused. "I'm guessing a cop is the strongest person you know."

"It's what I wanted to be as soon as I knew what they did."

"Did you know a cop when you were growing up?"

Olivia nodded. This wasn't where she'd thought the conversation would go. Very quickly, they'd segued into vulnerable territory. Instead of talking about what it was at home that she didn't want anyone to see, he'd found the reason why she'd become a cop.

"His name was Howard Barnes." She let out a breath. "I've never told anyone this."

"It's fine if you don't tell me. It's your story, Olivia."

She wanted to tell him, because it meant something to her that he was the one who knew—the only one. "I was six. Somewhere around there. My mom would drink at this bar, and she would leave me in the car outside with a blanket so I could sleep on the back seat."

His hand flexed in hers.

"Someone stole her keys and took the car for a joyride. There were two of them. They didn't realize I was in the back, and they were drunk. They ran the car off the road into a ditch and ran off. They left the doors open and it was cold."

"They left you by yourself?"

"That was the least scary part of what happened. I know how to be by myself." She took a breath. "Eventually a cop showed up. He scooped me out of the car and drove me to the hospital. They checked me out, and I told him what happened. He waited with me all night while my mom was sobering up enough to take care of me."

"They never put you in foster care?"

Olivia shook her head. "Social services in Benson came by plenty of times. But when she was sober, she was good, and she's one of those people who can talk their way out of anything."

"But that cop made an impression on you."

"It wasn't just that he found a deck of cards and taught me how to play a few games. Or that he got me a candy bar from the vending machine and made sure I ate a good breakfast in the morning. It was that I felt safe for the first time in my life. I was being cared for instead of being left alone or taking care of someone else."

She continued. "He came by regularly. I always had his card on me in case I was ever in a situation and I needed help. He made detective, and he and his wife would come to my volleyball games."

"He cared about you."

"He was the *only* one who cared about me. Sometimes I go visit at Thanksgiving. He's retired now, and his wife knits afghan blankets." Olivia usually worked on Christmas, and her mom would spend the day at a bar. "They're great."

"What happened to your mom?"

"Nothing. She and I share a house on Witherton Avenue."

Izan frowned. "You still live with her?"

Olivia didn't know how to answer that. Her mom needed

help. If Olivia left her alone, who would make sure she was... alive?

A loud voice echoed through the emergency department.

Olivia slid her hand free of Izan's. "Sounds like you're about to meet her."

"Liv-ya! Where you at, girl?"

She called out, "In here, Nicki."

Nicola Tazwell sauntered into the bay in skintight leather pants, a tight top, teased-out hair, and more jewelry than Olivia owned. Her earrings and necklace had Christmas hats on them, and her shirt had a racy version of an elf in full color with the little lights so she could make it flash. Olivia couldn't see her mom's feet but guessed she'd ignored the forecast and wore slingback heels.

Nicki set her hand on her hip, about to say something, when she noticed Izan. She looked him up and down. "Well, aren't you tall, dark, and handsome." She stuck her hand out. "I'm Nicola."

"Izan."

"Ooh. Exotic."

Olivia's cheeks heated. Not the way she'd thought today would go, but it was all out in the open now. Her secrets were free.

The question was, what would Izan do next?

TEN

I zan eased the car door closed. Through the window, Olivia gave him a look that very clearly said *Save me*, but there wasn't much more he could do. He rounded the front end of Nicola Tazwell's car and got in the driver's seat. Because Olivia had insisted he be the one to drive them home rather than her mom.

Ainsley was going to pick him up and bring him back to his car, in the parking lot of the hospital, since her shift ended shortly.

He pulled out, which meant he needed to look over his shoulder. Which meant he could glance back at Olivia. "Doing okay?"

He'd asked that question about thirty times, and she'd answered the same way each time.

"Fine."

Nicola reached forward and squeezed his shoulder. "She'll be just fine once she gets home. You should come in…have a drink with us. I'm sure Olivia will want to rest, but we can grill some steaks and get to know each other."

Izan didn't reply right away. He needed to think so he didn't insult her or make a promise he would regret. "I'm probably as tired as Olivia since I worked last night. With everything that happened today, I didn't have a chance to rest myself."

Olivia picked up right where he left off. "Sounds like we all need an early night. After all, I might be on medical leave for a couple of days, but there are dangerous men out there that need to be found. There has to be something I can do to help."

"Sounds exciting," Nicola said. "Maybe I'll call the girls and we'll go out searching. Find us a dangerous man."

Olivia let out an exasperated sound. "Leave it to the police. You could get hurt."

Izan pulled onto their street. The apartment complex was at the end, the same one where he'd nearly been blown up a few weeks ago. Amelia had dragged him out, then gone back for Zoe. Seemed like forever ago, but it wasn't that long. He'd had no idea at the time that it was where Olivia lived with her mother.

Olivia told him where to park, sounding exhausted but grateful. He wanted to offer to carry her inside, but her mom would probably request the same treatment. She'd been doing things like that since she'd shown up, but Izan tried to treat her like any civilian at a fire scene. Respectful, polite, and aloof—because he had a job to do.

He came around and opened the door for Olivia, holding out his hand. She took his hand and straightened out of the car. He heard a whispered "Thanks."

"Anytime."

Having a second they could phlisper to each other made him want to do it more. A lot more.

But her mother came over and broke the moment. "Izan!" She flung her arms around him, catching Olivia up in the hug as well. Pressing them both against him. "Hate to love you and leave you, but this one needs to get to bed."

She wound her arm through Olivia's and tugged her away, taking the car keys with her. "Don't be a stranger."

Yeah, not having her drive had been a good call. He wondered if Olivia had ever called a unit to pull over her mom for a DUI. Given how much it had taken for her to tell him about her mother, he figured she likely hadn't. Or she'd done it anonymously so no one knew it was Olivia who had called cops on her mom.

His sister pulled into the complex.

Izan slid into the passenger seat and, before he'd even buckled his seat belt, said, "Why does she still live with her?"

Ainsley twisted around to look at him. "Want to start at the beginning with that one?"

"Sorry." He ran both hands down his face and gave her the abbreviated version of what Olivia had told him about growing up with Nicola as a mother. "She's been neglected her whole life, always taking care of herself. Now she's an adult. She's a cop. Why does she still live with her mother?"

Ainsley pulled out of the complex. "Codependency?"

Izan didn't want to think of it like that.

"Olivia figures her mom will be safe if she's there to take care of her. Plus, she feels a little responsible for her."

"So it's about protecting her mom from herself and protecting everyone else from her?"

"Isn't that what you do? Protect the town from fire. Save lives with your medical skills," Ainsley said. "We all deal in our own way with where we've come from."

"I said something similar to her," Izan said. "But that was before I knew she still lives with her mother."

"Is it a deal-breaker?"

He didn't know the answer to that.

Ainsley said, "You're tangled up with a cartel. Maybe that's a deal-breaker for her."

"I'm not tangled up—"

She cut him off. "I know that, but I'm making a point. You have things you don't want people to know about who you are and where you came from. You've never brought anyone home to meet your family. Maybe she's just doing the exact same thing. Keeping her personal life private because she doesn't want to be judged. Or she was judged so many times, she keeps it on the down-low these days."

"If she'd agreed to go out with me, we could've talked through all these things."

"Would you have brought up the Sosas?"

Izan said, "Probably not. But is it wrong to want to be who you are now, not who you used to be?"

"So you've left that life behind?"

"I'm not sure it's left *me* behind. But yeah. Diego is dead, and Alonzo was in jail. The empire had been torn down, and even if someone is taking up leadership of the cartel, trying to rebuild things, it doesn't have anything to do with me. Until they decide it does."

"Easier to keep people at arm's length. It's why I became a nurse. So I could use what Mom and Dad taught us about always taking care of the little kids and making sure everyone was okay. But at the end of the day, I get to go home. They're my patients. They aren't part of my personal life and they shouldn't be. But I have to be careful I don't protect myself so much that I end up alone."

Izan needed a change of subject. "How are they?"

"Ewan and Blair's basketball team won the state championship. Archie just finished school for Christmas break, and he's working at that chicken place again until he goes back to campus. Caitlin thinks her boyfriend is going to propose on New Year's Eve."

"Thanks." At least one of them was keeping up with family business.

"They're all going to be at the church tomorrow night,

helping put up the decorations for Christmas. If you're not working, you could come and help."

He nodded but didn't commit to anything.

"And Junior is coming to Sunday dinner this weekend."

He whipped around to look at her. "What? You just met today!"

She grinned. "Not today. We've been dating for a month."

"A month. Wow. It's serious."

She slapped his arm. "I'm bringing him dinner tonight."

Izan wanted to laugh. "He's got stitches in his shoulder, so at least there's not much trouble you can get up to." He didn't even want to think about that. His sisters and romance? Not something he wanted to go near.

"You should bring Olivia with you on Sunday."

He coughed. "Not sure either of us is ready for that."

"Plus, there are criminals on the loose in your house."

He heard the edge in her tone and said, "It worked out. Olivia was there."

"He could've killed you." Her tone flattened. "I heard what happened when Olivia was telling those other cops. You nearly died." She turned into the hospital parking lot, bumping up the curb before she came to a stop in a space not far from where he'd parked. "Are you really going to stay at your house? He could come back."

Izan had to admit he wasn't looking forward to going back there. "I'll get some things and go sleep at the firehouse."

"Okay." She relaxed a fraction, but not much. She was worried about him.

"I'll be all right."

"That man could come back."

Izan tugged his sister over and gave her a side hug, kissing her forehead. "I promise I'll be careful, and I'll get somewhere safe."

The cops would be watching his house now that Sosa had

shown up there. But he figured that meant the escaped convict wouldn't be coming back anytime soon. Maybe never.

Fine by me.

"Invite her to Sunday dinner."

He chuckled as he climbed out of the car, then drove home and packed a bag. True to his word, he locked up the house and went to Eastside, where the shift on duty were eating dinner. Someone had left a Bible open on the table to the pages in Luke that detailed the Savior's birth.

Glory to God in the highest, and on earth peace, good will toward men.

He had to remember that God wanted to influence his life. God wanted to bring peace and favor to the journey he was on. Not just at Christmas, but all the time. Izan had spent so long trying to save other people, he'd forgotten that he was the one who needed saving.

It wasn't his job to save Olivia.

He knew what he wanted—and it wasn't that.

ELEVEN

The next morning, Olivia pulled into a space in front of the police department, Junior in the passenger seat. "Then she spent all night fussing over me. Coming in to fluff my pillows and bringing me more water, even though I already had four bottles." She rolled her eyes and glanced over at her partner. "Why do you look like you're going to puke?"

"Maybe because you drive like a race car driver." He reached for the handle.

"You should take your pills. You're due for meds, and you haven't taken them yet, right? Because you wanna be macho or some nonsense like that."

"Yeah, because when women fall for a guy, it's because he's helpless and can't sweep her off her feet."

Olivia turned the car off. "Some women might be into that."

"Pretty sure Ainsley isn't," he grumbled, climbing out of the car.

Olivia wasn't completely healthy right now either, but her headache was only low-grade. She walked beside Junior to the front doors. "What happened?"

"Nothing. She came over last night and brought me dinner, then hung out for a while."

"But you couldn't put the moves on because your shoulder hurt." She shot him a look. "It'll heal. That gives you time to apologize and show her that you can be vulnerable just the same as you can be a hero." She pulled the front door open. "A woman wants to know you're well-rounded, bro."

"What are you two doing here?" Basuto stood behind the counter in the bullpen, turned to a desk where he was moving papers around. "I'm just about to head out to the command center."

Olivia said, "We figured we could answer phones. Man the tip line."

He walked over to the counter and buzzed them in the door to the right, which got them behind the receptionist desk. Which meant he wasn't kicking them out. At least, she hoped he wasn't just letting them back so he could politely tell them to get lost.

"Far as I'm concerned, sitting here is the same as sitting at home." Junior perched on the edge of the desk, looking forlorn.

She wasn't sure if his bad mood was because he'd been injured and it hurt or because the woman he liked had seen him when he was injured and it hurt.

"We do need volunteers to man the tip line," Basuto said. "But it's over at city hall. I actually have a job I need you two to do. A little public relations job."

Olivia wasn't convinced. "Busywork?"

Basuto's brows rose. "You think I'd waste my time giving you a pointless errand just to get rid of you?"

She said, "No, Lieutenant."

"Good." He tore a piece of paper off a pad. "Go to this address. It's a wellness check. The mother believes something might have happened to her son, as he's not answering the phone and hasn't for at least a day."

Junior said, "That's not long enough to—"

Basuto cut him off. "Apparently that's unusual enough to warrant calling us. Knock on the door. See if he's okay. Call the mom and inform her. The number is on the bottom."

Olivia took the paper. "Yes, Lieutenant."

"Good." Basuto grabbed his jacket from the back of the chair. "When you're done, come back and ask the duty officer downstairs if he needs any lunch."

She nodded.

Basuto looked at Junior, who nodded also. The lieutenant said, "I'll be hoping we find these guys before I have to tell the two of you not to come back until you're cleared by a doctor."

Olivia wanted to argue that she only had a mild concussion, which meant a raging headache, and didn't need to see a doctor again. But she also didn't need to be back in uniform on shift for a couple of days. Okay, fine. Maybe more like a week.

But who wanted to take that much time off?

Her mom would be there *all the time,* and it was so awkward. Nicola did not know how to take care of a sick person. She'd only been so attentive last night because she'd wanted information about Izan and who they were to each other.

As if there was anything to tell.

Sure, they'd held hands in the hospital and told each other things they never told anyone else. She had, anyway.

But what did that make them now?

He hadn't asked her out again.

"Let's fill coffee cups before we go." Junior headed for the break room.

She followed because he couldn't carry more than one with his arm in a sling.

The drive to the address Basuto had given them only took fifteen minutes. She pulled up to the curb in front, badge on her belt. Gun holstered in her duffel, ready to be slid onto her belt.

Junior had a backup weapon since his main police-issued sidearm had been taken by the man who'd shot him.

"Doesn't look like anyone is home." She climbed out of the car, setting her gun in the spot she liked it. Being in plain clothes wasn't usual for her unless she was undercover, but she appreciated not being in uniform all the time. "You gonna go for detective one day? I'm thinking about it."

Junior glanced over. "Because this town needs another blonde police detective?"

She smirked. "We're going for a trio."

He snorted. "I haven't thought about it."

Too busy thinking about Ainsley, most likely. "Let's knock."

Junior used his good hand, but there was no answer. "Back door?"

Olivia nodded. She checked the front window as they wandered around the house, but couldn't see inside with the blinds closed. As she reached the corner, the neighbor came out.

"You lookin' for Ted?" The guy had no hair on his head and wore a T-shirt stained with engine grease. His fingers on the screen door were black around his nails.

"Have you seen him?"

The man shrugged. "Why do the cops wanna know?"

"We're just checking on him, that's all. When was the last time you saw him?"

"Coupla days, maybe? But I heard gunshots in there last night when I was comin' in. Figured he had the TV on too loud."

Olivia went back to the front door, lifted her foot, and kicked it in.

Junior went in first, gun ready in his off hand.

She followed him inside and wrinkled her nose immediately. "Yep."

"We need CSU here to collect evidence."

Sweat beaded on her forehead. "He turned up the heat

before he left." Doing that ensured the timeline the medical examiner came up with on when the murder had occurred would be off, because the temperature in here had fluctuated above normal.

"Found him."

"I'll clear the rest of the house, you call it in."

"Be careful."

She quickly worked her way through the house and made sure no one was lurking. It was clear except for the neighbor still standing in the doorway when she got back to the front hall.

"He's dead, isn't he?" The guy paled.

"If you're gonna be sick, do it outside."

The neighbor stumbled back off the step and headed for his house.

"Tazwell!"

She found Junior in the room with the body. What she'd expected to be a guest room or study had a boarded-up window and bare drywall on the walls that had been taped but not finished. As if, in the middle of a renovation, the homeowner had called a halt to the work.

"Check this out."

She moved to where he stood looking at boxes on the floor. Beside them was an open case with a rifle inside. The same gun that had fired at the van?

She said, "Did you open that?"

"The lid was knocked off when I came in. I didn't touch anything." Ramble crouched, pain in his expression. "Look at what's visible."

She peered inside and saw a black-and-white photo of a young woman. Bound hands and feet, lying on a bare mattress. Behind it was a bigger piece of paper, folded, that looked like schematics for a building. "Who is this guy?"

"That picture? She's one of Jason Vaynes's victims. I read the whole file after the breakout. The detectives always suspected he might've had an accomplice." He straightened and looked at the dead man lying face down in a pool of his own blood. "You think this is him?"

"Whoever killed him might've taken something."

"He left something as well." Junior indicated a gun on the floor a few feet away. "The murder weapon. My duty weapon."

Her brows rose. "He killed his accomplice with your gun and left it behind?"

"Not part of his plan, but maybe an added bonus. Take out the accomplice." Junior glanced from the boxes to the victim. "Then the path is clear for him to do whatever he wants."

"I don't like the sound of that." Olivia had been focused on Sosa, who was bad enough.

This Vaynes guy sounded deadly.

"If they aren't long gone from town by now," she said, "then we need a way to draw them out."

TWELVE

I zan took his coffee down the hall, not sure where he was going but too restless to sit at the firehouse and wait for a call. Thankfully his shift had started an hour ago. Being here but not working made him feel way too cooped up.

On the wall of the community noticeboard in the hall, he spotted a flyer for the church Christmas decorating party. His whole family would be in attendance tonight. All except him. Which was normal if he was on shift, but maybe Ainsley was right to nudge him about Sunday dinners—if only for the fact Junior would be there. Izan hadn't been to many lately, and not just because he was on shift a lot.

Bryce had his office door open. "Collins, in here."

Izan moved to the doorway. "Yes, Captain?"

Bryce leaned back in his office chair, an empty coffee cup beside his laptop. The whole room was maybe twelve feet by eight, but at least it was bigger than the lieutenants' offices. Bryce was moving up in the world, freeing up the chief because Bryce could show up as the commander of a scene. "You had a run-in with Sosa?"

Izan lowered the mug from his mouth and winced. "Olivia

was there. It turned out fine. Just a mild concussion, and Sosa ran off."

Bryce shook his head. "Penny is out looking for him, working with the police. She's determined to get him back behind bars as soon as possible."

"I hope they find him and all the others before someone gets hurt."

"She just messaged me. The cops found a body they think is Jason Vaynes's accomplice. Apparently Junior and Olivia were doing a wellness check because no one else was available."

Izan couldn't believe that. "They're both on sick leave."

"And if you were here but not on shift, and a certain kind of call went out, wouldn't you jump in the truck and go anyway? Because it would be all hands on deck."

Izan sipped his coffee instead of answering that.

"Exactly." Bryce eyed him. "For the record, they're both fine. No bad guys."

Izan was more relieved to hear that than he wanted to admit. "Just a dead guy?"

Bryce shrugged. Before he could say anything, the alarm rang through the firehouse.

"Rescue 5, Truck 14, Ambulance 21. Multi-car collision, mud slide, persons trapped. Multiple victims." The voice continued, detailing the location.

Izan left his cup on the floor in the hall, tucked by the wall, and ran through to the engine bay. He climbed into the truck just as Amelia closed her door, and Della hit the gas, pulling out of the firehouse in front of rescue squad. Lights and sirens going.

No doubt Captain Crawford would accompany them in his SUV with the department emblem on the side, acting as the scene commander.

"What's the situation?" Della asked, her grip tight on that big wheel.

Amelia scanned the information on the dash screen while the rain pounded down on the windshield.

"I didn't realize it was coming down this hard."

Izan glanced at Zoe, who sat beside him. "No?"

"It was only raining a little when I dropped the kids at the bus stop on my way here." Zoe peered out the window.

Amelia said, "Part of the highway washed out because the rain caused a mudslide near Ridgeman's Hill. Multiple cars. And the rain is only going to get worse. We'll need all the straps and gear we've got. There are vehicles washed down the hillside."

Izan worked the zipper up on his turnout coat under the seat belt and flipped up the collar of his jacket.

Della pulled over, the lights still flashing as they exited the truck. The early-morning sky hung over them with a thick layer of dark-gray cloud, rain drenching everything in sight. Across the road were expansive puddles of water. The mud that had washed across the highway carried debris, branches, and rocks with it.

Amelia yelled orders over the rainfall, and Izan ran to the edge to see over. The mud had washed down the hillside to the west, across the road and then over an embankment on the east side, where it had sent the cars down the hillside. He saw a couple of people hanging out their windows, waving. Terrified expressions on their faces.

Izan turned on his helmet lights and waved back. He made his way down a few feet, but his boots sank into the mud. He yelled, "Stay where you are! We'll come to you."

Ridge came up behind him. "You're going down." He tethered a rope around Izan's waist and connected it to a tree, using himself as a counterweight. "Good to go?"

Izan yelled back, "Yes!"

He felt the rope slack and started to walk down the hill, sticking to the area beside the flowing mud. The closest car had gotten itself hung up on a tree and wound up stuck.

Which was good, because it meant Izan could make his way over.

He reached the open window, and the woman in the front seat jumped out. He managed to catch her without them both going down, adjusting his hold on her. "Anyone else in the car?"

"Just me!" She whimpered. "I was going to pick up my kids, and now I'll be late."

"Let's see if we can get you partway." He had her shift around so she was on his back, and the rope tightened. He gave a hand signal, and they pulled him up while he walked, keeping him steady as he carried the weight of this terrified woman up the hill to the others. To solid ground, where she would be safe.

Once he'd deposited the woman at the top of the hill, he went back down to another car. Zack and Eddie did the same, the ropes controlled by truck firefighters. All of them working as a team to save people.

The next vehicle he reached was a pickup truck half buried in the mud. He didn't see anyone, so when he got close, Izan pounded on the side window. "Anyone in here! Can you hear me? Fire department!"

He tugged the driver's door open and braced one hand so he could grab his radio. "This one is clear. There's no one inside."

But the vehicle hadn't been cleared by any of the other firefighters. Where had the occupants gone? Because there was zero chance the pickup had washed down here with no one driving it.

He tuned out the shouts and realized what he was looking at.

Orange jumpsuits crumpled in a ball on the floor of the pickup.

"This is the escape vehicle." His hand shook on the radio. "The one the cops said they fled in. It's here." With no one inside it. Thankfully, because he had no desire to come face-to-face with one of those convicts. Especially not in a situation like this.

He looked around while rain soaked down his face and into the collar of his shirt.

Captain Crawford came back over the radio. "I'll inform the police they need to tow that into evidence. Any sign of the convicts?"

"I'll keep searching." Izan slid the door closed so the rain didn't wash away all the evidence. "Maybe they're here."

"Be careful."

Izan signed off, going around the van to another car farther down the hill. Who knew how far some of the cars had been washed down?

He spotted a couple of their firefighters making their way down the stable dirt beside the wash of mud and debris, going to the end of the devastation. They would find out how far the farthest vehicle had traveled and make sure every single victim was rescued. That no one was missed or forgotten.

Kind of like the way Izan had been rescued as a child. He hadn't done anything, but he'd been cared for and placed with people who had raised him in a good home.

Kind of like the way he'd been saved by Jesus Christ. Rescued. Set free. Cared for enough that God hadn't let him slip through the cracks to suffer destruction.

If Izan had the chance, he was going to share that with anyone who wanted to listen. He wanted the lost and forgotten to know that he'd been rescued, and they could be as well. He wasn't the Savior, even if he did that sometimes as part of his job, but he could point them in the right direction.

Toward the cross.

His feet slipped out from under him, and he slid through the mud to slam against the side of a Jeep. Inside the car, he spotted a terrified couple in the front seats. The driver, a male, rolled his window down. "Help us."

Izan nodded. "I'm going to get you out of there."

THIRTEEN

Olivia stood at the top of the hill in the rain, watching the pickup being dragged up toward them. The winch whined, forcing the truck through the mud. Finally it crested the lip onto the road, and the wrecker driver called back to his buddy, who shut off the winch.

She'd told Junior to stay in the office and had come alone to do evidence collection. After the day they'd had, he should be home in bed. But no one was willing to stay on the sidelines when multiple convicts were out, loose and able to hurt people.

The next time they found a body, it might not be that of a bad guy. It could be the body of someone innocent caught in the crossfire. In the wrong place at the wrong time. Because the police hadn't found the convict fast enough.

"Need a hand?"

She glanced over at Izan in his full firefighter gear. "You look exhausted."

"I could use a cheeseburger." He shrugged, taking a drink from a water bottle. "But I'm good."

"Sure." A cheeseburger sounded good.

Olivia pulled on a pair of the gloves she used for evidence collection and said, "Just don't touch anything."

"I doubt you'll get much in the way of prints from that."

"That's not what I'm after, though I will be dusting for prints. They take weeks to be run, and we need these escaped convicts caught before the results come back."

Wind blew along the highway, flipping up her collar. She had a rain jacket on, the hood pulled up over her head. The wind whipped her hood back, so the rain soaked her hair and face. But what else was she going to do? It was far too windy for an umbrella, and she needed both hands.

She had evidence bags and collection tools. Olivia bent into the car, which shielded her from the pouring rain. But it did nothing to keep her warm. Even with base layers on and a sweater over her long-sleeve shirt, she was still chilled—and she hadn't even started.

The first orange jumpsuit had the number on the back that she knew belonged to Mackey. Blair Mackey had been coercing foster kids to steal for him like he was Fagin from *Oliver Twist*, even going so far as to take the life of kids he should have cared for. The whole thing turned her stomach. This wasn't a man who should be out on the streets, loose so he could profit from his disgusting tactics. He only cared about money. He didn't value human life at all.

Olivia tucked the jumpsuit in an evidence bag and sealed it. She marked her notebook with the relevant information.

Someone else would be doing a deep dive on fibers and trace evidence. She didn't have the patience for it. Olivia would much rather kick a door down and throw cuffs on the bad guy.

"Do you guys have any idea where they all ran off to?"

She glanced at Izan, who was watching what she was doing, and then turned back to continue putting jumpsuits in bags. "We know that in the days before the breakout, Mackey received a series of calls from the same number. There was no call the day of the breakout. The number belonged to an unregistered phone."

"That's like a burner, right?"

She nodded. "It's possible it belonged to the officer we believe is their accomplice. There's a theory that Rainy Athers might've been having an affair with Mackey."

"A prison guard and a convict? Are you serious?"

"It happens," she said. Thankfully not that often, and it was usually squashed before things could get anywhere near this far. "It's not unheard of. She might've gone dark side and helped them escape so she and Mackey could be together. The others just happened to be in the vehicle. The sad part is that her partner was caught in the middle, and he's in critical condition. A man could die simply because this woman couldn't keep her feelings professional."

"That's horrible."

"It's life." She shrugged and turned to him, holding another evidence bag. "Unfortunately, things aren't always the way we want them to be."

"I'm ready for Christmas. That's all I have to say."

She stared too long at his jaunty smile. "Christmas?"

"Yeah, we get this all wrapped up and it's nothing but decorations, eggnog, hanging out singing Christmas songs. All of it."

She shook her head. "I didn't peg you for being a Christmas fanatic."

"The Collins family might not know so much about Hispanic culture, and I didn't grow up speaking Spanish at home, but they are *excellent* at Christmas. They all go crazy." He grinned. "In fact, they'll be at the church tonight, helping decorate. I might go since I'll be off shift. Hey, you should come with me." He nudged her shoulder.

"A tempting offer."

"But you're busy?" His expression lost a little of the excitement about Christmas.

"I don't know what time I'll be finished with this." She turned to him. "But if I'm free, maybe I'll be there."

He grinned. "That would be great."

"You're ready to introduce me to your parents?" Wasn't that a milestone in a relationship? They seemed to have suddenly jumped to warp speed, going from a first date to meeting his parents. Getting to know each other. That meant he wasn't messing around.

His eyes flared. "I mean…if you want to meet them."

"You already met my mother." She turned back to her task, gathering the rest of the pile of clothing. Underneath, she found fast-food wrappers. They could trace the restaurant and get security footage. Find out who was in the vehicle—whether they'd gone through the drive-through or come inside the restaurant.

"If you want," Izan began, "maybe we could get something to eat before the decorating. Or after."

"Maybe we could," she echoed. "Just not from this place." She held up the evidence bag.

Izan said, "I've never liked that place. Their fries are overrated."

Olivia smiled. "Then you've got yourself a deal. Or a plan."

"Or a date?"

She nodded. "Okay, a date."

He leaned in a little, almost like he was thinking about kissing her. To their right, someone yelled, "Collins!"

He stiffened and turned to the side. "Yes, Lieutenant?"

Amelia had her hands on her hips again.

Olivia said, "She does that a lot, doesn't she?"

Izan turned back to her. "Gotta go. Duty calls and all that. Text me later when you're done?"

She nodded and watched him jog away, pulling out her phone. Under the hood of her jacket, she called Junior.

He answered before the second ring. "Please tell me I can leave."

"Ha. You stay put. You were shot."

"I'm bored."

"Then run this license plate. Tell me who the truck is registered to." She went to the front of the vehicle and read off the numbers and letters. "Although, if they abandoned it, then we can almost guarantee it won't lead to them. Otherwise, we'd have never found it."

"You think they got washed down from the highway and ran off?"

Olivia said, "I spoke with a witness who said the truck came from up the hill and washed down with the mud. So I think they abandoned it on the side of the highway and tucked it up in the trees. When the mudslide happened, it got washed across the highway and down with the other cars."

"Maybe they didn't plan for anyone to find it. They thought they'd hidden it well, and they took off in street clothes to who knows...Okay, the search result populated. That truck belongs to Richard Wallace."

"Any relation of Damien Wallace?"

Junior was quiet for a second. "His brother. The guy is a plumber, uses the truck for work. I'm gonna call Detective Ridgeman. She'll want to interview him again. Find out if he knows where we can find Richard."

"Get me an address. I'll go talk to him." She looked at her watch. "If I can get that done, I'll make my date with Izan."

"A date? With Izan?"

"Oh shush."

"Are you kidding?" Junior said. "This is *huge*. It's *epic*."

She rolled her eyes. "I'm out here in the pouring rain. Can we be done with this ridiculous conversation so I can get back to work before I'm soaked through to my bones, please?"

"Since you asked so nicely."

Olivia sighed. "It's just a first date." Where she was going to meet his parents—which she would *not* be explaining to Junior. "It's not that big of a deal."

She hung up on Junior so she could have time to take a shower. Curl her hair.

Okay, fine.

It was a big deal.

But so was getting this done and finding those escaped prisoners. Otherwise, she wouldn't be able to enjoy the time off as much as she would if the world was a little safer.

So Olivia got back to work, trying not to think about kisses.

FOURTEEN

Izan had been on a roll after the best dinner ever. In fact, he'd have said he *was* on a roll...until he pulled into the parking lot.

Olivia stopped in the middle of talking about her afternoon after he'd left the scene. She said, "What is it?"

"Looks like they're all here." He pulled into a space.

"There's only a handful of cars here."

He winced. "And most of them belong to my siblings and my parents." He spotted another couple of cars—the pastor and the church custodian. Why had he thought this was a good idea? Things had seemed great earlier, chatting with Olivia in the rain. Now his stomach flipped over.

"We can do something else. Or you could drop me at the station and come back by yourself."

And everyone would know he'd chickened out. "No way." He wasn't going to be a coward. Ainsley had probably told them all he was bringing Olivia tonight, and they'd shown up so they could see her. *Worst idea ever.* He said, "Besides, I want to know if you found that guy. The convict's brother."

She unbuckled her seat belt. Rain on the windshield quickly

blinded the view. Without the wipers on to clear it, they were suddenly cocooned in a world of their own. Almost like no one else existed. It seemed for a moment as if it was just the two of them.

Kind of like it had at the restaurant, when he'd been listening to her talk about police training and the other officers in her class at the academy. Watching her face light up as she described the pranks they'd played on each other.

"You're sure?"

"I'm good." He twisted to her and rested his arm on the center console so he could lean closer. "If you are."

She eyed him with a little suspicion. Maybe this wasn't the right moment to talk about work. It did feel like something entirely different was happening.

Which, of course, it was.

Izan had decided to simply show her the real him. The guy who said what he was thinking and let it all hang out.

"I'm good."

"That's good." He studied her lips. They'd curled up endearingly as she spoke. He wanted to press his lips to hers and see what she tasted like. If it was as good as he thought it might be. "I'd rather sit here though. We're going to get soaked running to the front door."

"You didn't used to do that when you were a kid?"

"Sure, but now I've got a good reason to stay in the car."

"Oh?" Her lips curled up again. "And what reason is that?"

He shrugged, trying to keep things playful. "You."

She was focused on the manhunt, wanting to help, but she was also on medical leave—so there were limited things she was allowed to do. Detective Ridgeman had accompanied her to the house where Damien Wallace's brother lived.

"So I can tell you about my day?"

"You can tell me whatever you want," Izan said. "But did you find Wallace's brother?"

"The house was empty. Thankfully, I didn't find a second dead body today. It's never easy, no matter how many times it happens."

Izan hadn't intended for the conversation to go this way, but nodded. "We see some pretty harrowing things on callouts. People who got hurt, mangled in all sorts of ways. When it's a child is the worst. It sticks with you."

She reached over and took his hand. "Makes you want to hold the people you care about close."

"You can hold me close anytime."

She shook her head, chuckling. "We should go inside before this conversation gets any worse."

"I thought it was going well."

She laughed.

Yeah, he wanted to kiss her. "Let's go."

If he did kiss her, then he'd have to figure out how to stop. Otherwise they'd be out here in the car for who knew how long. He'd rather deal with the anticipation of their first kiss than have to cut it off and meet his parents with a flushed face and his cheeks pink from embarrassment.

"Ready?" He reached for the door handle.

She flipped up the hood of her jacket. He raced around the car and snagged her hand. They ran to the front doors of the church like that, spilling into the building, giggling and out of breath.

The entry was empty of people, his shoes echoing off the floor with a hollow sound. He pushed open the doors to the sanctuary and found a small group of about a dozen people sitting in the first couple of rows.

A dark-haired man stood in front of them holding a gun.

Olivia flinched, patting her pockets. Searching for her…"My gun is in the car."

Izan hadn't taken his attention off the man. "Alonzo, what is this?"

He walked ahead of Olivia and saw one of his brothers turn to watch him come over. Olivia could figure out how to call this in, get help here. He needed to distract Sosa so that she could do her job.

He needed to draw attention to himself.

"What are you doing?" Izan spread his arms wide.

"Jogging your memory." Alonzo shifted the gun to point it at Izan, then moved his arm to aim at Izan's mother.

Izan stiffened. "About what? What do you want?"

The guy should've been halfway to Mexico by now. He could've run, but he was still here. In town. Thinking he had unfinished business. Or that he knew this area well enough he could hide...and do whatever he wanted.

"You know what I want. So give me Diego's money, and I won't kill these people. Your *familia*." He said the last word like it was a slur.

"They're more my family than you are." Izan was going to keep him talking until the police got here. "They raised me. Cared for me. Now you're going to threaten them. That only means you know they mean something to me." They meant *everything*. "If I had your money, I'd give it to you. Because their lives are worth more than some stupid money I don't even care about."

"Then tell me where to find it."

"Leave with me. We'll take my car," Izan said. "I'll take you to the money."

His family reacted. Mom whimpered, and the others moved to look at him. Someone gasped.

Apparently he was a good actor, because they didn't know he had no idea where the money was. He'd never had it and wasn't going to be able to produce it. What he needed was for the Collins family not to be in the line of fire.

He felt Olivia move behind him, and his phone was tugged from his back pocket, where he always kept it. She didn't have his password, but she could make an emergency call. Get the police here.

"We can go right now." Izan motioned with his head. "No one has to get hurt."

Olivia grasped a handful of his shirt and slid his phone back in his pocket. Did she think the police could track him if he went with Alonzo? At least one of them was thinking ahead, because he had no idea what he was doing.

Alonzo said, "I get that money. It's mine. You aren't family."

"That's right, I'm not. I don't want Diego's money. I never have." That, at least, was the truth.

He earned his money fair and square. Izan had no idea what had happened to the money his birth parents had stolen from Diego Sosa. But the man had killed them both for it. Alonzo knew enough to presume Izan had it, though Izan had no idea what gave Alonzo that impression.

Alonzo held the gun on Izan and dragged Ainsley to her feet with his other hand. "We'll take just one with us. For insurance."

Ainsley gasped. "Izan."

"Your brother will make sure nothing happens to you." Alonzo leaned in and smelled Ainsley's hair. "But that doesn't mean we can't have some fun in the meantime."

Izan flinched, taking a step toward Alonzo. "Let her go, or no deal."

Alonzo chuckled. "You think you have any say in this?" He lifted the gun and pointed it at Ainsley's throat, kind of like the way he had with Izan.

Izan's throat tightened reflexively. He knew exactly what it felt like being held like that. Helpless and unable to do anything for the risk of getting shot in the head. Lights out.

No, that wasn't how his family was going to lose Ainsley. Not right before Christmas, and not at any other time. The second they got out of here, he was going to jump Sosa and finish this.

"You don't need her. You'll have me."

Olivia stepped out from behind him. "And me. There's no way anyone will come after you with a cop as a hostage. Izan and I will go with you, and you'll get that money."

Alonzo dragged Ainsley along with him. "I don't need a cop."

He whipped the gun over and pointed it at Olivia, already pulling the trigger.

FIFTEEN

Olivia saw it coming. Time seemed to slow down. She moved behind Izan, dragging his arm around because pulling was easier than suddenly pushing against all that strength. She needed him out of the line of fire.

They spun around together and landed on the floor, gunshots overhead. A steady beat of two...three...four shots. Alonzo stopped firing.

The ringing in her ears quit, the smell of gunpowder in the air. Alonzo was chuckling. "That was impressive."

Hmm. Not as impressive as what she was going to do next.

The entire plan had been foiled. All her attempts to shake her head and silently order Ainsley and Izan's young-adult-aged brothers to stay in their seats and not intervene were hanging by a thread.

She scrambled out from under Izan and stood. "You aren't taking that young woman anywhere."

Olivia should've worn her vest for this date. She should've been carrying her gun.

Now she had to rely on backup to solve a problem she

could've solved on her own. But wasn't that the point of being a police officer? She didn't have to do anything alone.

Alonzo's eyes narrowed.

Ainsley's expression shifted as well, but in an entirely different way. Olivia clocked the slight movement as she adjusted her stance and then twisted. Ainsley rammed her elbow back into Alonzo's side, hammering his abdomen so that he doubled over. She brought her elbow up again and slammed it down onto his back.

Olivia raced to him and grabbed his gun.

But Alonzo was already scrambling up. He ran at her, but one of the boys stuck his leg out and tripped him. He fell onto Olivia, and her back hit the carpet of the church aisle. The gun dropped from her hand.

Alonzo reached for it.

Izan dove on him, dragging him to his feet. Izan pulled his fist back and hammered Alonzo in the face with a punch that sent the guy spinning around.

The door slammed open, and a crowd of boots pounded into the room. So many it sounded like thunder. Like the sound of *backup*. "Police! Hands on your head!"

Olivia lay back on the carpet and just breathed.

Ainsley slumped down into a seat on the end of the pew, hand on her chest. Breathing hard. Her face pale.

Officers ran by Olivia, and she shifted to the side so she didn't get stepped on. Alonzo was secured and cuffed.

She sat up, her head swimming. Okay, fine. It was pounding.

"You good, Tazwell?" That was Lieutenant Basuto. He stood over her, a disapproving expression on his face.

She lifted both hands. "I didn't do anything."

He shook his head, then held out his hand. "You need an ambulance?"

"No." She grabbed his wrist, and he helped her to her feet. Basuto let go, and she glanced at Izan. "Good?"

"I am now." He touched his chest and let out a long breath.

The cops led Alonzo back down the aisle, clearing out of the church. Olivia held out her hand, and Izan took it. She tugged him over to the row behind Ainsley and they sat. "Are you okay?"

His sister nodded. The other family members gathered around.

Someone yelled, "Ains!"

Ainsley shot up out of the seat and ran down the aisle to meet Junior, racing in with a haggard look on his face. His arm still in a sling. He hugged Ainsley, looking as relieved as Olivia felt that this was over.

Olivia chuckled. "I'm fine too. Thanks for asking."

Izan put his arm around her, and she leaned her head on his shoulder, not quite feeling like she could sit still. "Adrenaline," she said on a breathy exhale.

He kissed her forehead.

An older couple sat in front of them—Izan's parents. The other siblings got up, hanging out in the aisle now they were free to get up from their seats.

"Mom, Dad. This is Olivia."

She lifted her head from his shoulder. "It's really nice to meet you guys." She held out her hand and shook with them. Brenda and Sean, they said their names were. "Really nice."

Brenda smiled. "You stood up to that man."

"Saved two of my kids," Sean said. "Means I owe you."

Olivia shook her head. "I was just doing my job." But it was more than that, wasn't it? "I care about Izan a lot. I wasn't going to let Alonzo take him anywhere." She glanced over her shoulder, where Ainsley and Junior spoke quietly to each other, still in their embrace. "Junior is my partner."

Brenda smiled. "It'll be good to have more heroes in the family. Can't have too many if you ask me." She glanced at her sons, twins but not identical. They reminded Olivia of a much younger version of Bryce and Logan. The kind of boys who would grow up to be heroes, like so many of the men Olivia knew.

"Agreed." Izan squeezed her shoulders.

She looked at him. "You realize we're still on our first date, right?"

Izan's father chuckled. "Didn't take me long to know Brenda was the one. That's for sure."

"We've all heard the story plenty," one of the boys said.

"I'd love to hear it." Olivia smiled.

Brenda got up. "He can tell you while we decorate. These wreaths aren't going to hang themselves."

The family dispersed, finding decorations. Discussing where they were going to be hung around the sanctuary.

As if just moments ago they hadn't been held at gunpoint by a man who could easily have killed one of their family—or all of them. As if life simply moved on, or you got on with it.

"They're pretty amazing."

Izan said, "It'll hit them later. We can get ice cream or put a movie on and all pretend we aren't crying."

"That's how you all process your fear?"

He shrugged against her. "Christmas will help. All being together and relaxing. Remembering the reason for the season and being thankful we have each other still."

"Sounds magical."

"Want to join us? Be part of the Collins Christmas celebration?"

Their faces were close, and she realized they were whispering like Ainsley and Junior. Olivia scanned the dark brown of his eyes, soaking up the affection she saw there. "I'd love to."

Izan leaned down and touched his lips to hers, gently exploring. As if he had all the time in the world.

In a way, they did.

This was only the beginning, but if they stuck together and

looked out for each other, if they treated this start like a fragile thing to be tended, they could watch it grow into something strong, with a solid foundation. The fact it started here in God's house gave her the confidence to trust that it was His plan for them.

A Christmas like no other.

Maybe even one that would last forever.

RESCUED TRUST

MICHELLE SASS ALECKSON

He's risking his career to save her. She's risking her life to trust him.

Officer Anthony Thomas has spent years crafting the perfect image—until one mistake threatens to destroy his career. Now he's stuck on protection duty for a woman who'd rather face a serial killer alone than accept his help.

Firefighter Della Nixon survived once, but the scars run deeper than anyone knows. When the sadistic killer escapes prison with revenge on his mind, Della's past comes roaring back—along with a devastating secret that could destroy everything she's fought to rebuild.

But the killer knows Della's darkest secret—the lie that put him behind bars. Now he's determined to expose her truth to the world, even if it means burning down everything in his path.

With a blizzard closing in, can they outrun a killer and face the secrets that could destroy them both?

ONE

One failure was all it took to destroy an image Officer Anthony Thomas had spent years trying to build. With a chance at redemption in his grasp, they wanted to pull him off the search for the escaped prisoners? How else was he supposed to rebuild the reputation he'd lost and prove he had what it took for a promotion?

He shook off the rain as he stepped under the tent canopy. The flimsy shelter was better than nothing against the incessant downpour, but the dropping temperatures would wreak havoc on the manhunt. First the flooding. Now ice. Hopefully whatever the sergeant wanted wouldn't take long so he could get back to it.

Anthony snagged a disposable cup and filled it with coffee from the plastic carafe. "What did you need, Sarge?"

Sergeant Aiden Donaldson looked up from the plastic tabletop scattered with maps and grids. "Ah, Thomas. Need you to head to the firehouse. You're on protective detail." His gaze fell back to the maps.

"But we have two more prisoners out—"

"Save it. Not my decision." He let out a long sigh, gave a slight shake of his head. "I do what I'm told, same as you."

Anthony barely caught the grumbled words.

"These are dangerous criminals. Mackey? Vaynes? And I'm supposed to go babysit someone?"

Sergeant Donaldson stood straight. "Our job is to protect and serve. That's what you'll be doing."

Anthony swallowed the bitter coffee. After he'd let Sosa get away, he didn't really have a chance at convincing his superior of anything. Not that anyone had said anything. But if they were pulling him off the hunt, the message was loud and clear.

Maybe if he put in a little time making nice with whatever big shot claimed they needed protection, he could get back to doing real police work and finding the convicts. The kind of work that would show he was detective material.

He unclenched his jaw. "Who am I protecting?"

"Della Nixon. Firefighter. Know her?"

Anthony barely kept his jaw from dropping. "In passing."

She was newer to the Truck 14 crew. The stunning firefighter definitely caught his eye when they were on scenes together. Dark, olive-toned skin, big brown eyes, and midnight-black hair that always looked silky, even after being smashed under a helmet for hours...Of course he noticed her.

The first time he'd seen her, he'd tried to introduce himself and stumbled over his own name and walked away. Which was probably for the best. She clammed up whenever he was there. And he wasn't one to stick around where he wasn't wanted. "Why does she need protection?"

"She testified against one of our escaped prisoners. Jason Vaynes."

"The serial killer?"

"That's the one. Apparently, even before he escaped, she was receiving threatening notes. I'm not convinced they're from him, but now that he's on the loose, the chief wants someone on protective detail twenty-four seven. That's you."

"Aw, come on, Sarge. Why me? You know I'm better suited to chasing down Vaynes and Mackey out here. I should be—"

"Do you understand your assignment, Officer?" Sergeant Donaldson folded his arms. A tilt of the head and narrowing of the eyes, and Anthony's appeal died on his tongue. He knew that look.

This was what he got for screwing up. For letting Sosa get away.

Babysitting duty.

He swallowed. "Yes, sir."

"Good. Get to the firehouse right away. You're there until I tell you otherwise."

Anthony walked back out into the rain. Ice coated the deep puddles in the grass and the edges of the sidewalks he crossed to get to his cruiser in the parking lot. They'd have to move their temporary checkpoint station indoors soon. It had been just over forty-eight hours since the accident-slash-escape, and the weather only grew worse by the minute.

And yet, out here in the bitter cold was where he wanted to be. Where he *should* be.

"Where are you going, Thomas? Got mud on your shoes?" K-9 Officer Cole Stuart chuckled as he turned up the Sherpa-lined collar of his coat.

So Anthony liked to take care of his clothing. Image mattered. He paid good money for quality and wouldn't apologize for it. But he would gladly muddy all his Alexander McQueen sneakers for a chance at bringing down these criminals.

"Nah, got reassigned on protection detail."

Stuart sucked in a breath through his teeth. "At least you'll stay warmer than the rest of us roughing it out here." He opened up the back of his SUV and rubbed down his partner, Titan, a German shepherd.

"I'd rather be out here doing real police work." Showing the department that he had what it took. "Keep me updated?"

"Sure thing." Cole gave him a clap on the shoulder and left with the dog.

Anthony held back a sigh and opened his own door. Might as well pay his dues.

This is what I get, isn't it, Lord?

He should've been the one to bring in Sosa. He'd been on the task force last spring when the man had blown up a hotel, kidnapped the governor's family, and tried to set up a whole cartel in Last Chance. He knew how slippery he could be.

But when he'd had his chance yesterday, he'd blown it. Anthony had been on his trail when Sosa went and held his friend Izan Collins, fellow officer Olivia Tazwell, and a few others hostage in a church while they were decorating for Christmas.

Talk about killing the Christmas cheer.

Not that he was a fan of the holiday. But still. Some things should be sacred for the kids. And it was Anthony's fault that it had escalated that far. He should've caught Sosa before the guy had a chance to terrorize again.

But now, instead of righting that wrong, he was back at the bottom. He pulled up to the firehouse and made his way inside. Zoe Lewis, in her firefighter uniform, held a ladder while paramedic Kianna Russell hung a strand of Christmas lights from the ceiling in the lobby.

"Looking good, ladies." Anthony stomped the water and mud off his shoes on the rug.

"Who, us? Or the decorations?" Kianna's playful smirk was beautiful and harmless. They'd established a good friendship, but both knew they'd never be a couple.

"Both, of course." Anthony moved over to take the ladder. "Here. Let me do that."

"You don't think Zoe can handle a ladder?" Kianna tipped her eyebrow up, almost daring him. "Or are you just trying to hit on us?"

"Can't a guy be a gentleman once in a while? Besides, Zoe is married, and I know better than to make any moves on you. I know when someone's out of my league."

Both of the women laughed.

"I suppose you'd be better at holding the ladder steady than decorating that table with the garland." Zoe looked up at Kianna "What do you say?"

"By all means, put the man to work. Oh, and don't forget to put up the poster for the toy drive. The collection box should go over by the reception desk. I'm almost done here."

Anthony held the ladder while Zoe arranged greenery.

Kianna came off the ladder, and they moved it to the other side of the door. It didn't seem right to be standing around while the others did all the work. "Why don't I hang the lights?" Just add *interior decorator* to his résumé. Right under *babysitter*.

He needed all the goodwill he could get. If it made a positive impression on these ladies, hopefully it would help break the ice with Della. Show her he wasn't a complete doofus who didn't know his own name. And if she put in a good word for him with the police department, it could help him get out of the doghouse.

"You really wanna hang the lights?" Kianna asked him.

"I always have time to help out our friendly neighborhood firefighters. And in the name of gender equality and all, you can hold the ladder for me."

Zoe chuckled from the other side of the lobby. "Why don't you sweet-talk Alice into some more thumbtacks, and we'll see if she thinks you qualify. She's pretty strict with the office supplies."

"Alice? Of course she's careful about who she trusts with office supplies." Anthony moved over to the reception desk and leaned in toward the woman behind it. She had a no-nonsense vibe with her salt-and-pepper hair pulled back in a low bun. "But you can trust me. I am a police officer after all."

Alice narrowed her eyes. "So I hand over the thumbtacks, and what will I get out of this arrangement, Officer Thomas?" A little twinkle in her eye gave her away. She was enjoying this.

"I was hoping—"

"Alice, I'm waiting for a police—" Della Nixon walked into the room and froze at the sight of Anthony.

He stood tall. "Hi, uh, hey." He cleared his throat and tried again. "I believe I'm the one you're waiting for." He put on his full-watt grin.

Her lips dropped into a frown. "Guess they aren't taking me seriously after all."

TWO

Della had finally reached out for help, and this was what she got. She marched out of the room before she said something else she'd regret. They'd sent Anthony Thomas to protect her? The man spent more time flirting than doing his actual job! Well, flirting with everyone except her.

Not that it mattered *at all* what he thought about her.

But if the department had sent the officer who looked more like a cover model of a men's fashion magazine than a bodyguard, were they really taking her seriously?

Her conscience pricked. *And why should they?* She *was* a liar, after all.

The notes showing up in her mailbox, and even in her locker, said so. Which gave more credence to the threats they contained than she could ignore. Because only one other person alive knew about her lie. And if he found her?

No. She couldn't go there.

Della walked into the break room and grabbed a sponge. She scrubbed a spot of dried coffee off the counter.

With the first few anonymous letters, she'd been able to hold it together. Jason Vaynes had been safely locked away in prison, where he couldn't hurt her anymore.

Then he'd escaped.

So she'd swallowed her pride and called on the police. She was scared, and she was big enough to admit it. She would *not* be his victim again.

And here she'd laid it all out to the nice officer on the phone, only to be mocked now with the arrival of Officer Thomas.

The same Officer Thomas now standing in the doorway.

"Ms. Nixon, I don't think we've officially met before, and yet I get the distinct impression that I've offended you somehow. I assure you, I'm here to help."

Oh, he was handsome and suave all right. He filled out the dark-blue uniform to perfection. Capable, strong shoulders and a trim but solid figure. The dark hair he kept neatly styled contrasted with the most startling shade of blue eyes. Eyes that seemed to laugh and shine too bright to take life seriously. She'd heard more than her fair share of his serial dating escapades from some of the others. She refused to fall for his flattery.

She dropped the sponge and looked at him. "You're right. We haven't met before, but I've heard about you."

A tic in his jaw and the slight tightening of his smiling lips were the only hints that her implied barb had hit its intended target. She wasn't usually this forthright, like ever, but she was barely holding on here. She didn't have time to tiptoe around anyone's ego. Not when her life was on the line.

"I don't know what you heard, but I take my job incredibly seriously. I'm here to help keep you safe." He stepped into the room.

"Hmph. The precinct's poster boy?" She focused on another spot on the counter and attacked it with her sponge. "I have a serious threat on my hands."

"Who said a person can't be attractive and capable at the same time?" He gave a nonchalant shrug, but the challenging spark in his gaze tripped her up a second. "*You* pull it off. Heard you rescued an octogenarian from a house fire last week."

He was good. She'd give him that. But that blue-eyed gaze bored right into her, setting off a warm swirling she felt all the way down to her toes.

She struggled for words. *Sheesh!* A few pretty compliments and she was falling apart.

He could pounce, finish her off with a well-placed placating remark, but instead, he leaned in. "Give me a chance before you write me off completely. I want to help."

At least he wasn't easily scared off. She needed someone to watch her back. Someone who wouldn't scatter at the first sign of trouble. His persistence could be an asset.

If she could trust him.

"Fine." She grabbed the coffee mugs from the drying rack and stacked them in the open cupboard. Anything to hide the shakiness in her hands.

"I know you talked to someone at the precinct, and my sergeant said you were the one who helped put Vaynes behind bars, but it would help me know what we're working with if you can walk me through this from the beginning. Do you mind telling me what happened?"

Of course she minded. But he was right. It was only fair she give him a chance. And maybe she *was* coming down too hard on him simply because he was sophisticated and happened to be one of the few men in Last Chance that had a good sense of style. Even if he did date a lot, she never heard anything bad about his police work. And he did seem genuinely concerned.

Who was she to turn down any kind of aid? She needed all the help she could get.

And she had to admit, desperate times, desperate measures and all that meant she couldn't be picky.

She folded her arms across her chest. "Can I trust you?"

He held her stare and gave her a small nod. He didn't flinch, didn't look away. "I'm here to help. I don't want anything to happen to you."

A hint of peace settled in her soul. Like a starving person, she would take the tiniest morsel offered.

Okay, Lord, I'm going out on a limb here.

She grabbed a water bottle, and they sat at the small round table, off to the side. "What do you need to know?"

"Start at the beginning. You were captured by Vaynes. Along with your friend, right?"

"Yeah. Lily."

"And how did you two know each other?"

She slowly traced the top of her cap. "I met Lily in college. She didn't have any family, and we got really close. So that summer, when I came back here to stay with my grandma, she came with me. We worked a day job at the grocery store and then at a bar in the evenings."

"What bar?"

"The Black Barrel"

"The one downtown?"

Della nodded before continuing. "Jason Vaynes was a regular there. He was there every shift Lily and I worked. I knew he liked her. He was always staring at her. But she didn't think much about it. She had a boyfriend back at school, and Jason never did anything. Just always ordered a beer and nursed it until closing, when he'd pay his bill and leave a big tip."

"Then what?"

She swallowed hard and gathered enough gumption to get the rest of the story out. "One night when Lily and I had the closing shift, we had car trouble. It was after two a.m. I should've noticed the lights were out in the parking lot, but...I didn't. Everything after that gets hazy—" Della closed her eyes, willing back the stinging tears that wanted to escape. She didn't want to relive the horror. But she needed Officer Thomas to understand the danger here.

"I woke up and had no clue where we were. Lily was sobbing, saying we had to escape. But he kept drugging me. When I was awake, I was chained to a bed, and Lily would be passed out. I don't remember how long we were there. His prisoners. But I know the last shift I worked was July twenty-ninth, and the day I escaped and woke up in a hospital was August twenty-ninth. A month to the day."

"And Lily?"

The name still brought a shaft of pain through her chest. Her friend had sacrificed everything for her.

"He'd broken her legs. She knew she wasn't going to make it. She was so adamant that I get away." Della paused to take a sip. "She used the drug that he'd given me on him. It knocked him out. I didn't want to go, but I promised her I'd get help and come back for her. I couldn't let her sacrifice be for nothing. So I left. But whatever it was that he put in me messed me up. I ran from the cabin where he held us and found the highway, but I was so malnourished and dehydrated that I passed out. By the time I came to and was able to direct the FBI to where he'd kept us, Lily was already dead."

"I'm sorry." His voice was gentle. Sincere.

Della looked up. His eyes weren't glinting or mocking. They stayed steady and true as he held her gaze.

"That took a lot of guts to get away and go for help. They caught him, right?"

"They did. And I testified. He was sent to prison, and I've been trying to move on and not let him take anything else away from me. But now he's out there, free, and he's coming after me."

"If he's smart, he'll get as far away from Last Chance County as he can. His face is all over the news and social media, so he's more likely to be caught here, where everyone is on the lookout. What makes you think he'll come after you now?"

There it was. The doubt. It would come out sooner or later.

Maybe it was an innocent question, one he thought was simply procedure. Or did he think she was paranoid? That was a possibility too. Guilt ate away at her and messed with her head more than she liked to admit. But reality was, she'd gotten away while Lily had perished, and every single day, she had to live with that.

And it couldn't completely be paranoia. She had proof that Vaynes was after her.

"I know because he told me so. He's been leaving me threatening letters for the last month."

Officer Thomas frowned. "But he was in prison until the escape."

"I don't know how he was getting them out, but I know they're from him. The first one showed up on my doorstep. So I got a security camera. Then they showed up on my car, left on my windshield when I was out at the store or at church. One was left in my locker, here at work. He said he won't leave until he finishes what he set out to do."

"How do you know it's him and not someone trying to play a sick joke or bully you? Not that it's okay for anyone to do that, but how can we be sure it's really Vaynes?"

"Because there's things he says that only he would know."

Officer Thomas seemed to consider her words, studying her from across the table. "All right, then. Will you show me the letters?"

Finally, they were getting somewhere.

THREE

The beautiful Della Nixon was hiding something. Anthony had been a cop long enough to see the signs. But there was genuine fear in her captivating face. Which only cemented the twist in his gut that said he was in the wrong place. He should be out hunting down the criminal responsible for tormenting her and killing her friend.

The trauma was real. So what was it that she *wasn't* saying?

He'd have to familiarize himself with the details of the case, but he didn't doubt that Jason Vaynes belonged behind bars, never to be allowed to walk freely in society again. Maybe getting to know the details of Della's case would help him track Vaynes down if he could get back out there. And that meant seeing these letters.

"You believe me?" Her eyes narrowed as she stared him down.

"Is there a reason I shouldn't?"

She shook her head. But her thumb tucked itself into her fist that rested on the table.

Interesting.

"Well, let's see them. Where are they? At your place?" He

hoped his expression didn't show the questions or suspicions lurking in his head.

"I brought them here."

"Why didn't you show them to the police?"

"He was in prison. So there wasn't really anything he could do but mess with my head. Until he escaped."

It sounded good, but there was still something Anthony couldn't quite pin down about her. "We'll need to classify them as evidence, but there might not be much we can get off them in terms of evidence if you've handled them already." He stood, ready to see these threats for himself.

"After the first one, I was careful not to touch them without gloves. I kept the envelopes and letters all in a plastic baggie. Just in case. And the police officer I talked to said he was sending someone here while I worked, so I brought them to give to you."

That showed some forethought at least, but the chain of evidence was already tainted. Still, he wasn't going to let anything, big or small, go without tracking down every possible clue.

He was, after all, here to protect her.

And if he so happened to catch a serial killer and restore some goodwill with his department, so be it.

Della led him out of the small break room and down the hall. Loud voices cheering over the unmistakable sound of sports announcers meant a bunch of the crew were watching a game in the lounge. A quick peek as they walked by, and he saw Penny Mitchell there, on Bryce Crawford's arm. He'd worked with them last spring to put Sosa away the first time. What would they think if they knew how badly he'd messed up?

But it was Chief Conroy Barnes's opinion that mattered most. Anthony wouldn't make it to detective if he didn't do some damage control and prove that he had what it took. He'd been cultivating CIs and trying to prove himself for too long to miss the mark now.

But in the back of his mind, his father's voice lingered, the disappointment clear in his aloof glance when Anthony had shown him his rock collection.

The boy won't amount to anything. Just look at him.

He had banished that voice long ago, only to hear it incessantly since losing Sosa. Anthony shook the memory away as they approached the women's locker room.

Della stopped outside the door. "Let me check and make sure no one is inside."

He'd have to trust that she wasn't tampering with the evidence any further. She seemed almost desperate for someone to believe her, so it didn't benefit her to mess with the letters any more than she already had.

He waited in the hall until she opened the door and left it propped open. "Come in."

He followed her to the middle row of gray metal lockers. She spun a combination lock and opened the one with her last name on it. A feminine scent, exotic and floral, wafted over him. A down coat and rain boots took up most of the space. On the top shelf rested a clear makeup bag holding an array of dainty bottles and brushes. Della pushed the coat aside and opened a brown leather purse. She dug through it, then paused. "What—"

She snatched the bag and brought it out of the locker. She mumbled something as she opened the bag as wide as possible and continued to dig.

She finally looked up, her face pale.

"What is it?"

"They're gone. Someone stole the letters." She gripped her bag tight enough for her knuckles to go white. "I promise you they were here in my bag when I started my shift this morning."

If she was lying, the wobble in her voice was some of the best acting he'd witnessed.

He kept his voice calm and steady. "You sure you didn't forget them in your car, or they might've fallen out?"

"They were here. I made sure of it." She spun and dug into her locker.

Looking over her shoulder, he watched. Nothing behind her coat or under her boots. Nothing on the shelf with her products and makeup.

She faced him, lifting her chin. "I promise you, I had them."

He gave a slow nod, not wanting to completely discount her, but also not yet convinced. "So where are they?"

"Obviously they've been stolen."

"You sure your locker was closed completely this morning? Locked?"

"You watched me unlock it. I gain nothing by lying to you."

"I never said you were lying. But under stress, we space out. Overlook stuff. Maybe we should check your car. Or see if one of your coworkers found them and turned them in to the receptionist. Just in case."

"I'm telling you, I had them *in my bag* when I got to work this morning. I double-checked. Someone broke into my locker and took them."

"Why would anyone do that?" He knew most of the crew. They wouldn't stoop that low.

"To mess with me? How should I know?"

Those furrowed brows? Yeah, she was angry now.

And although she was probably hiding something, maybe this wasn't it. It didn't really make sense for her to fake the letters' disappearance. Unless she'd never had them in the first place. But to what end would she lie about that?

"All right, then, is anything else missing?"

Her shoulders relaxed a smidge at his question, almost as if his belief in her really mattered. "I'll check." She turned back to her locker, this time methodically moving the products on her top shelf, scanning the locker from top to bottom. Her breath caught.

"What is it?"

"My hairbrush and"—she swallowed—"a picture."

"What picture?"

"The picture I had of Lily." She pointed to an empty spot inside the door. "It's gone."

FOUR

A deep chill sank into Della's bones, sending an icy shiver throughout her body. This was bad. No one else knew about the letters. No one but Vaynes and whoever he'd had delivering them before he escaped.

And now she didn't even have proof that they existed. That the threat was real.

But it was the missing hairbrush and picture that drove it home.

Vaynes was on the hunt, and she was the prey.

"You're sure they're both gone?" Officer Thomas actually looked slightly concerned as he studied her.

She could only nod. She clenched her jaw tight, trying to stop the tremor going through her.

She pointed to the empty spot where the snapshot of her and Lily at the lake had hung. The tacky putty she'd used was still there.

Officer Thomas leaned in, studying the door of the locker. "Okay, the missing photo is concerning. Why the hairbrush? Any significance?"

Della sank to the bench, closed her eyes. She didn't want to remember.

But she had to. For Lily.

"Vaynes...he, uh, he had a thing for long hair. He would cut locks of Lily's. I think he kept the hair as trophies, but they never did find where he had them."

"Mmm. Someone could've borrowed it and not put it back. But"—he released a long sigh—"let's see what security cameras caught."

So he still didn't believe her. She shouldn't be surprised. "There's no footage from inside the locker room. People change clothes in here."

"We'll look at the hallway footage, everyone going in and out. Are you certain the brush and photo were here when you started your shift?"

She looked him in the eye. "Positive."

"All right. Let's go view the footage." He followed her out to reception, where Alice helped them access the video feed from this morning. She then left to give them privacy.

"Here you are, entering at 7:20 a.m. Let's see who else enters the locker room." Anthony hit play.

Della hoped it was a sick joke. A prank. She zeroed in on the screen, watching for anyone to go into the room after she'd exited at 7:28. If there was a reasonable explanation, she was all for it. But no one else went in.

Nothing.

"Play it again. Slower. Someone was in there." She shoved the words out through her clenched teeth.

He went back and played the feed at a slower rate. "Nada. There's no one that goes into the locker room after you."

"I'm telling you, someone took the letters. Stole my hairbrush and swiped that picture. And they did it today, because it was all in my locker this morning."

Anthony leaned back in the office chair, one eyebrow lifted. "How? There's no proof."

"Except my missing stuff!"

He nodded toward the screen. "Then tell me why I'm not seeing anyone going in or out of the women's locker room."

"I don't know! That's what you need to find out. Maybe the footage was tampered with."

"Or maybe you're scared. Stressed. Forgetting a few details like where you set your brush down. Either way, the footage doesn't lie. There are no missing chunks of time. I watched the time stamp."

"It's him. It's Vaynes. I don't know how, but he's been here. He's messing with me. It's all part of the game."

Della paced, desperately trying to get ahold of herself. She couldn't let him get away with this.

But Officer Thomas did not look convinced. He stood and pulled out his phone. "I don't know that Vaynes was here, but I'll request his case file and see what I can find. I'll be here for the rest of your shift. You're safe. So try to relax." He flashed a condescending smile at her. "Where can I get some coffee around here?"

Sheesh, be a little more convincing, why dontcha? "The break room."

Bryce Crawford stuck his head in the door. "Hey, Della. Patterson is asking for you. She's in the storage room."

Officer Thomas stood. "Yo, Crawford, what's the coffee situation here? Decent?"

Bryce smirked. "Guess it's your lucky day, 'cuz I just brewed a new pot."

The guys walked off in the opposite direction. Della marched back toward the storage room. Basically, she was on her own. The police department had sent their token officer and figured that was enough.

Clearly, they didn't understand the threat.

Amelia Patterson looked over from the fire extinguishers that lined the top shelf when Della walked in. "Did you find what you needed in the surveillance footage? Alice told me you were reviewing this morning's recordings."

Should she say something? She was still new to the job—the rookie, despite the fact she'd been here for months. She didn't want to come across as a weakling. And chances were, if Officer Thomas didn't believe Della, neither would Amelia.

Besides, if Vaynes was here, it was obvious who he was after. And if he wasn't, she didn't want to put everyone on their guard only to be the girl who cried wolf.

"It wasn't what I thought, but it's fine."

"Okay…" Amelia paused, studying her for a moment. "So is everything still set for the toy drive next week?"

"Everything's going as planned."

"Good. We got another box of donations." She pulled out a big cardboard box, a couple Nerf guns and Barbie dolls sticking out of the top. "They still need to be wrapped."

"I'll get to it."

"Let me know if you need help. With anything."

Della nodded.

"I mean it, Nixon. We're here for you. If you're having a problem, I want to help." She paused, as if waiting for a response. "So, what's going on that has you so jumpy? Is it something to do with the letter you had a few weeks ago?"

"It's the whole escaped convict thing. It's got me on edge."

Understanding flickered in her lieutenant's eyes. "Vaynes. I remember that case. I never put it together. But you were one of his victims, weren't you? *That's* why you have police protection?"

"Yeah. Though I'm not sure Officer Thomas is taking me seriously. We didn't see anything on the surveillance, but I know someone was messing with my locker."

"Have you talked with Penny Mitchell?"

"Bryce Crawford's fiancée?"

"She was on the *Sosa* case last spring and almost died trying to capture him. Why don't we bring her in? An extra pair of eyes couldn't hurt. And if something is going down in our firehouse, I wanna know. We can put her private investigating skills to work."

"Sure."

They found Penny and Bryce in his office. As the captain for the firehouse, the guy who reported directly to the chief, it was probably best Crawford was on board and informed about what was happening. Della explained the situation to them, and Bryce bristled when she mentioned the missing items from her locker.

Penny's usual smile fell into a tight-lipped grimace. "Well, he's not going to take anything else. You don't go anywhere alone, 'kay? Not even in this building. Is this why Tony is here?"

"Officer Thomas?" Della asked. "He's my police protection, but I don't think he's convinced."

"I know Tony. He's a good officer. I'll look into the case with him and see what I can do to help track down Vaynes." Penny pushed off the desk she was leaning against.

Bryce stood too. "I'll take a look around the perimeter. Penny's right though. Don't go anywhere by yourself." He left the office.

Della took a full breath for the first time in days. Maybe she wasn't quite as alone as she assumed. It certainly felt good to have her coworkers take the threat seriously.

Amelia studied her a second. "Why don't we go wrap some of those presents? Might as well stay busy."

Her smile was probably meant to be reassuring. But nothing could make Della forget that Jason Vaynes was on the loose and had her in his crosshairs.

FIVE

Anthony tried to concentrate on lifting the fingerprint off the locker. "You don't have to watch over my every move, you know. I've done this a few times." He glanced over his shoulder at Penny Mitchell.

She stood behind him, eyes narrowed as she observed. "Gotta make sure you're doing it right."

He knew better than to read anything into that tease in her voice. She was head over heels for Bryce Crawford, and if he wasn't mistaken, her wedding was coming up soon. Not that he hadn't done his fair share of flirting with her months ago, when she'd assisted the department with the Sosa case. But she was engaged now. He knew it wouldn't go anywhere, which made it safe, harmless fun.

No chance of getting hurt again.

"Don't you have a case? Or someone else to bug?" He lifted the tape off the locker and pressed it onto the white cardboard.

Before she could answer, his radio squawked. "Think we've got something." Sounded like Jessica Ridgeman's voice. As detective, she was probably running point on a section of the search. A search he should be a part of. "Path east of the river. Footprints and—"

Anthony turned the volume on his radio off. If it wasn't attached to his vest, he'd be tempted to chuck it across the room.

"Whoa there, buddy." Penny spoke as if she were placating a child. "What's up with that grumpy face? Aren't you glad they're on the trail?"

"Of course I'm glad. I hope they catch them." He shut the lid to the fingerprint case a little too forcefully.

"Then what's the problem?" The childish banter was gone. It was his friend Penny asking in earnest.

"I should be out there. Tracking those prisoners down. Not... sitting around waiting for something to happen."

"What you're doing here is important, Tony. That woman is scared. She's been through hell."

"I know, Pen."

"She doesn't think you're taking her seriously. Why is that?"

"When I didn't see anything on the footage, I was skeptical. And maybe I still am. Stress and anxiety can mess with memory. Make people see things that aren't there. Even forget things."

How many times had he lived through it with his mom? All the times she was convinced of aliens or intruders—what did the doctor call it? Psychosis brought on by stress. She'd manufactured stories that had nothing to do with reality because his dad had left.

Della *had* been through hell. He'd read the file. And knowing the man who'd caused it was now on the loose could trigger all kinds of anxiety. But he still had the sense that there was something she was keeping in the dark.

So maybe originally he'd dismissed it. "But I'm doing my due diligence." He sealed up the kit. "Fingerprints are ready to be processed. Despite my gut telling me there's something she's hiding, I'm investigating this like any other case. And I'm not going to let anything happen to her."

"I know you won't. You're a good man, Tony. Even if you don't like Christmas."

"Who told you that?"

"Olivia Tazwell said you're the only one not doing Secret Santa at the office."

"You're gonna get on my case about that too? Don't you have more important things to do? Plan a wedding. Find a missing person." He chuckled, desperate to throw off any inquest about his dislike of the holiday.

"Someone's gotta keep you on your toes."

Anthony moved to the door and held up the fingerprints. "I'll have someone from the station pick this up. Where's Nixon now?"

"With Amelia, in a storage area. I'll show you."

Penny showed him to a small room in the middle of the building. Without windows, it was a little dark. Shelves of extinguishers and air tanks lined one wall. Paper products filled another. Della stood alone at a table in the middle of the space, wrapping a children's board game.

Penny left to find Bryce while Anthony walked in with his case. "I've got the fingerprints from the locker. I just need a set from you to compare. You probably have one on file, but couldn't hurt to do a more recent one."

Della looked up from her taping. "We can do that here." She finished her present and set it aside.

Anthony pulled out the ink pad and got to work.

"So...you believe me?" Suspicion laced Della's words.

He deserved it. He believed she was scared. He believed she had a legitimate reason for that fear. He just wasn't sure Vaynes was skulking around the firehouse when the man could be hitchhiking to Canada. But he also wanted Della to know he was a good cop. "We want all our bases covered."

She studied him a beat and nodded. She placed her first finger on the ink pad. Anthony helped to place the print in the corresponding box. The second he touched her smooth skin, a sensation almost like an electrical pulse ran up his arm.

Okay, that was weird. Keep it professional, Thomas.

Her hand was warm, fingers long and slender. It had been a while since he'd held a woman's hand. Everyone liked to think he had an active dating life, but the truth was, he didn't want to get that close to a woman. Close enough where she could take what was left of his heart and demolish it. He'd rather keep things light and casual. Safe.

So, better shove aside whatever that reaction was and move on.

He finished taking her prints and closed the kit. "I'm not sure how long it will take to get results."

"I understand." A pause. "And thank you for taking this seriously."

He still wasn't completely convinced that Vaynes was harassing her. But he'd hate to miss something. Again. And it could be someone else messing with Della. Either way, he had a job to do. He would do it to the best of his ability.

"I'm not going to let anything happen to you." He looked her in the eye. This was at least something he could promise and deliver on.

High-pitched alarms sounded. "Rescue 5. Truck 14. Structure fire."

"That's us," Della said. "We've got a call."

"Then I'm coming with you."

"You're coming with us?"

"Your job is to put out the fire. My job is to watch your back."

"Okay." She gave him a hint of a smile, the first he'd seen from her—at least, the first one she'd ever directed at him.

And oh man, was it ever enticing.

SIX

Della drove the fire truck and pulled up to an old building in the downtown area. At least this was one instance she had control. She was the one behind the wheel. Zoe and Izan sat behind her while Amelia rode up front. Lights from the other emergency vehicles flashed red and blue in the driving rain and sleet. Officer Thomas's car was probably one of them since he couldn't ride on the truck.

Izan Collins jumped out. "Let's stop this fire from taking out the whole block. These buildings down here are old."

"Hey, Izan, you bringing a date to the Christmas party? I heard you got pretty cozy with Olivia Tazwell during that hostage situation at the church." Zoe plopped her helmet on and grabbed the tank with her number on it.

Della watched for his reaction as she hiked up her own air tank and tightened the shoulder straps. Even with Izan's tanned skin, a blush crept through.

"What can I say? Being trapped together makes the heart grow fonder. She finally agreed to go out with me." He tried to play it off, but that grin, the one that had his dimples popping out in full force, was there. He'd had a thing for Olivia for a long time, but it hadn't gone anywhere. But something must've changed, since the word was they were now officially a couple. "So we'll be there. How about you ladies?"

Zoe shrugged as she pulled her irons—a Halligan tool and crowbar—out of the truck compartment. "I'll be at the party with my boys. My husband is still deployed. I hear Kianna is looking for a date."

Della checked her air tank. "The party is next week. Isn't she cutting it close?"

"Which means she still has a few days to decide." Zoe tugged her gloves on and turned toward the building.

Della wasn't even sure she'd stay long at the Christmas party. For sure she wasn't going to worry about a date. But the toy drive—now, that was her baby. She wouldn't miss it for anything. And the sooner they put out this fire, the sooner she could get back to her preparations. "Let's do this."

Gray-green smoke poured out of the front windows of a shop, but no sign of flames yet. Not from the outside. The discolored billows were enough reason for concern. Something toxic was burning. At one time, the building had been a café, then a thrift store. Now it was an insurance office with a couple apartments above it.

Della and the others found Lieutenant Patterson talking with Bryce. As captain, he would be the scene commander on this call.

The lieutenant pointed to the building and yelled over the sirens and alarms. "Rescue Squad 5 is going to the back while you fight the fire up front."

"You got it, boss." Izan grabbed the hose while Zoe and Della attached one end to the truck. Once they were ready, the trio stepped toward the building, but Officer Thomas approached. "Nixon, make sure to stay between Izan and Zoe. I would go in there if I could, but—"

"Don't worry. We watch out for each other." Della pulled her SCBA mask on, then the helmet.

"We got this, Tony. Let her do her job." Izan's voice came through the speaker in his mask.

Anthony backed away but didn't look happy about it. Maybe he was taking the threat more seriously than she thought. He actually seemed pretty concerned about her. But for now, they had a fire to put out.

Izan wedged his Halligan tool into the door frame. "Hit!"

Della aimed the flat axe head and swung. The one hit was all it took. The door flew open, allowing thick gray clouds to pour out. Della followed Izan and crawled under the smoke hanging from the ceiling. Zoe, right behind her, should have the hose head. They got to work, assessing the fire, finding the main source around the corner of the front room and in an old kitchen.

"Let's get water on it," Izan called out. Zoe passed up the nozzle. Once situated, they called to start the water. Izan aimed the hose while Zoe added more slack as needed.

Della blocked out the chatter from the other teams on the comms and called over the radio that they were ready for water. She stumbled on a rug and readjusted her grip on the hose. She shut her eyes a quick second, which only made her dizzy.

"You okay, Nix?"

"Is it just me, or is the smoke getting thicker?" She didn't need anyone thinking she couldn't do her job. She pushed all the discomfort aside and focused once more on the fire. Her eyes stung, but she could see the indicator lights on her mask. Green lights. Plenty of air. So why did her eyes burn?

They stepped farther into the kitchen, dragging the heavy hose with them. Della tripped and fell to one knee.

"Hey, you o—" Zoe stopped mid-sentence. She leaned over to help her up. "Della, get out of here. Your mask is filling with smoke!"

"What?"

No wonder her eyes hurt so much. She blinked them, trying to stop the burning as she stumbled out of the building. She ripped off her helmet, and even without loosening the straps, the mask hung off the side. She gulped the fresh air.

Anthony and Bryce ran over, Kianna Russell at their heels with an oxygen tank.

"What happened?" Anthony asked, his voice tight, rain dripping off his coat and hat.

Bryce helped free Della from her air tank. "Something's wrong with the SCBA. Her mask had smoke in it." He inspected the mask and valves. "Here. Look at the straps. They were cut partway. If they're hanging on by a few threads, it wouldn't take much for you to lose the suction you need for a good seal."

"Why don't you take some oxygen? We don't know how much smoke you inhaled." Kianna handed her the mask.

Della held it but didn't put it up to her face. "I inspected the whole thing this morning. Everything was fine."

Kianna pushed the mask onto Della's face. "Focus on your breathing."

Crawford and Officer Thomas shared a look.

"Go back and check the footage. I inspected my unit first thing." Her voice sounded muffled under the plastic covering the lower half of her face.

"It's okay, Nixon. We're on your side. Try to relax." Kianna looked up from taking her pulse.

"Easy for you to say. You don't have a serial killer after you." She stared down Officer Thomas. He still didn't look convinced. Like she'd sabotaged her own equipment? "You have to believe me though. I don't skimp out on my inspections."

"I didn't say I don't believe you." Anthony cocked his head sideways. "I'm trying to understand what happened and why a serial killer would sabotage your equipment."

"What happened is someone tampered with her mask."

Bryce looked around them, eyes narrowed as he studied the crowd gathering outside the police line. Even in the horrible weather, people gawked. "We shouldn't be out in the open like this."

"He's right." Officer Thomas moved to block her from the crowd's view. "Think you can walk?"

"Of course I can. I'm fine."

"Russell, is she okay to sit in the back of the ambulance?" he asked Kianna, as if Della couldn't speak for herself.

Her friend nodded. "I can bring the cot."

"I don't need a cot." Della wasn't going to be rolled anywhere when she had two capable feet.

Bryce carried her damaged mask over to Amelia while Kianna and Anthony walked Della over to the truck. She kept her head down, the oxygen on. Anthony wrapped an arm around her shoulders as he helped her up the steps of the ambulance. She couldn't tell if he was simply standing between her and the crowd or if he was afraid she'd keel over, but for a moment she felt safer. The next deep breath came easier.

She sat on the cot while Kianna took her pulse again and set an O2 meter on her finger. "Your numbers look okay. How are you feeling?"

She could handle a little burning of the eyes. "I was hardly in there that long."

"I want you to rest here, and I'll check your numbers again later. If everything is normal, I'll release you back to duty." Kianna moved to the front seat and chatted with her partner Trace while she typed on a tablet.

Della tried not to look at Officer Thomas. He stared out the window, eyes sharp and focused on something intently. She'd never really seen him like this. Usually it would be in passing, when the fire was out or the dangerous situation averted. In those moments, he'd flirt and joke around. Well, with everyone else, at least. He'd approached her once but hadn't said anything before moving on. She'd assumed that's what he was always like, one of those happy-go-lucky types that let others do the heavy lifting while he scoped out a date for Friday night.

But in this moment, he was vigilant. Quiet. Intense. There was nothing lighthearted about him now, from his tense lips to his hands flexed in a fist as he leaned against the door of the ambulance.

"Do you see something?" she asked him.

A muscle in his jaw flexed. "Not really. Between the rain and smoke, there's not much to see."

Della dropped the mask and sat up. "I should be out there. With my team."

"You need to stay here." He glanced over, a soft nod in her direction. "But I know what you mean."

"You ever been injured on the job? Unable to work?"

With one more glance out the window, Officer Thomas sank into the bench running along the side of the truck. "Not injured. But...I screwed something up on a job, and now, instead of being out there tracking Vaynes and Mackey down with the rest of my team, I've been reassigned."

Ah. The pieces came together. "You're stuck babysitting me."

"Aw, come on, Nixon. Don't say it like that. It's not personal. It's just—" He grunted, snatched his black beanie off, and ran his fingers through his hair. The combed hairdo now loosened, left his wavy dark locks to fall across his forehead. She'd never seen him so disheveled. It was almost as if she were seeing the real Officer Thomas. The man with*out* the mask.

"Then what is it?"

His blue eyes locked onto her. "I let someone get away. Now everyone else is fighting the elements, trucking through mud and rain and ice because I botched up. And here I am in a cozy firehouse all day, plenty of hot coffee at my disposal, watching over a beautiful, capable woman who's already surrounded by a team of fighters, while everyone else tries to clean up my mess. Hardly seems fair."

Beautiful? Capable? That's how he saw her? Usually he seemed to avoid her. There was a lot she didn't really know about Officer Thomas. But she'd heard the rumors. "The joke around the station is that you don't like to get your clothes dirty. You have a collection of expensive shoes that cost more than I make in a year, and you're saying that you'd really rather be out in the miserable cold and mud hunting down criminals?"

"I want to prove that I'm a good cop." He shrugged. "And I look for deals on quality shoes. Never pay full price." He winked at her.

Maybe she'd misjudged him.

"Officer Thomas, I—"

"It's Anthony."

A beat passed. Her pulse kicked up a notch.

"All right…Anthony. I just wanted to apologize for this morning. I was…a little harsh."

"A little?" He quirked an eyebrow. "Either that or you did a horrible job trying to flatter me by calling me the precinct's poster boy. I mean, I like a compliment as much as the next guy, but you really need to work on your delivery."

She released a rueful chuckle. "Okay, I was a lot harsh. I didn't think you were taking the threat seriously."

His lips hitched up into half a smile as he smoothed his hair back. "I might be a little skeptical about who or what the threat is, but I'll make sure you're safe. I promise."

She'd have to watch herself with a handsome smile like that, but she couldn't deny he did care about doing his job well.

"Okay. And you can call me Della."

SEVEN

Something about the way she looked at him sucked all the oxygen out of the ambulance and made him feel like a teenager with a crush again. Anthony would have to watch himself in any confined spaces he shared with Della Nixon.

You can call me Della.

A warmth for once in her brown-eyed gaze, instead of an icy dismissal, felt like winning a well-fought-for prize. Maybe because from the first day he'd seen her on the job, he'd known she was completely out of his league, striking him dumb and unable to complete a simple sentence.

Kianna gave her the all clear, but Lieutenant Patterson sent her back to the firehouse with Anthony instead of letting her help with the cleanup once the fire was out. "I need you to finish wrapping those gifts and getting the final details ready for the toy drive."

It was a safer option, so Anthony didn't dispute it, but Della seemed frustrated by her boss's command. He held an umbrella over her head as they rushed to his car. He cranked the heat and headed back to the station. She shivered on the passenger side, glaring out the window at the sleet and freezing rain. Maybe he could help her focus on something else.

"Tell me about this toy drive," he said. "Sounds like it's a big deal."

She turned toward him. "How have you lived in Last Chance and not heard about the toy drive? We do it every Christmas."

Oh, right. A Christmas thing. He should've picked a different subject. He tried to keep his smile nonchalant. "I'm not really into the whole Christmas thing."

"The *Christmas thing*? I thought you went to church with Collins and some of the other guys."

"So?"

"Christmas is one of the most important holidays in the church. God coming down to earth and all? That seems like a big deal. You sound like you'd rather have a tooth pulled. Without pain medication."

Anthony tugged on his collar. "I believe that the Son of God taking on flesh is a big deal. But I've never been big on the commercialized version—people spending more money than they should on over-the-top presents, outlandish displays of obnoxious yard decorations, overeating super unhealthy food. Doesn't seem much like celebrating the birth of Christ."

"I can see that, but…I dunno, I guess I think more about families coming together, people gathering to celebrate something good for once, decorating and bringing light to dark places. The toy drive is just trying to give children in tough circumstances something special, to show them that they matter. We decorate the firehouse, the trucks, and someone will dress up as Santa and hand out presents. And for these kids, one toy can really make a difference. It's my favorite part of the holiday."

"Really?"

She smiled. "Yeah. In fact, I'm in the process of becoming a foster parent so I can help kids out that really need it."

The tenderness in her voice struck him deep. Seeing the holiday through her eyes, well, it was what he'd wanted Christmas to be when he was a kid. For a few months, he'd been in the foster system himself, waiting for his mother to be released from psychiatric treatment. The fact that Della wanted to help children in similar situations impacted him more than he was ready to admit.

"Well, I would hate to disappoint children. Do you need help with anything?" If he could help Della forget her troubles for a bit, it would be worth it.

"I do still need a Santa…" She smirked from the other side of the car.

He shook his head and laughed. "Uh, that's a hard no. I'm not jolly enough for that role. But if you need a grinch, I'm your guy."

"It was worth a shot." She smiled at him, a little glint in her eye. "But I don't think of you as a grinch. Green isn't your color."

"You don't think so?"

"I mean, you look good in any color but—" She cleared her throat, mumbled something under her breath. "I'm gonna stop talking now."

"What was that?" he asked. "I must be hearing things, because it kinda sounded like you think I look good."

Her cheeks flushed bright red. "Shut up and keep your eyes on the road. At this rate, your ego won't fit through the cargo door at the station."

"Yes, ma'am." Anthony grinned. With a lot of effort, he pulled his focus back to what was happening outside. Her blushing smile almost had him reconsidering the Santa thing.

Almost.

It certainly had him considering other things. Like asking her out, if he could pull the words together. Probably not the best timing while protecting her, but he couldn't deny the hope that welled up inside. Hope that if he did ask, maybe she wouldn't brush him off.

Back at the almost empty firehouse, they shed their wet jackets and gear and got to work in the small storage room again while waiting for the others to get back. Della measured out wrapping paper and cut while he folded and taped. Their pile grew until she pulled another box out.

"What else happens at this toy drive?" Anthony put a sticky green bow on a LEGO set they'd wrapped.

"We'll have a big meal for the kids and their caretakers here at the firehouse. Some games and crafts too. Santa is the big finale. After the guests leave, we have our work Christmas party. It's fun."

She glanced up at him through her dark lashes, her lips tipping up into a slight smile like she was going to say more— and froze. She swayed, her body listing to one side before she caught herself on the edge of the table.

"Della, are you—"

She swallowed hard. Closed her eyes. "I just got really dizzy."

A wave of nausea hit Anthony. How had he not registered the onset of a headache?

His migraines often came on hard and fast, but he usually felt one before it was this bad and took his meds to stave it off. He must've been distracted.

The whole room tilted. For a quick moment, he looked up, trying to figure out what was going on. "Up there. What's that?" He pointed to the barely visible cloud of white gas dropping into the room from a vent.

Della started to look up but then fell to the ground before Anthony could catch her.

"Della!"

Whatever it was coming through that vent, it wasn't good.

Air. They needed fresh air.

He dragged Della to the door. Collapsed against it. The knob didn't budge.

Locked in.

His legs refused to work. Anthony dropped down to the ground next to Della. Her eyes didn't open when he tried to rouse her. She moaned, clutched her head, and curled into a ball.

Thoughts didn't form. But pure instinct had him pounding on the door. They needed out. Now.

Help. He needed to call for help. Anthony reached for his radio.

Not there. He'd set it on a charger when they came inside.

Phone? His hands felt heavy and clunky as he searched his pockets. His vision blurred, blackness creeping in on the sides. He pounded the door again.

They were trapped, and he was losing consciousness.

Some protector he'd turned out to be.

EIGHT

As she lay on the floor dying, Della could've sworn she heard a laugh. A familiar, evil laugh. She was close enough she kicked at the door. But with everything swirling in and out of focus, maybe it was only a horrible nightmare. The pain sure felt real. Each pound on the door sent a shockwave through her skull. They needed to get out. She couldn't breathe.

Anthony's eyes rolled back into his head as he leaned against the thick metal door.

Lord, help. And please don't let him get away with this.

Because no doubt Jason Vaynes was behind all this.

Footsteps on the other side of the door stopped. The knob jiggled. Anthony fell into the hall. Della tried to move but couldn't. Strong hands dragged her out of the room.

"What happened?" Penny Mitchell's face blurred.

"CO2," was all Della could get out.

"We need oxygen!" Penny called down the hallway before dragging Della farther away from the storage room. More footsteps sounded as Della closed her eyes and concentrated on pulling in each breath. The cold from the linoleum floor seeped through her shirt, chilling her back and legs.

Someone shoved a plastic oxygen mask in her hand and held it over her nose and mouth. "Try to breathe slow and deep."

Della looked up to see Kianna yet again shoving an oxygen mask in her face. Penny held one out to Anthony, who'd also made it farther out into the hall and away from the storage room. Trace propped him against the wall next to her. After a few minutes of fresh air, they moved to the back of the ambulance, where they both rested and stayed hooked up to the oxygen monitors and tanks. Eventually, the nausea and dizziness faded.

Voices and sounds from the cargo bay came in through the open back doors of the ambulance. The rest of the crew must be back from the call.

Penny came up to the rig, wearing gloves and carrying a fire extinguisher.

"Is that what I think it is?" Anthony sat up on the cot.

"If you think it's a carbon dioxide extinguisher that was fixed in the ventilation system, filling the room with poisonous gas and trying to kill you both, then yes."

A chill ran down Della's spine. Vaynes.

"I went back to the women's locker room and looked at the vents in there. There's one big enough a man can fit in it."

"You think that's how our killer got in the building?" Anthony asked.

Penny nodded. "I tracked the system through the building and found where it was probably accessed. Found some threads of fabric caught on a sharp corner."

"Okay then." Anthony blew out a short breath and looked at Della. "You were right. Someone *is* trying to kill you. And with that missing photo, I think you're also right in assuming it's Vaynes." He shook his head a little. "I just don't get why the guy would go through all these elaborate plans if he simply wants revenge. There's a lot of easier ways to kill someone."

Penny set the extinguisher on the ground and sat on the bumper of the ambulance. "Vaynes has a sick mind. Insane. He would rather mess with his victims and torment them. It's worth the risk of getting caught to him because it's all about the game. And I spoke with the warden at the prison. His cell is one big creep-fest all about his obsession to torture and kill a fire-fighter. I think it's safe to assume it's Della."

A sheepish look crossed Anthony's face. "Sorry I didn't believe it at first."

Della sat up and let the words sink in.

He believed her.

Relief rushed in, easing some of the burden she'd become so accustomed to that she didn't realize the weight of it until it was lifted. For a moment it was almost euphoric.

But the voice she couldn't escape was right there too, and everything crashed in even harder.

You lied. In a court of law. You lied after swearing on the Bible that you would only tell the truth.

And the desperate urge to defend herself rose up.

But I had to. I had no other choice. I couldn't let him get away with it.

And now, if she told the truth, she could lose everything Lily had fought so hard for.

Because it was *Lily*'s dream to go into social work, to become a foster parent and help kids that had no one else. A dream Della shared and wanted to fulfill on Lily's behalf. But it would be hard enough to qualify as a single woman. If she had a felony on her record…

Nothing she did drowned out the incessant conversation in her head. Over and over again, like some horrific carousel ride.

Chief Macon James marched up to the ambulance. "What's this I hear about a serial killer trying to take you out?"

Della straightened. "I'm sorry, Chief. I—"

"You don't need to apologize. I'm just worried. Are you okay?"

Why did it feel like she should apologize, like it was her fault? The weight of the lie grew, pressing on her chest. "I'm much better now. I'll get back to work, sir."

"No way. You and Officer Thomas need to get checked out at the hospital. I won't make a bad situation worse."

This time Anthony shook his head. "I'm goo—"

"You will both report to the hospital and get a doctor's all clear before returning to work. Understood? And I'm not beyond calling Chief Barnes, just in case you think of going around me." His look was one of concern but also unrelenting firmness.

"Yes, sir," Della said.

Anthony nodded and slumped back on the cot as soon as Chief James walked away.

"Come on, you two. I'll give you a ride over there." Penny removed her gloves and pulled out her phone. "I think Andi is working. I'll see if she can get you in and out quickly."

"Who's Andi?" Della whispered over to Anthony.

"Bryce's little sister. She used to be a paramedic, but now she's working as a nurse and applying to med school." He hopped out of the back of the truck and helped her down.

The nausea was almost gone, but the pounding in her head and weakness in her muscles couldn't be ignored.

Three hours and three ibuprofen later, Della had her medical clearance. Andi walked her down the hall. "I hope next time I see you it will be under better circumstances. Tony said he's waiting for you in the lobby. Right through those double doors there." She left her with a friendly wave.

It took more effort than normal to push open the door into the lobby, but at least she was on her own two feet. Two feet that felt clunky, but still, she was upright.

"Doing okay?" Anthony stood up from the blue padded chair

in the lobby. His light touch on her arm seared through the fabric of her uniform.

Crazy how a simple touch and empathetic blue eyes could almost turn her into a blubbering mess.

But Vaynes had been close. Too close to taking her out. Della couldn't shake the chill from the time she'd spent lying on the cold cement floor in the firehouse. Surely that was the only reason Anthony's touch warmed her, affected her so deeply. She swallowed past the lump in her throat and pasted on an attempt at a smile. "Blood work came back fine. You?"

"Same." He pushed his hair back. "Bryce brought my vehicle, so I'm at your disposal. What now?"

"The only thing I want is a slice of deep-dish olive and sausage pizza, and bed." She rubbed her arms, trying to generate some heat.

Maybe she didn't even need to eat. Not with the huge pit in her midsection growing by the second.

But there was no way she could actually sleep. Not with Vaynes out there.

"The captain assigned another cop to watch over your place tonight, but—" Anthony's thumbs hooked on his vest, but he didn't finish. He might've been grinding his teeth together the way his jaw flexed.

"What?"

He looked at her, all sense of playfulness gone, his gaze intense. "It's personal now. I don't want you out of my sight until Vaynes is back behind bars. And don't you live with your grandmother?"

"She's spending the winter with friends in Arizona. I'll be fine."

"Maybe it would be better if we both stayed at the firehouse tonight. Night shift will be there, and whichever officer they assign to us can stick around too. I know I'll sleep better if you're protected by more than one person."

She hated how the weaker part of her melted at his words. Someone looking out for her? Someone believing her?

But he was just trying to do his job. She should remember that. He was a better cop than she'd given him credit for. She couldn't read anything more into it.

"I can sleep at the station. There's more I can do for the event next week, but you should go home, Anthony. You're off duty now."

"I'm not gonna sleep well at my apartment, wondering if you're safe. You're stuck with me, Della. At least until we catch this guy." His handsome smile—and yeah, it was a true Anthony Thomas smolder—only made her feel worse.

She turned away from him and stared at the poster promoting proper handwashing techniques. "Well, maybe you shouldn't be stuck with me. You don't deserve to be targeted by a serial killer. You were hurt because you were with *me*. Go home."

"Hey." His voice was gentle. A warm hand cupped her elbow as he moved to face her. "You don't deserve it either. I know this move. Probably even invented it."

"What are you talking about?"

"You think if you push others away, you're protecting them. But it's not true. Isolating yourself makes you more vulnerable because you have to face whatever it is alone. Together, we'll have a better chance of protecting others and capturing Vaynes. So let those of us who care help." He gave her a teasing smirk. "All right?"

She rolled her eyes but chuckled. "You don't have to be so nice."

Anthony sighed. "If I had done my job night before last, we might not even be in this situation. I have a lot to make up for."

"You mean Sosa?"

"Yeah. It's the second time that guy's gotten the upper hand on me. He hurt people I care about." He looked at her, his gaze earnest and sincere. "I'm not gonna let it happen again."

Della nodded and tucked those words around her heart as they drove back to the firehouse. The words wandered around her head as she went through her nightly routine and washed her face.

He hurt people I care about. I'm not gonna let it happen again.

Did that mean he cared about *her*?

For a fleeting second, she was tempted. Tempted to lean on someone else for a change. Tempted to relax her guard. Tempted to see if there was anything more to Anthony Thomas than a handsome face and gallant words.

What-ifs rolled through her mind as she brushed her teeth and her hair. She lay in bed and stared at the tiny green light shining on the smoke detector on the ceiling.

Okay, yeah, she could see Anthony might be someone she could care about too.

But if he knew what she had done, he might not feel so inclined to help her. He upheld the law, tracked down criminals.

He should take her in and lock her up too.

She sat up and punched her pillow into shape. If only she could fix her life as easily. Being locked up and behind bars might even be an improvement with the way fear had a choke-hold on her. Maybe if she could unload the burden, tell the truth, she'd finally find some peace in the quiet of the night.

She'd told herself she'd lied for Lily's sake. That any price to pay was worth it. But she hadn't known back then the heavy burden and inner turmoil she'd shackled herself to. Now, if the truth came out, she could kiss the opportunity of doing foster care goodbye. She needed to take this secret to the grave.

But she couldn't get Anthony out of her head as she lay back down.

He hurt people I care about. I'm not gonna let it happen again.

She pictured Amelia helping her wrap presents.

I mean it, Nixon. We're here for you. If you're having a problem, I want to help.

Penny and Bryce were tenacious. She hadn't known them long, but she had no doubt they weren't going to let this matter with Vaynes drop, no matter what.

So maybe the whole world didn't need to know her secret. But maybe she could trust a very select few. People who would understand why she'd lied. People who would keep the truth to themselves.

They'd have to, or she could lose her job, her chance at being a foster parent. But if they could be trusted, maybe sharing the burden would release the building pressure inside enough that she could sleep again.

NINE

Anthony stayed at the firehouse despite Della's protest, but there was no way he could sleep just yet. Not that he was fishing for compliments or gratitude, but the more he insisted on helping Della, the more he could feel her pushing him away.

Finding Penny and Bryce sitting alone at a table in the break room, he asked them about her. "I tried to apologize for not taking the missing items seriously and everything but"—he crossed his arms and leaned against the counter—"I get the impression she's pushing me away. Like I offended her or something. What gives?"

Bryce looked at Penny and shrugged. "Don't ask me to explain women. This is all you."

Penny chuckled as she poured two mugs of coffee and offered one to Bryce. "Not everything is about you, Tony. She has a demanding job, both physically and mentally. And being a woman, she's got a lot to prove. She probably doesn't want everyone looking at her like she's the weak link. She might be trying to save face. Not look like a victim."

"I suppose that makes sense. I just thought…" Anthony

stared down at his Dolce & Gabbana black sneakers. He felt a little more put together in his own clothes. His straight-leg blackwashed jeans and Stone Island sweater were the right mix of casual comfort and style. But he still didn't have the words.

"What? Surprised she's not falling at your feet and flirting back with you?" Penny gave him a pointed look.

Bryce laughed.

"Aw, come on, guys." He pushed off the counter and stood, facing them both. "I'm trying here. And I'm telling you, my gut says something else is going on. Like she's hiding something, or there's more to it than she's telling us."

"You're right."

The three of them spun around to see Della standing in the doorway. Even in her joggers and cropped sweatshirt, hair loose and falling down in shiny black waves, she was gorgeous. No makeup or stiff uniform to project a sense of formality, just Della.

She slumped into a chair and brought her leg up, her arms wrapped around the one knee while the other leg dangled down. "I can't do it anymore," she whispered. Her eyes were a little red and puffy, like she'd been crying.

Anthony's heart tugged. "Della, we're here to help you. You don't have to do this alone."

Penny reached over and gave Della's arm a little squeeze. "What's going on, Nix? What were we right about?"

Della looked up and swallowed hard. "I lied."

"About what?" Penny asked.

"Vaynes."

The room went silent. Only the sputter of the coffee maker and whir of the fan could be heard.

The misery on Della's face and the tears shimmering in her big brown eyes hit Anthony in the chest like a battering ram. He stilled, not wanting to spook her and stop the confession.

After a shuddering breath, Della continued. "I never saw

him. I lied on the stand and said I did, but I didn't. I never actually *saw* Jason Vaynes when Lily and I were captured." She blew out a long, shaky breath.

How long had she been carrying that around? More questions flooded Anthony's mind. "Are you saying it was someone else? That you falsely accused him?"

Della's head shot up. "No! It was *him*. I know it was. Like I told you before, he kept me drugged most of the time I was captured. And he had a creepy mask on anytime he came into the room where I was chained. But I could hear his voice. Hear Lily begging and screaming. And when I was awake, Lily told me everything. It was the same guy from the bar. She described him."

"So it was still Vaynes who did it," Penny said. "Why did you lie?"

"I have no doubt it was him. But I knew. If I took the stand and told the truth, that I never actually saw him, as drugged up as I was, there was a good possibility his lawyer could discredit me. The prosecutor told me there wasn't a lot of physical evidence tying Vaynes to the crime scene. I realized my testimony was vital to putting him away. And I—" She paused a moment. "I couldn't let there be any chance of his getting away with it. Not after Lily died to help me escape." Tears tracked down her face as she looked up at Anthony.

He could understand it. How many times had his own testimony as a cop been twisted or misconstrued, allowing a criminal to go free? He couldn't imagine what it would've been like for Della to take the stand under those circumstances and have her witness torn to shreds.

The injustice of it burned, to know Vaynes had done the unthinkable to vulnerable young women and could've gotten away with it. Because she wasn't wrong. It happened more than it should. And even now, he ran loose, still tormenting Della.

He approached the table slowly and sat across from her.

"I can't imagine what you've been through. I can understand why you did it. Probably would've been tempted to do the same in your shoes. But regardless of your case, he's still a convicted criminal who escaped and needs to be brought in. He still attempted murder today—twice, if he's the one who tampered with your mask and set off that extinguisher. So yeah, our focus needs to be about bringing him in. And I'm definitely not going to let him get near you again."

Della's shoulders lifted and pulled back, maybe helping her take the first full breath she'd taken in a long time. Her eyes were clear and focused, no more shadows or darkness hiding in them.

But he also had to tell her the truth. "But once he's captured, Della, we'll have to face the truth about the perjury. We can't keep hiding."

"I know it's the right thing to do, but my grandmother and I are in process to become foster care providers. If I'm charged with perjury, it will be a felony on my record, and there's no way they'll accept me. Not to mention I could lose my job."

Bryce set down his mug. "You're right. And it will take a lot of guts to come clean. But sometimes the right thing is the hard thing."

"And some good legal counsel will help too." Penny squeezed her hand from across the table. "But more than that, *God* can do amazing things with the broken pieces of our lives. We don't want to limit Him. When we choose our way over His, it's really about our lack of trust. And that lie is gonna eat you up from the inside out."

Della blew out a long breath. "It already has." She looked up at them with tears hovering on her lashes. "But I'm scared. What if they let him go free? What if I lose everything?"

"You won't lose us." Anthony needed her to hear him. He was finally seeing the woman behind the aloof mask. He could see how fear and trauma would make her think that lying was the only option. But he didn't want her to have to live that way. "The truth will set you free, Della. And whatever happens, we'll stand with you come what may. For now, let's keep you safe and capture Vaynes."

"You guys are gonna help?"

"You're one of us, Della. We take care of our own." Penny looked over at Anthony and Bryce. "Right, guys?"

"Right." They answered together.

Della's eyes lit. No more shadowed expressions. She'd always had determination, but now there was something more. Now there was hope. "I've got an idea."

"That's what I'm talking about." Anthony grinned. "Spit it out."

Della laid both of her hands flat on the table. "We use me as bait."

TEN

Della was done being a victim. She was done lying. Done waiting. So she laid out her plan to the others.

Anthony balked. "Are you crazy? Putting yourself out as bait for a serial killer?"

She'd thought he'd be impressed. Maybe even eager. "You want to catch him, don't you? I mean, that's all you've been focused on."

"Yeah, but not by risking your *life*." He turned to Penny and Bryce. "Tell her she's crazy, guys. This is not the plan."

Bryce narrowed his eyes like he was actually considering it.

Penny studied Della. "I dunno. Let's not write it off when we haven't even heard the details yet."

"We don't need details. We need a new plan." Anthony pushed off the chair and paced.

"Penny's right. We should at least listen to what Della has to say. The weather is awful out there. There's a ton of people trying to track Vaynes down and getting nowhere. So maybe we lure him to us. Let's hear her out."

At least Bryce was on board.

Anthony, however, didn't look happy about it, but he stopped pacing and folded his arms against his chest. He had street clothes on, and yes, the man had style. His outfit was not off the Target clearance rack like hers. But she knew he really cared about protecting her and bringing Vaynes in. So after all his talk of wanting to do anything to capture these escaped convicts, why was he so reluctant now?

It wasn't because he actually cared about her, was it?

Stop it, Della. Do not go there. Just lay out the plan.

After a self-shakedown, she began. "Vaynes is after me. Why don't I go back to my place alone tomorrow evening. You guys set up a perimeter. My neighbors next door are gone until after the holidays, so you could wait there. Instead of him taking us off guard, we'll be ready and waiting."

"And we're supposed to let him come after you? What if he gets past us? What if he decides game over and just wants to kill you before we can get there?" Anthony glowered.

"He's a serial killer. He's all about the torture. He'll take his time." Penny tapped a finger on the table.

"Oh, that's comforting." He paused. "Have you forgotten? I hate to admit it, but he's smart. He's evaded us for days already." Anthony straddled a chair, a whiff of his designer scent distracting Della for a moment.

But she couldn't lose focus now. "So I'll wear some sort of tracker. We can set up cameras."

"Don't you think he'll be expecting a trap like that?" Penny asked.

"Maybe. But why not try? I go about my normal routine, and we post undercover cops in each place I go. I don't live an exciting life. It's pretty much work, the gym, church, and home. He'll strike at some point, but we'll have people waiting."

Anthony shook his head. "I don't like the idea of putting you at risk like that. And I'm not sure the chief will go for it. All extra resources and manpower are going into the search for Vaynes, Blair Mackey, and the missing prison guard. I doubt the department will want to pull people off the search."

"There's three of us right here, and I bet we can get a few more on board." Penny sipped her coffee. "Jude would help."

"Who's Jude?" Della asked her.

"My former partner from when I was with the ATF. He's married to Bryce's sister Andi."

An ATF agent sounded promising. "See, we can make this work. I just don't want to hide in the dark anymore. I'd rather keep working and doing my normal thing."

Bryce seemed to be mulling it over. "If we stay in communication, we can tag team, someone always there wherever she goes."

Della read the room. Penny and Bryce seemed on board. But Anthony's lips were still pressed into a thin line. She needed to sell this.

"See? I'm not really baiting Vaynes as much as living my normal life, with some carefully selected bodyguards watching over me." He still didn't look convinced. "And we'll still have one cop on protective detail."

Penny set her coffee down and leaned closer. "And then maybe that person looks distracted, and we create an ideal situation for Vaynes to make a move."

"I think you guys are nuts." Anthony's slight shake of his head didn't bode well.

Bryce clapped him on the shoulder. "That's okay, Pretty Boy. We can handle this without you." He rubbed his hands together. "Let's come up with a schedule and plan."

"I'm not going to sit back and *not* help," Anthony grumbled as he switched his chair around and scooched it up to the table. "If there's a rotation, I better be in it."

That was more like it. Despite Anthony's objections, she did feel better with him watching her back and being a part of her security detail.

But she needed to remind herself he was only doing his job and to keep her heart out of it. Because if she let herself think there was anything more to this protective vibe she was reading, she'd be as delusional as a grown adult still believing in Santa Claus.

ELEVEN

Anthony woke early the next morning. Not that he was at all rested. How could he be? His friends were crazy. Taunting a serial killer? It was asking for trouble. But clearly, he was outnumbered. Still, if they thought he was going to sit by and watch, they were wrong. He wasn't going to leave Della's side until Vaynes was back in prison.

In a straitjacket.

Or better yet, secure in some black site detention center built to withstand terrorist attacks and earthquakes.

At least Della looked like she'd gotten some decent sleep after they'd talked. Even at the firehouse, with plenty of others around to watch over her, he couldn't relax his brain enough for some REM.

Della sat on the other side of his squad car, her presence adding to the ultra-alert vibe running through him. He was on the clock already, but Della's shift didn't start until this afternoon, so they headed to the gym. And he might go mad if he thought about the risk they were taking, so he better find something else to talk about.

"Do you work out every morning?" he asked her.

She set her pre-workout drink in the cupholder. "Yeah. I know I can use the gym at the firehouse, but it's easier for me to stay focused when I'm not on call. I know I won't be interrupted this way."

"That takes a lot of dedication." His admiration for her continued to climb.

"I don't have a choice. I have to stay in shape. It's a job requirement. The second I go lax, I let my team down. And I fought too hard to be a firefighter to lose it by slacking off."

"Did you always know you wanted to be one?"

"No. As a kid I had a very different plan. After my parents died, I decided I was going to become rich and open up orphanages back in India, where my grandmother is from."

Anthony pictured young Della Nixon ready to take on the world. "And how were you going to do that?"

"Fashion design. I actually went to college for it."

"Really?"

She chuckled. "Should I be offended that you find it so surprising?"

"No. It's just such a drastic change from fashion designer to firefighter–foster mom that I didn't see it."

"Yeah." Her voice grew soft. "Well, a lot changed after… everything with Vaynes."

Of course. "What made you decide on firefighting, then?"

"It was one of the firefighters that found me. The woman stayed with me until paramedics arrived. She was the first sign of hope after days and weeks of torture. The first sign that I was going to be okay. I want to do that for others. On their worst days, I want to be a sign of hope that they're going to make it."

"Now that, I can definitely see. It's a pretty hardcore job too."

She smiled at him. "Yeah, it is. I never felt prouder of myself than when I passed that qualifier test. It was the hardest thing, physically, I've ever done."

"It makes—"

Anthony's phone rang.

He glanced down at the name on the screen and quickly denied the call.

For a moment he waited. The road noise did nothing to cut the tense silence in the car.

"Do you need to call her back?" Della's words were soft. He probably looked like a jerk, refusing to talk to his own mother.

But, "No need."

Talk about ruining the moment. His mother had a habit of doing that.

"So...I take it you're not close?" she asked. He glanced over. She gave him a sheepish smile. "Sorry. I saw it was your mother. You don't have to explain anything."

The muscles in the back of his neck throbbed. The beginning of a headache if he didn't take meds soon. But none of that was Della's fault. He sighed. "I'm not on the best of terms with my mother. It's complicated."

"I get it."

"You do?" He glanced over.

"Well, not really. I'd give anything to talk to my mom again."

Yep. He was a world-class heel. But he was a sucker to hear how real families functioned. What a childhood could've been if he'd had a normal mother and actual father. "What was your mother like?"

"She loved color. She was an artist. She told the most wonderful stories and fairy tales. And any time I was scared, we would play a game. It helped calm me."

"What game?"

"We would list names or titles of God using the alphabet. I would be so busy trying to come up with one for the letter Q that I'd forget whatever I was afraid of."

"She sounds pretty special. Was your father into art too?"

"No, he was a scientist, but he adored us both. They gave me an amazing childhood."

"I wish I could say that."

Without thinking, the words had fallen from his mouth. A wish he'd wished for so long, for a different childhood. Della said nothing. But a warmth on his arm made him look down to find her mittened hand resting on his arm.

"I'm sorry it wasn't."

Aw, great. He couldn't have her pitying him. Now he needed to explain. "It's not like my mom didn't try. She's not a bad person or anything. It's just—" How did he put it? "When people are kind, they would say she marches to the beat of her own drum."

"So she's eccentric?"

"Very. She was born in the wrong era. She would've made a great hippie."

"A hippie?" Della asked. "Like she wears bell-bottoms with peace signs or something?"

"Oh, her wardrobe was definitely part of it." Anthony winced, remembering her outrageously ugly shawls and scarves over long, flowy skirts. The dirty overalls she often wore as she worked in her garden and the thrifted outfits she would make him wear. "But we also lived on a small farm, off-grid. She homeschooled me. We had our own little world. If she went into town, it was usually to protest something. She was caught up in conspiracy theories, convinced of everything from aliens to nanorobots in the water supply and stuff like that. You name it, she was probably on board with it and on a mission to educate the public too."

"She sounds like quite the character."

That was a nice way of putting it. And Della's soft smile melted some of the resentment inside. "You could say that."

"And your father? Was he ever in the picture?"

"In the beginning. But they fought all the time, and eventually he left us when I was nine."

"I'm so sorry."

"I'm better off without him. He wasn't really interested in being a father. But it hit my mom pretty hard. She had to be hospitalized for a while, and I had to live with another family and go to public school after being homeschooled my whole life. Talk about an eye-opening experience."

"That had to be traumatic for a little kid."

He tried to shrug, but his shoulders were too tense. "Yeah, it was rough for a chubby kid with long hair and weird clothes, who wasn't ever allowed to watch television."

"You? Chubby and awkward? I can't picture it."

"I was. And the kids were relentless. It was right before Christmas, and they couldn't believe I'd never heard of Santa Claus. They thought *I* was the alien. One day I even ran away and called my dad at work, begged him to pick me up. He refused. He said, 'I told her you'd end up some weirdo with the way she was raising you. She made her choice and I made mine. Better get used to it, kid. I'm not your dad anymore.'"

"Oh my word, Anthony. That's awful!"

"I got over it. It just…it just really messed with my mom, you know? She never fully recovered, and even today, she can be detached from reality. She takes everything too far. She'll become paranoid about harmless things. So every phone call is an emergency. And I love her, I really do. But I know I can't feed into her delusions."

"That's got to be rough. Do you think she's lonely?"

"Good news is she has kind neighbors that help her out. I know if there was a real problem, one of them would call me."

"But what about *you*? She probably misses you if you're her only family."

"After we get through this case and Vaynes is behind bars, I'll go check on her. But for now, we have to stay vigilant. I don't want to scare her."

"Right." Della nodded. "I wouldn't want her to get caught up with this if Vaynes is tracking me." She paused. "But when this is over and you do go to visit, if you want someone to go with you, I will. Maybe she could use another friend."

"You would do that?"

"Of course. So she's a little quirky. Everyone could use a friend. And I happen to like quirky people."

If Della followed through on that, she'd be the first of his friends to meet his mother. Maybe he shouldn't be so embarrassed by her, but the few times his high school buddies had seen her, they'd been cruel behind her back. And he'd never brought home any dates, too scared that by the end of the visit, she'd be touting the need for revamping the education system so that her future grandchildren wouldn't be brainwashed. It took a special kind of person to mesh with Kimberly Thomas.

But something about Della made him wonder. Would she really be as accepting as she said?

TWELVE

Della tried to shore up enough courage to face Vaynes, but her heart went out to Anthony. No wonder he cared about his image so much. Maybe it even explained his lack of Christmas spirit. An experience like that made a lasting impression on a kid. It made her grateful for her own upbringing. And only spurred on her passion to help children in similar circumstances.

It was the whole reason she wanted to go into foster care and why she loved the toy drive event. Maybe she'd see if Anthony would attend with her. If anything could melt a grinch's heart, it was seeing the joy on a child's face when they received a gift they weren't expecting.

And maybe it wouldn't be so bad to have a date this year for the firehouse Christmas party.

But it wasn't about that. They'd just met.

Right now, she needed her game face on.

They walked into the gym. It wasn't anything fancy, but the big windows looking out toward the mountains gave the space an airy feel, despite being filled with ellipticals, treadmills, weight machines, and the smell of perspiration.

"Do you think this will work?" she asked Anthony in a low voice.

"I hope not."

She almost missed his grumbled reply. "I'll be fine. Just go get your coffee like we planned. The place is two doors down."

"I don't like it." His facial expression didn't hold back. His hands fisted on his hips, and the way he swept the room over, not missing a thing, screamed vigilant cop. But she needed Anthony to leave so Vaynes would approach. If the man knew her routine, he'd show. The plan was for her to linger close to the exits and in the more secluded areas. She'd even do a stretching routine in one of the empty classrooms. Penny would keep her in sight the whole time.

"Penny's already here, over in the corner at the rowing machine, and isn't that Officer Ramble at the free weights?"

Anthony gave her a stiff nod. "Yeah, but his arm is in a sling. He's still recovering from a gunshot wound."

"But he's close and can sound the alarm if needed. Which means I'm covered. Now go get your coffee and take your time coming back." She pulled her hair back into a high ponytail while she spoke.

"Anything else, your highness?"

Was that a smirk underneath all that huff?

"Yeah, one of those power smoothies with an extra immunity boost."

He just stared at her.

"Anthony, go. I'm fine." She physically spun him around and pushed him toward the exit. "Enjoy an espresso while I work out. I don't want you staring at me while I sweat."

He finally left, and Della moved to the stationary bike in the farthest corner. She did a rotation of weights, and after that, core exercises, but no sign of Vaynes. She jumped at every little sound. Maybe she wasn't quite as brave and ready to face her worst nightmare as she said, but at least she was trying. Putting herself out there.

But after an hour and a half, her muscles were burning, her shirt was drenched, and her nerves were shot. So much for thinking the exertion would relieve the pent-up frustration. She really couldn't justify staying any longer.

After a quick shower, with Penny covering the women's locker room, Della met Anthony back by the gym entrance.

"Any sign of him?" He handed her a green smoothie.

She let out a sigh of defeat. "Not a thing."

"Let's get some lunch—some real food and not something you have to slurp—at Backdraft. Take your mind off things for a while." Anthony took her gym bag from her hand. "Bryce and Izan will be there, watching from a distance."

"Does that mean you'll leave me alone again?"

"Maybe. If Penny will watch the back exit from her car."

Della finished her smoothie on the quiet ride over. The Backdraft Bar & Grill was a local favorite and a packed house with the lunchtime crowd. The smell of smoke was welcome here, with its signature barbecue meals and smoked brisket. The hostess led them around a group of rowdy construction workers, sat them in a cozy booth, and left them with the menus. After confirming Bryce and Izan were a few tables away, Anthony stood.

"I've got a phone call to make. Order me a coffee if the server comes?" he asked.

"I'll ask for decaf. You're jumpy enough as it is."

He didn't laugh as he walked away. Probably he was as wound up as she was.

Della watched as he paced near the hostess stand and pretended to talk. Or maybe he really did call someone. Either way, this was her shot. She wandered down the short hallway by the restrooms, the most logical spot for Vaynes to grab an unsuspecting victim. She lingered in the dark shadows, studying the pictures of firefighters and firehouse memorabilia hanging in the halls. Nothing. She quickly used the restroom and washed her hands. Back in the hallway, she made her own fake phone call, one ear open and focused on hearing anyone approaching.

A couple of women in business suits passed her by. A mom with a toddler too. But no one else. Finally, she gave up and sat back down in her spot. Anthony was already there, and the server waited to take her order.

This was not going well.

Not that the lunch with Anthony wasn't pleasant, but the longer they went without a sign of Vaynes, the more her gut churned. By the time they were done eating, she was already exhausted from the hypervigilance.

She shouldn't have ordered the extra-spicy wings. Not that she'd finished them. The rest of her basket lay off to the side of the table while Anthony actually finished his big salad. Only his breadstick remained. Chatter from around them died down as the lunch crowd thinned.

"Della, we'll get him." Anthony rested his hand on hers but then snatched it away quickly. "Whoa. Your hands are pure ice." He grabbed both her hands and rubbed them lightly. "We need to warm these up."

It was such a simple thing, but the gesture brought tears to her eyes. Tears she willed to stay put, even if they stung. And for a moment, she rested there in the softness and concern in his gaze. Letting out a slow breath, she held his stare. "Do you really think we'll find him? I don't know if I can—"

"We'll find him."

Whether it was the confidence in his words, the tenderness in his touch, or those unwavering baby blues, Della believed him.

And oh, she was liking this hand-holding thing way more than she should.

He's only trying to protect me. Don't get sucked into this!

Because eventually, Anthony would have to move on to a different case. She couldn't read anything into it. At all.

But she could no longer deny that she wanted to. She cringed inwardly to think of how callously she'd treated him when he'd first shown up yesterday. Talk about a one-eighty.

"So, what now?" she asked.

"I've got an idea." Penny appeared out of nowhere and slid into the booth next to Della. She glanced at their hands but didn't say anything. Instead, she helped herself to the fries Della hadn't eaten.

"Do I want to know?" Anthony lifted an eyebrow.

Penny just grinned.

"Great." He sighed. "Okay. Let's hear it."

Penny bumped Della's shoulder. "See, he acts all tough, but he's actually a big ol' sw—"

"Spit it out, Pen." Anthony let go of Della's hands, but she didn't miss the slight blush that bloomed on his cheeks and neck.

"Jude and another buddy have been watching Della's house. No sign of anyone approaching it all day. I say we give Della *my* car and she drives home alone and we see if Vaynes shows up."

"Absolutely not." Anthony leaned away from the table. "It's too risky. She'll be too exposed."

"Hear me out before you get all huffy." Penny snagged another fry and popped it in her mouth. After chewing, she continued. "You and I can follow at a distance. She has a tracking device in her shoe. We have an established perimeter. That's minimal risk."

"And if he tries to shoot her as she gets out of the car?" Anthony asked.

Penny leaned in. "He's not a shooter. He's a serial killer. He wants to be up close to his victims so he can mess with their minds. That's how he feels powerful."

"What about the carbon dioxide? That wasn't up close and personal."

"He was probably watching from that vent. As soon as you were both knocked out, I bet he would've taken Della and left you there to rot. All of it, though, is meant to terrorize his victims, remind them that he can get to them."

"Oh, well, that's reassuring." Anthony jammed his fingers through his hair, messing up his gelled hairdo. He probably didn't even realize he was doing it. "Look, I'm her protection detail. And I say it's too risky."

"We gotta give it a shot, Tony. And we'll be watching her. Tracking her."

He stared Penny down as he took a sip of his water. Maybe he was actually contemplating the idea. Then he turned to Della. "What do you want to do?"

Good question.

She looked at Penny and Anthony. They were giving up their day to watch over her. And others were out there fighting the freezing weather and awful conditions, tracking down these escaped convicts. She *was* cold. And weary. And...done with being afraid.

She finally found the words. "I just want this over with."

Anthony closed his eyes a second and then focused on her a moment before his gaze shifted to Penny. "Fine. But I'm in charge. The second we see Vaynes, we move in. We don't *let* him get close. Not this time."

Penny stood. "All right. Let's do this."

Hopefully, this time it would work.

THIRTEEN

Anthony must be going soft, just like Penny had teased. He never should've agreed to this. He tried to loosen his death grip on the steering wheel of his squad car as he peered through the windshield. Penny, on the other hand, hummed along to the radio. She had tuned it to a country station as soon as she'd slipped into the passenger seat, like she owned the place. Like they were out for a leisurely cruise and not trying to catch a killer.

His wipers were at full speed, yet he could barely see Penny's burgundy SUV through the freezing rain and sleet. Della was keeping it at a good speed at least. Nothing reckless or unsafe. Still, he didn't like this idea.

"So…" Penny let the word linger. "You and Della?"

"What about it?"

"Don't bite my head off, Tony. I'm just saying, you two looked pretty cozy over lunch. I wasn't interrupting anything, was I?"

"Like that's ever stopped you before."

She laughed. "My, my. I don't know that I've ever seen you

this surly. You're usually one of the most chill and upbeat people I know. You must really like her."

Anthony lost all words. There was no comeback to throw Penny off the scent. She was right.

"What's not to like? But here I am, letting a serial killer try to nab her. What's wrong with this scenario?"

Penny laughed.

"It's not funny," Anthony growled.

"Sure it is. The great Anthony Thomas has finally fallen. And for the record, you have my wholehearted approval. Della is tough, but she's one of the good ones. I think you two would be perfect together."

"We're just working together. We haven't even been on a date."

"You've never asked her out? She's probably the one single woman in Last Chance you haven't."

"That's not true."

"Oh, it is. When I first moved here, Andi warned me all about you and Bryce specifically. Of course, I didn't listen and I fell for Bryce anyway. However, everyone knows that you, my friend, only date a woman for a few months, then you're on to someone new. So if you try to pull that on Della, you're going to have to deal with me."

"Can we just focus on keeping the woman safe and out of Jason Vaynes's hands for now?"

"Yup. You're a goner."

He wasn't even going to answer that.

"You're following too closely," Penny said. "Back off a little."

"I can hardly see with this rain. I'm not letting her out of my sight."

"She's almost to her house. We can go past it and backtrack on the next street over. Jude is watching over there. If we take his spot, he can use the neighbor's house like she said."

Anthony hated being this far from Della, even though they had her on an open phone call, just muted. They could hear the upbeat Kelly Clarkson song she was listening to on the car radio. She parked in the short driveway in front of a yellow cottage-style home and killed the engine. Anthony drove past her and kept going.

"See anything?" he asked Penny.

"Nothing." She looked down at her phone. "Jude is moving into place."

Good, because this was when Della was most vulnerable. Moments of transition were the hardest to protect. Anthony should probably thank God for the awful weather, which could only deter Vaynes. He wouldn't be able to stay outside watching for any length of time. And Anthony would have to trust that Jude and his buddy were vigilant enough that Vaynes didn't sneak past them.

"Maybe I should do a quick sweep of the house before she—"

"She's fine." Penny nudged him with her elbow. "We're listening. We're tracking her."

Right. Anthony sped up and turned left. He turned again when he found the narrow alley Della used to access the detached garage. The squad car blocked the alley, but he and Penny would have enough room to get out if needed. It gave them a mostly clear view of Della's backyard.

"So now we sit and do nothing." Anthony grabbed his pack of gum. At least he could keep his mouth busy.

"Nothing but wait for a serial killer to show up." Penny sounded way too chipper for this.

Anthony said nothing. He turned the volume up on the phone they were listening on.

Over the next few hours, darkness crept in. By five o'clock, the sky was black, and the temperatures had dropped enough to turn the freezing rain to thick snow. Anthony had to keep the car running to keep the windshield wipers on. There was no movement except a random alley cat dodging the snowflakes, looking for shelter.

Finally, Della spoke to them over the phone.

"I should be glad he didn't show, but I'm only getting more impatient. Are you seeing anything?"

Penny took the phone off mute. "Nothing."

"I guess I'll get ready for my shift, then. I'll leave for work in half an hour."

"Sure." Anthony was glad to hear her voice and, for some reason, wanted her to hear his. "We'll follow you once you leave."

"Okay, I'll let you know when I'm ready."

He was ready to see her again *now*, and to have the protection of the security system at the firehouse. Twenty-nine more minutes to go. He settled back into his seat. Even rested his head for a moment.

"What's that?" Penny pointed through the windshield.

Anthony sat up straight. "Where?"

"On the other side of Della's house. I saw movement."

Anthony removed his service weapon from its holster and bolted from his car.

"Tony, wait!" Penny hissed from somewhere behind him.

He probably should've grabbed his hat, but it was too late for that. The movement in the shadows spurred him. He squinted through the thick snow and made his way down the alley.

A figure dressed in black slid around the corner of the next house down. Anthony sprinted after the person. "Stop! Police!"

The person paused and looked back before darting between houses. Definitely male. Average height and weight. But the man's black beanie and neck warmer hid most of his face. No sign of a weapon in his gloved hands.

Anthony ignored the cold seeping down the collar of his coat and kicked up his speed a notch. The pounding of Penny's footsteps sounded from behind him.

Just as the man reached the driveway in front of Della's neighbor's house, Anthony made his move. He lunged and wrapped his arms around the man's torso, knocking him down to the ground.

The man flailed. "Get off me!"

Anthony flipped the guy over and whipped the hat off his head.

Not Vaynes. It was just a kid lying there in the snow, barely sixteen by the looks of him.

"Who are you, and what are you doing?" Anthony didn't have time for this.

"Nothing! I swear!" The kid held up his empty hands in surrender.

Anthony stood and yanked the boy to his feet. "Then why did you run?"

The boy's shoulders slumped. "I'm grounded. I was sneaking out to see my girlfriend. She lives a couple streets over."

"You've gotta be kidding me."

Penny ran up to them. She looked at the kid and chuckled. "What's going on?"

Before Anthony answered, he heard Jude's voice on the radio Penny was carrying. "Everything okay?"

"All clear. False alarm," Penny told him. "Stay where you are."

"Copy that."

Penny clipped the radio back onto her belt. "So, what did I miss?"

"Romeo here is sneaking out of his parents' house." Anthony let go of the kid and brushed the snow off his pants. "I'll escort him back home. You should get back to Della."

"Yes, sir."

Anthony didn't have to look up at Penny to hear the smirk in her response. And it didn't take much convincing for the kid to cough up his address. Anthony walked him home and spoke to the parents. By the time he got back to the squad car, he was soaked to the bone. He shivered in the driver's seat and didn't look at Penny.

"Well, that was exciting." She must've found it pretty humorous by the sound of it. But Anthony didn't have time for fun and games. He ignored Penny and spoke into the phone.

"Della, are you ready to go?"

"I'm heading out right now."

"We'll be right behind you." He pulled out of the alley and waited.

"That was a complete waste of time." He'd sat in wait for hours, and they were no closer to finding Vaynes than they had been before.

Penny only smiled. "I don't know. It was kinda nice to sit and watch the snow and see all the Christmas lights."

If he sounded like Ebenezer Scrooge, he didn't care. "Bah humbug."

FOURTEEN

One look at Anthony walking into the firehouse, and Della couldn't decide between laughing and crying. His uniform was soaking wet from the waist down. The handsome smolder was gone and replaced by lips thinned into a scowl. The guy'd had no clue what he was in for when he was assigned to protect her.

Penny looked like she was trying to hold back a chuckle. "I'm gonna update Bryce. See you guys later." She winked at Della as she walked past.

"Why is Penny winking at me?" Della asked Anthony.

"Because she likes to torture me? Who knows." He tugged his hat off and finger-combed his thick, dark hair.

"You must be cold. Want some coffee?"

"Anything hot will do." He actually smiled at her briefly. "Thanks."

It only stirred up the crazy sensations swirling around her middle. She hated seeing him so discouraged.

But she liked having him near. Maybe once he warmed up, she could gather enough courage to ask him to the Christmas party. It would be nice to have a date for once.

Zack Stephens and Ridge Foster were chatting with Kianna in the break room when they walked in.

Ridge's eyes went wide. "Yo! What happened to you, Thomas? Catch the serial killer?"

Anthony conjured up a light chuckle and told them about the teenager he'd tackled in the snow. But the smile he gave everyone didn't reach his eyes.

She poured him a mug of hot coffee and started a teakettle for herself. She didn't need any more caffeine at this point. She was already on edge.

How much longer was her life going to be on hold? People were giving up their holidays and being pulled from their jobs to watch over her. At least now she had work to focus on.

The teakettle whistled right as their tones went off on their phones.

"Fire Truck 14, Rescue 5, report to house fire on East Twelfth Street. Unknown number of occupants. Two-story structure."

Della listened to the rest of the details as they jogged out to the bay. Anthony ran beside her. "Are you sure you're okay to do—"

"This is my job, Anthony. Remember?" She stepped into her firefighter pants and pulled them up by the suspenders.

"I'll be right behind you."

She paused a moment and caught his blue-eyed gaze focused solely on her while everyone else rushed around. The crazy thought of asking him to the party, right now, flitted through her mind. But that was dumb. This was horrible timing. Instead, she leaned over and kissed his cheek. "I know."

Before she could catch his reaction, she stepped into her boots and grabbed her coat. Ridge yelled that he was starting the truck. Anthony left, and she pushed away all the distractions.

She couldn't control Vaynes. Couldn't do a lot of things, but right now she *could* do this. She inspected every piece of gear and equipment before she put it on and jumped into the truck behind the wheel. She could navigate these roads and fight this battle. She could do her job.

Amelia sat in the passenger seat and helped call out directions while Della peered through the thick snow coming down. She drove through one of the more rundown neighborhoods and pulled up to an old two-story home. The Craftsman sported a sagging porch, neon graffiti on the front door, and narrow dormers on the second story, which currently spewed smoke.

"I'm surprised this place hasn't burned down before now," Zoe said as Della parked. "I hope the snow stops it from spreading to the other houses. They're so close together."

"I dunno. It might be an improvement." Izan's voice carried over from the back seat. "There's a lot of shady stuff that goes on here. Might be better to burn it all down and start from scratch." He called in to the radio that they were on site.

As soon as Della was out of the truck, Anthony was there. Snow fell around them. "You'll stay in the middle again? Between Izan and Zoe?"

His concern was sweet, but she had to stay on task. "I'll be fine. And yes, I'll be the communications person and stick close to the others."

He nodded and squeezed her hand, then stepped back and let her go. So much was happening between them. It was fast.

But it settled deep into her soul. This was a good thing.

So as soon as she was done with this fire, she was asking him out. And she was going to forget about Vaynes and move on with her life. Maybe he really had left town after his failed attempt with the CO2.

She grabbed her air tank and tools and joined Zoe and Izan, who stood with Amelia. "What's the plan, Lieutenant?" Zoe asked.

"Izan, you take lead with the hose. Nixon, you stay on the radio while Lewis feeds the hose as needed. Neighbors say it's a rental. No idea if anyone is in there or not. There's a car parked in the garage, so Rescue 5 is here and will be on standby. You stay on the fire and call if you see anyone. They'll be ready to help evacuate."

They didn't waste any more time. After setting up the hose, Izan marched up the crooked steps. Hopefully the porch would hold them. With the rot and missing boards, they'd have to tread lightly.

It didn't take much to open the front entrance. Izan took the hose and led the way, crawling under the thick smoke through a living area. Della followed, weaving around a dingy couch and scratched-up coffee table.

"Looks like the fire is in the kitchen, off to the right. Stay close to me." Izan's voice came through her speaker. He stood and readied the hose. "All right."

"Start the hose," Della called into the radio.

The hose went rigid. Izan aimed the water into the heart of the kitchen. Flames engulfed the whole room. "I need more pressure."

Della relayed his request and looked around. "I'm going to check out the next room and see if we need to call Rescue in."

Zoe gave her a thumbs-up. Della checked the door of the next room. Her thermal imaging showed it to be cooler than the other spaces. Using her Halligan tool, she knocked the door open. With the thick smoke, she relied completely on the TIC. No body or heat source registered on the screen. She moved back to the living room and found another den. Empty. She glanced up the stairs. A shadowy figure moved through the smoke.

"This is Last Chance County Fire Department. Stay where you are so we can help you."

No one appeared.

Was she seeing things? Her TIC showed the shape of a person at the top of the stairs. Someone was standing there.

Why didn't they move? Were they scared? Confused? Not surprising if they had smoke inhalation.

"It's okay. Come on down." She used the voice speaker in her helmet and readied her radio. She should call in Rescue 5. But before she could say anything, the person moved down a step.

"That's right. Stay low and follow my voice." Della climbed the first few stairs. If she could lead the person out the front door, they wouldn't even need Rescue.

Smoke obscured her vision, but on the TIC screen, she could see the person coming toward her. They were still walking upright.

"Stay below the smoke. It's better if you crawl down," she called out through her speaker.

Whoever it was ignored the instruction.

"Seriously, stay low. You shouldn't breathe in the—"

Out of the smoke, a man appeared on the stairs. A breathing mask covered his face, but she knew those soulless eyes.

Vaynes.

Before she could scream, he knocked her radio out of her hand and grabbed her. A sharp pain in her neck sent a burning throughout her body and then...blackness.

FIFTEEN

Anthony felt nothing. Not the snow, not the wind, not his toes. Maybe he was simply numb from the freezing temps, but until he could see with his own eyes that Della was okay, he would ignore everything else. Especially all the things she'd set off with that quick kiss to his cheek, back at the firehouse. There were so many questions he wanted to ask her, but all he could think about at the moment was the most important one: Was she okay?

The gnawing in his gut had only intensified since they'd pulled up to the dilapidated Craftsman. But he tried to stay out of the way as other fire crews rushed across the small lawn in their black gear. Flames crawled up the right side of the building. Hoses crisscrossed the snow from the fire hydrant at the street to the crews fighting the blaze from outside.

But Della was inside. Inside where he couldn't see her. He stuck close to her lieutenant. Patterson would be in communication with Della, but since her request for more water pressure, he hadn't heard her voice.

"Is she okay in there?"

Amelia looked up from the water gauge she was checking. "Back off, Thomas. She's a good firefighter."

"I know, but…it's been a while."

"They're busy, you know, doing their *job*."

"And I'm doing mine. Something feels off here. Can't you have them check in? Then I'll back off."

"Okay, okay."

Amelia spoke into her radio. "Truck 14, check in. We okay in there?"

Nothing but static responded.

"Collins, Nixon, Lewis. How's it looking?"

After a moment of silence, finally Amelia's radio crackled. "Collins and I are fine. I don't have line of sight on Nixon. Got any more water pressure?" It must've been Zoe. The voice was female, but not Della's.

"I'm giving you all I got," Amelia spoke into the radio. "Why isn't Nixon responding? She should be giving the updates."

"She's checking the next room. We heard her talking a moment ago."

Anthony's gut clenched tighter. "She can't be alone. They need to stay together."

Amelia waved Anthony out of her face. So maybe he was invading her personal space. But Della. Where was she?

He took a tiny step back. "Get visual confirmation that she's okay. Please."

"Nixon, where are you? You should stick with Collins and Lewis."

No response.

Amelia cleared her throat and tried again. "Lewis, check on Nixon. Collins, you handle the hose."

"I'll go find her," Zoe said. "She might be helping someone and have her hands tied up."

Anthony grabbed the radio from Amelia and pushed the

button. "She can't be alone, Zoe. I need to hear her voice, and you need to stay with her. Della, if you hear me, speak up—"

Amelia yanked her radio back. "Anthony, I get that you're worried, but if anyone is going to order them around, it's me. They're fighting a dangerous fire in there. We have protocols."

"Does that include letting someone go alone into a different area? Why isn't she answering the radio?"

"I don't know. But before we jump to conclusions—"

"Lieutenant? Lewis here. I'm not seeing Nixon. The smoke is super thick, but she was supposed to be in the next room. She's not. Want me to check the rest of the house?"

Anthony almost snatched the radio again, but Amelia swerved away.

"I'll send Rescue in. Zoe, get back to Collins and watch his back." Amelia ran over to Bryce. "Nixon is missing in the house. Get someone in there to find her."

Ridge Foster, Rescue 5's lieutenant, grabbed a tank and mask. "I'll look for her myself."

"I'm coming with you." Anthony reached for another air tank.

Patterson stayed him with a strong grip on his arm. "Anthony, let him do this. He's trained. You're not. You go in there unprepared, and we'll have two people to rescue."

Ridge jogged off toward the front entrance of the house. He joined Eddie Rice, who waited by the front door.

Anthony's hands froze on the metal air tank. She was right, but…"I can't just stand here doing nothing."

"That's exactly what you're going to do. I'll call Bryce over if I have to." Amelia stared him down. "But there *is* something you can do. You can *pray*."

Anthony shoved the tank back in place on the truck and marched a few feet away. Yeah, he should trust these firefighters, who considered Della their family. He shouldn't be so angry at Amelia. But Della was in there and *not* responding.

Still, the prayer thing was true.

But he was having a really hard time believing it. What did that say about his faith?

A loud, piercing alarm sounded from inside the building.

Anthony grabbed a firefighter walking by, struggling to drag another hose. "What's that noise?"

"Sounds like a PASS alarm," he said.

Anthony picked up the wet hose and helped tug it toward the house. "A what?"

"A personal alert safety system. All the fighters have them. Means the person hasn't moved in thirty seconds."

Della.

Anthony dropped the hose. Amelia and Bryce were right there.

Bryce grabbed him by the shoulders before he could sprint to the burning building. "Don't even think about it, Thomas. I know you're tasked with protecting her, but Rescue is looking for her. That alarm will lead us right to her. Wait."

Part of him knew this. But logic was not sounding so logical right now. He should be there.

"Bryce, come on." He didn't even care if he sounded desperate. Begging.

"I can't let you in, Thomas. Hold back. And pray."

Amelia and Bryce weren't going to relent. He could see it in their stances. But Amelia did go in to help. All Anthony could do was wait.

And fine. He'd try to pray.

But the only words that he could conjure up were woefully insufficient.

Lord, help her. Keep her safe. Please.

Bryce must've recognized his compliance. He stood next to him as they faced the front entrance together. The piercing alarm stood out among all the other sounds. Sirens on the trucks still ran. Voices yelled across the lawn.

The fire still roared, now shooting out the chimney on the roof, sending sparks and smoke up into the sky. The falling snow did nothing to extinguish it. The streams of water from the hoses only created sizzling steam as the fire laughed at them and grew stronger.

Zoe's voice sounded over Amelia's radio. "We need another hose in here. Collins is trying, but it's not enough."

The captain spoke into his unit. "We'll get the other crew in there. Foster, any word yet?"

"The alarm is coming from upstairs. Second story. Heading there now." Ridge's voice came through clearly.

But it wasn't nearly fast enough.

Bryce called Kianna and Trace over. "We need EMS on standby. Possible unconscious or injured firefighter."

"We're ready."

Anthony checked his watch. Five minutes now. "Why haven't they found her yet?"

"They have to be thorough. Give them—"

"Found her!" It was Ridge on the radio.

"Status?" Bryce asked.

"Unconscious. Back room in northwest corner. Bringing her out now."

Kianna looked at Trace. "Let's get the cot."

Anthony could only stand there and count the seconds. There were too many of them as far as he was concerned. The paramedics were back with the cot right as Ridge and Eddie spilled out of the front entrance, carrying Della between them. Turnout gear and her mask obscuring her face. But her dark braid swung in the air until they set her on the cot.

She was too still.

Anthony rushed over, but the others crowded him out. He followed them to the ambulance, where finally, he could at least stand at the foot of the cot as they lifted her in. Kianna removed the mask while Trace checked for a pulse. Kianna froze.

"What?" Anthony yelled. Why did Kianna look so confused? And more importantly, why wasn't she doing anything?

Trace dropped his hand from the patient's neck. "I can't find a pulse."

"Try again!" Anthony gripped the sides of the ambulance door, ready to launch inside and start CPR himself.

But Trace only shook his head. " She's dead."

The words barely registered when Kianna spoke. "But it's not Della. I don't know who this woman is."

SIXTEEN

Della's moan echoed. Where was she? Her head hurt too much to open her eyes. Her body shivered. She curled into herself, needing to conserve whatever warmth she could find. She finally cracked one lid open. Stark cement walls and a dirt floor. The lone light bulb dangling on a cord from the ceiling gave out meager light. Not enough to push back the darkness creeping in from the corners.

She had to get out of here.

With shaky arms, she pushed her torso up. The thin sleeves of her work shirt did nothing to fight off the chill. Looking down, she had her uniform pants on still, but only socks on her feet. What happened to her turnout gear? Her boots?

More importantly, where had Vaynes taken her, and how was she going to escape?

"So, you're awake." The raspy voice followed by the sound of footsteps descending a staircase sent a shockwave of ice through her body.

She tried to inject confidence into her words. "You're not going to get away with this."

He laughed, the mirthless sound bouncing around the empty

room. "I have, and I will. We have unfinished business. You cut our last game short. And I've had plenty of time to dream up new ways of playing."

He didn't move closer to her. He stayed in the middle of the room, outside the faint light from the bulb.

It took everything Della had to hold eye contact. But she refused to back down. She refused to show the fear that ricocheted through her. She dug deep to find the anger, anything to push aside the hopelessness. She couldn't let him see how much he affected her. It only fed his appetite.

She *could* focus on getting information and escaping though.

"Where are we?" she asked.

"Somewhere no one will find you. Not for a very long time." He smiled and circled around the light, sticking to the shadows. "Had quite the time getting up here with this weather. And it's only getting worse. So if you think you're going to sneak away and flag down help, think again. We're too remote. If I don't kill you, the elements will. But that's not really something I'm anticipating. I took precautions."

He said "up here." So they must be in the mountains outside of the city somewhere. She'd much rather take her chances with nature, but she kept the words to herself. She needed more information.

"What are you going to do with me?"

He moved close enough to reach out and touch her hair. Della pulled away, but not fast enough. His grip tightened, and he yanked her head up close enough to smell his foul breath in her face. "We're going to set the record straight."

"What record?" She could barely breathe with him right in her face, but she couldn't let him know that. He needed to keep talking.

"The official court record. You know, the one you lied in. That's cheating. That's against the rules."

"You killed Lily. That's murder. You got better than you deserved when they sent you off to prison."

He wagged his finger in her face. "That's not how we play." He released her hair and stood. "But no matter. We'll make it official. Show the world that you lied. Then we'll even the score."

That didn't sound good. The man was sick. But these were the same phrases he'd used in the notes. No doubt he was the one who'd written them. "How did you send those letters to me from prison?"

Vaynes's sinister smirk grew. "What letters are you talking about?"

"You know which ones. The ones you stole out of my locker. Isn't that cheating too?"

"I couldn't have evidence just sitting around to be found. I know you called the police. They needed to see that you're a liar. You can't be trusted."

"Who delivered them in the first place? You were in prison."

Vaynes yawned. "I would love to keep this conversation going, but I have more to prepare."

"Oh, so you don't know." Maybe she could taunt him into spilling more.

But he just shrugged. "I don't. Mackey took care of that for me. It was part of our agreement."

Mackey? The criminal who had escaped along with the other guy and Vaynes. "What agreement?"

Vaynes's grin grew full force. "Who do you think planned our escape?" He moved closer. "Mackey might think he was the mastermind, but he couldn't have done it without me."

He was dying to show how cunning he was. She needed to goad him into revealing more. What was the other criminal's name? The one that had gotten away from Anthony.

Della remembered. "I heard Sosa was behind it all."

"Sosa? That man is worthless. I am the brains of this operation. And enough stalling. I have work to do. But I'll be back to get you. Soon."

He climbed the wooden steps and shut the door. As soon as he was gone, Della stood. The room swirled around her, and her legs shook. She fell against the wall to hold herself up. She waited for the dizziness to pass and tried again. But whatever Vaynes had injected into her still coursed through her body, sending swells of nausea to crash over her. But it was her spirit that was truly in distress.

Her heart cried out.

God I need You! I can't do this anymore. I can't hold up under the weight of this lie. The darkness is about to swallow me whole, and I'm so afraid. I've been letting fear dictate my words and my actions when instead, I should've trusted You. I should've told the truth and left it in Your hands. You're bigger than the court system. You're bigger than Jason Vaynes. And so if this is the end, I want to be clean before You. I need Your forgiveness. I thought justice was up to me. But it has always been Yours.

I'm so sorry I didn't believe Your word that the truth would set me free.

Della rested her forehead on the cold wall, willing her head to clear.

Instead, she slumped down to the ground and passed out again.

She awoke to find herself blindfolded and sitting in a chair with her hands bound. Her chin rested on her chest, her neck craned at an uncomfortable angle.

"Now you will know the truth. You called her a hero, but I'll show you what she really is."

Who was Vaynes talking to?

Della lifted her head. Whatever Vaynes had covered her eyes with had left a slice of visibility. Della studied the old wooden floorboards beneath her feet. Two electrical cords ran next to her chair. The room here wasn't any warmer—in fact, it felt bigger, more cavernous. Icy drafts sent shivers throughout her body.

But somehow, even in the cold darkness, she felt lighter. Unburdened. She didn't know what would happen, but she knew who she belonged to. Where she would go if this was the end of it all.

But she didn't want it to be the end.

"Now our trial can begin." Vaynes ripped the blindfold off.

Della squinted, trying to protect her eyes from the bright light flooding them. A phone on a tripod stood next to the construction light trying to blind her.

Vaynes wore a black robe and stood behind a podium with a gavel in hand. "It's time you had your day in court, Della Nixon."

SEVENTEEN

Anthony had failed yet again. First, he'd let Sosa get away. Now, Della had been missing for five hours, taken under *his* watch. Here, he wanted to bring these convicts in, prove he was ready for more responsibility and to become a detective. Instead, he should be turning his badge in.

Permanently.

Where was the "light" in this that he was supposed to see?

Chatter buzzed all around him. The bullpen wasn't usually this busy in the middle of the night. Then again, they didn't usually have the chaos of three missing convicts and a kidnapped firefighter thrown into the normal caseload.

"Will you stop the pacing already? We'll find her." Officer Junior Ramble glared over his computer screen at Anthony. "Why don't you do something helpful like track down any other known associates of Vaynes?"

"You think I haven't done that already? Dead end. Every single one of them. The guy was a loner. No record of visitors at the prison. No calls for him. Nothing. There's no clue as to where he found the deceased woman that was in the house. I've gone through all the missing persons reported and still haven't

ID'd her. And the trail Penny and I followed in the backyard led nowhere. Vaynes had a getaway vehicle."

"And we now know what it is." Penny slapped a paper on the desk in front of Anthony. "Black 2006 Ford Explorer."

"How'd you find it?" Anthony asked.

"Canvassed the neighborhood and something finally paid off. Caught this image on a nearby security system. That's Vaynes in the driver's seat. I already ran the plates. The SUV was stolen. The owner is out of town for the holidays. He was crankier about being woken in the middle of the night than to hear about his stolen car."

"Let's put out the BOLO. I'll get that started." Junior took the paper and ran off.

Penny grabbed a candy cane off Olivia's desk. "How you holding up, Tony?" She kept her voice low, calm as she unwrapped the candy. Somehow it helped him, to see her keeping it together.

"Any minute, I'm sure, the chief will come out here and call for my badge."

"That's not true."

He pushed his hair back off his forehead. It was probably a mess right now, but he didn't care. "I screwed up. That's not the kind of image the department wants for its officers, let alone detectives."

"You were hoping to move up?"

Anthony nodded, staring out the windows at the bleak darkness. "Guess I can kiss that goodbye."

"Hey." She waited until he made eye contact. "This job is about way more than image. *You* are more than the image you've been trying so hard to project."

"And what's that?"

"The image that says you have it all together. You have everything in control."

Anthony huffed.

But Penny didn't stop. "You're a good man, Tony. You have heart and integrity. I'm sure the chief knows that. No one is asking you to turn in your badge. Besides, everyone has cases like this. You think Basuto or Donaldson haven't had their fair share of bad guys slip through their fingers?"

"Maybe. At this point, I just want to find Della."

"Me too." She gave him a sad smile. "I know it feels like there's no hope right now, that evil and darkness are winning. But that's not the last word."

But it sure seemed that way. He'd prayed. So where was God in all this?

"I get—"

"Hey! Look at this! He's made contact." Detective Savannah Wilcox called out from the other side of the bullpen. "He sent us a file." She pointed a remote at the smart screen hanging on the wall. Within seconds, a video played.

Della sat in the middle of the shot, tied to a chair. Dirt smeared her face. Her silky hair was tangled and half falling out of a braid. She didn't look too banged up. Then Anthony noticed her hand. It was strapped to a table, two of her fingers mangled and bloodied.

What in the world had he done to her?

Anthony's hands fisted as Vaynes came on-screen. He wore a long black robe and faced Della. "Are you ready to tell the court what you've done?"

Della lifted her chin. "I said I would. Just turn yourself in and I will."

"You know what you have to do." Vaynes held a hammer over her hand, ready to strike.

"Let me go." Della's voice shook, sending a tremor of fury through Anthony.

"Where is this coming from?" he yelled over to Wilcox.

"It was sent to us. I'm trying to trace the email." Savannah kept typing as the video played.

"Is it live?" Penny asked her.

"Maybe. I'm looking."

A scream brought all attention back to the screen. Vaynes had done it. A third finger lay broken.

Anthony slammed his fist onto the desk.

She was at the mercy of a killer because he'd failed to do a simple job. He'd failed to protect her. Why wait for them to ask for his badge? He didn't deserve it.

"Tell the court the truth. You promised to tell nothing but the truth." Vaynes walked behind Della and yanked her head up by the hair. "Look into the camera and tell them."

"The truth is you killed Lily."

He lifted the hammer again with his free hand. "You know what I'm talking about. Tell them! I'm not going to stop until you tell them the truth."

She looked straight into the camera, her voice wobbling. "I lied." Tears mixed with blood ran down Della's beautiful face. She dragged in a breath and continued. "I said that I saw him, but when I was abducted, I never saw his face." She closed her eyes, and her shoulders drooped forward.

"So what you're saying is, you committed perjury." Vaynes let go of her head but stayed there, speaking right behind her ear. Loud enough for the camera to pick up. "You never saw your captor's face. You were drugged the whole time. He wore a mask. Isn't that right?" Everything within Anthony wanted to lunge through the screen and take Vaynes down himself. But it was the sight of the woman he was growing rather attached to being tortured that broke his heart. His failure had caused this. He never should've let her out of his sight.

Anthony was not a violent man, but he'd never wanted to hurt another human being more than he did right now. The darkness pressed in on his very soul.

God, where are You?

Suddenly Della opened her eyes. Narrowed them slightly.

She lifted her chin and looked straight at the camera. "The only way you would know that I didn't see his face, the only way you would know about being drugged or the mask is if *you* were there." Her lips went tight a second before she threw her head back into Vaynes's skull with a loud cry. Then the video cut out.

"Where's the rest?" Anthony rushed over to Wilcox's desk. "What happened?"

He needed to see, because suddenly, scenarios of Vaynes torturing Della in retaliation stormed all logic and clear thinking.

She pounded on the keyboard. "I don't know. That's it. It was cut off. In the email, Vaynes is demanding that his case be thrown out. He says he'll be in touch."

Penny sprinted over with the candy cane still in her mouth. "Play the video again. We need to look for clues. Figure out where they are."

This time, when Savannah played the video, Anthony studied the background. But his eyes kept wandering back to Della. The pain, the terror there, left him shattered.

Oh God, keep her safe.

The final spark before she threw her head back gave him hope.

She was a fighter.

But she needed help, and he wasn't there.

But I am.

A gentle voice inside pushed back the panic and despair. It didn't get much worse than this kind of darkness, Della at the mercy of a killer. But what had Penny said?

I know it feels like there's no hope right now, that evil and darkness are winning. But that's not the last word.

The LED candle display in the window caught his eye.

"Tony, did you see anything?" Penny's question shook him out of the haze.

"No, play it again."

God, help us to see what is hidden in the dark. Shine Your light. Help us to find her.

This time, Anthony stayed focused on the background and surroundings. "The building looks old. Check out the wooden walls behind her." Peeling white paint and gaps between warped planks showed the building's age.

"Where do we have old wooden buildings like that?" Junior was back and watching the video with them.

"Who knows? He could have her in an old barn out in the country, or downtown in one of the historical buildings," Savannah said.

Historical.

An emblem on a podium off to the side caught Anthony's attention. He stilled. "I know where she is!" He ran to his chair and grabbed his coat. "It's Sagebrush City."

"Sagebrush City?" Olivia walked in, already wearing her winter gear, carrying a bunch of coffee orders.

"It's a historical mining town, up in the foothills. A ghost town. It's open to tourists in the summer, but no one would be out there now." Anthony checked his weapon.

"I've never even heard of it, and I grew up here." Junior threw his coat on over his sling as they all ran for the parking lot. "Are you positive? We could be way off track if we're wrong here."

"My mother used to sell produce there. Spent a lot of time there as a kid, so yeah, I'm sure. That emblem is the city seal." They rushed outside, the freezing precipitation hitting them in the face. "We'll need chains. The road is going to bad with the ice and snow."

But at least he knew the way.

Hang on, Della!

EIGHTEEN

Provoking a serial killer by breaking his nose might not have been the most brilliant move. Here, under the blinding spotlight in an otherwise dim room, Vaynes off doing who knew what, Della could see that.

It had been her last-ditch effort for justice and retaliation. As much as she had been ready to tell the truth, she hated doing it on Jason's terms. She had hoped to leverage what he wanted to convince him to turn himself in.

Dumb idea.

The spark of defiance that had inspired the move must've evaporated into the night. Now she was stuck with the reality of the situation pressing in on her like a relentless chokehold.

She was going to die.

"God, where are You? Remind me of the truth."

The whispered prayer escaped her lips but did little to fill all the dark space around her.

Vaynes probably knew that leaving her anticipating his retaliation was a much more effective torture than anything he could do physically.

It was working.

Her body trembled. At this point it could be the shock or the cold or the fear. Who knew? But the longer he left her here, the more bleak the situation grew. The agony from her mangled fingers, throbbing down her arm, was unbearable. She couldn't stop the tears if she wanted to. Her body hurt so much she'd almost welcome Vaynes knocking her out at this point, except for the fear of waking up to something even worse.

I could really use a rescue, Lord.

Remember my names.

Names?

Her breath caught. Her mother's game.

Almighty, Bread of Life, Creator. Deliverer. Emmanuel.

Della paused. Emmanuel. God with us.

Her heart lifted at a quiet voice inside.

You are not alone.

But she sure felt like it.

She'd been alone for a long time. She'd thrown herself into work, the foster parent process, volunteering, all trying to fill the darkness that plagued her. She'd turned down outings with coworkers and even acquaintances at church. She was much better at serving and teaching and working than connecting with others.

But nothing had shaken the shame of not being there for Lily. Lying on the stand. Call it survivor's guilt or whatever. She'd lost her parents and best friend. Another loss would have destroyed her. It had seemed easier to do life on her own.

But look at where that had gotten her.

A picture of Anthony filled her thoughts, his blue eyes concerned, his dark hair messy from dragging his fingers through it. He had to be going out of his mind.

Too bad she hadn't asked him out, gotten to know him sooner.

She hadn't known him long, but over the last couple of days, she'd learned a few things about the handsome officer. Despite the clothes and the Casanova reputation, he wasn't the kind of guy to sit back and do nothing. Even now, he was most likely searching for her. And then there were Penny and Bryce and the others. They were probably doing everything they could to find her.

Maybe there was reason to hope after all.

And it wasn't only these friends.

She claimed she believed in God Almighty. And He was Emmanuel, God with her, right here. Right now.

She wasn't alone.

All right, Lord, time to stop believing the lies. Remind me of the light of Your love. Fill me now. And lead Anthony and the others here. If not to rescue me, may they at least capture Vaynes before he can hurt anyone else. Please.

A wave of energy thrummed through her. No need to stay here scared and helpless. She needed to use this time to free herself, to help them find her. If there was a way to send up a signal to them...

Della peered into the shadowed corners and studied the room. The longer she did, the more her eyes adjusted. The building was old. Almost cavernous with how empty it was. An old-fashioned cot sat behind bars of a little jail cell in the corner. Next to the cell was a sturdy wooden desk, an ink stand with a feather sticking out of it sitting on top. Ancient "Wanted" posters were tacked to the wall. They all looked like props in a Western movie. A lantern even sat on a barrel in a different corner, with burlap sacks arranged around it.

The lantern.

It might work as a signal. Hopefully it had something flammable in it. But she had to get to it. The wooden chair she was tied to was on the flimsier side. If she could free her arm from the table she was strapped to, she could maybe find a way to escape. Signal for help.

Without Vaynes holding the straps tight around her arm,

she'd managed to loosen them a little. She couldn't move her hand without excruciating pain shooting up her broken and bloodied fingers, but she had to. He could come back at any time.

Della bit down on her molars and yanked her shoulder away from the table, screaming inside at the burn shooting up from her hand. But her arm, already bloody and now sweaty too, finally slipped out of the straps.

That was one limb she could use. But with the broken fingers, there wasn't much she could grasp. There was no way to untie the knots trapping her other wrist or undo the duct tape around her ankles and chair legs. But she could scooch the chair out of the construction light's reach and look for a weapon or tool. Bit by bit she hopped the chair over the cord stretched across the room and made it to the desk. Nothing there to use. But the lantern might be useful. Using her thumb, she hooked the wire handle of the lantern and lifted it to her nose.

One whiff told her it was kerosene.

Now she just needed something to ignite it. If there was a way to get outside and set a small fire, someone would call the fire department, right? Della moved toward the double doors across the room.

"Where do you think you're going?" Vaynes roared.

She yelped as he caught the back of her chair and dragged her to the middle of the room.

He knocked the lantern out of her hand, sending it crashing to the floor. Splintered glass shimmered while the kerosene puddled and spread across several of the wooden planks.

No!

"Now look at what you've done." Vaynes grew still. He threw a case on the table and opened it. The light glinted off the metal tip of a needle in his hand.

She couldn't be drugged again.

She threw her weight back and forth with what little give she could find. Every instinct screamed to get as far away from him as possible.

Vaynes stepped closer. She thrashed harder, tipping her chair. She fell to the side, her free arm barely escaping being crushed. But in the fall, one of her legs broke free. With it, she kicked at Vaynes, catching him in the chin, then the chest.

He fell over, knocking the light down to the ground and flooding the room in darkness. But sparks caught the spilled kerosene and quickly ignited. Flames licked the floor, growing taller by the second.

Vaynes didn't move.

She had to get out of here.

Della kicked, scooting herself and the chair farther back. With her free arm and leg, she pushed herself as far away from Vaynes and the fire as she could until she'd positioned herself against the wall, by the double doors that had to be the main entrance. But already, the table she'd been strapped to in the middle of the room was ablaze. A wall of flames cut her off from Vaynes, but she couldn't free herself from the chair. She couldn't stand.

But she could kick.

Having lost her sock in the fray, she kicked at the door with her bare foot. It didn't budge.

She screamed and kicked again. She had to get free.

Smoke rolled off the low ceiling. Della coughed and continued to beat at the door.

The smoke grew thicker, the flames danced closer, and Della's muscles screamed for relief. A coughing fit overtook her. She lay on the floor, still strapped to the chair, and gasped for breath. The fire was only a few feet away, but she had nothing left. Her kicking must've broken something in her foot. She couldn't move it anymore.

As she lay there, a voice called her name. It was faint, maybe only a figment of her imagination. Hopefully someone would take care of Grandma Priya. Her thoughts grew fuzzy.

This was it.

There would be no foster care, no honoring Lily's sacrifice. No chance to get to know Anthony.

But then a draft of cold, clean air rushed over her as the doors flew open.

"Della!"

She pried open her eyes to find Anthony standing over her. He lifted her, chair and all, and carried her into the snowy night.

"Set her down, Tony." Penny pulled a multitool from her pocket and cut the tape and rope, freeing Della's other limbs. As soon as Della was free from the chair, Anthony scooped her up in his arms. Someone, maybe Penny, tucked a coat around her. Shouting, sirens, and flashing lights swirled around them.

And there was Anthony. The warmth from his body fighting off the chill in hers.

This wasn't a dream. He was real. He was here. She smiled.

Finally safe and sheltered, Della rested her head against his chest and succumbed to the blackness overtaking her.

NINETEEN

Anthony raced back to Last Chance as quickly as the treacherous roads would allow. As grateful as he was for the break in the weather that had allowed the medevac helicopter to land and take Della, he hated that he couldn't ride with her. And now the storm system was back even stronger as he fought to get to the hospital. He wanted to be there when Della woke. Wanted to tell her the nightmare was over.

Vaynes was dead. No one had been able to reach him in the burning building, though Bryce had tried. The building was a total loss, but thankfully the rest of Sagebrush City was safe.

There was a lot more to tell her.

Like how much he liked her. How he wanted her to meet his mother. That he would gladly don a Santa suit if it brought joy to children and made her event a success. He rehearsed the whole list while he drove to the hospital and then waited in the lobby. But hours later, when he was able to step into her room and see for himself that she truly was alive and awake, he forgot it all.

She sat in the bed, propped up at an angle, early-morning

light shining through the window. Her eyes met his and her full lips tilted up into a weak smile. "You came."

Even with the croak in her voice, it was still the most beautiful sound he'd ever heard. He walked up to her bed and took her free hand in his. Her wrist had been bandaged, but her fingers fit perfectly entwined with his. Her other hand was in a cast and rested in her lap.

"I've been so worried about you," he finally said. Not the most eloquent opening, but it was true.

"I'm okay."

"Really?"

"The doctor says I'll make a full recovery."

His eyes landed on her cast, the IV lines, and the bandage wrapped around her wrist. "I'm sorry we didn't get there sooner."

"You came just in time. You saved m—"

"Knock, knock." A nurse came into the room. "I'm just taking vitals." She walked over to the bed. "Is this the police officer you were telling me about?"

Della nodded. "This is him. Officer Anthony Thomas."

"So you're the one who saved this young lady? Aren't you the handsome hero. No wonder she swooned in your arms." The nurse chuckled.

Anthony's cheeks flushed hot. "It wasn't just me. There's a lot of people who made it happen. A lot of people who care."

"Well, the paper has your picture on the front page. All the nurses are saying you deserve a medal. And it's gotta be good PR for the police department."

"I was just doing my job. The important thing is that she's safe."

"She's blessed to have people looking out for her. The doctor even wants to discharge her later this morning." The nurse kept chatting until she finished taking Della's vitals and left.

A stillness settled in the room. Della picked at the blanket folds on her lap. "Did you mean what you said?"

"What?"

"That rescuing me was just doing your job?"

His first reaction was to play it cool. But he stopped, shook his head. He was done trying to hold on to that image. "I said it so she'd stop gushing."

Della chuckled. "She was laying it on pretty thick. I bet you get that a lot."

"Not really. But if you want to know the truth, I really care about you, Della." She was more than a job, more than getting a promotion or showing his superiors he was worthy. She was way more than the notoriety of catching a serial killer.

He might as well lay it all out there and be honest. "I'd like to spend more time getting to know you."

Her lips turned up in a slow grin. "I know a great way to do that."

"You do?"

"I still need a Santa for the toy drive. And I can't think of a better person than the police department poster boy. Especially now that you're a headliner."

Anthony threw his head back and laughed. "You're never gonna let me live this down, are you?"

"Nope. But—" She dropped her gaze, then looked up at him shyly through her thick lashes. "You can totally say no if you want to but...um, would you like to accompany me to the firehouse Christmas party?"

He reached for her hand again. "I'd be honored."

And for the first time in many years, he had something to look forward to this Christmas. Hope for the future, and someone special to share it with.

RESCUED HOPE

LAURA CONAWAY

She doesn't need her heart broken again. But he might just be the one to heal it…

K-9 Officer Cole Stuart has two missions: catch killer Blair Mackey and convince EMT Kianna Russell to give him a chance. Two years of hunting a monster, months of gentle pursuit—both seem impossible until one violent winter storm changes everything.

EMT Kianna Russell keeps her heart locked away for good reason. She's already lost one person she cared about to Mackey's violence—her foster student Jaxon—and been betrayed by a man she trusted. When Mackey escapes, she can't stay on the sidelines, even if it means partnering with the devastatingly attractive K-9 officer who sees through every wall she's built.

Trapped together in a deadly manhunt, their carefully guarded hearts are about to be tested.

As blizzard conditions turn their hunt into a fight for survival, they discover they're walking into a trap years in the making. Mackey has an accomplice with inside access, and suddenly they're not the hunters—they're the prey.

With a traitor in their midst and innocent lives at stake, survival depends on complete trust.

Racing through treacherous mountains against time, Cole must prove his love is worth the risk while Kianna faces her deepest fear—trusting a man who could shatter her heart. Because when their enemies close in, only faith will keep them alive.

Will their love survive the storm... or will they lose everything before they've begun?

To my Lord and Savior who came into the world to provide the best Christmas miracle and is the true Light and Hope. Soli Deo Gloria.

"In his name the nations will put their hope."

MATTHEW 12:21 (NIV)

There was no going back to the good ole days for Cole Stuart. But that didn't have to be true for the rest of Last Chance County—so long as he caught the escaped convict.

Detaining Blair Mackey would be the best gift this holiday season, but it would require a Christmas miracle. The job was proving to be the quest of the year—follow the shining star to the culprit, except Mackey's location continued to shift.

"Ice and snow won't stop us, right, Titan?" His breath puffed in front of him thanks to the early-morning temps hovering at twenty degrees Fahrenheit. Cole opened the back door of his cruiser, and his K-9 partner barreled out. He unhooked the German shepherd's leash, and the dog stared up at him with his brown eyes.

Cole zipped up his police jacket, then donned his winter gloves. This time of year made him grateful for the layers to his uniform that held the heat inside. The last thing he could afford right now was frostbite. Anything that would delay being out in the field to find Mackey. A mix of rain and snow flurries pelted his face, and he kept his gaze downwind. He pulled up his hood and lowered his sunglasses to block out the sun's glare.

"Just got to the east side of Crest Forest. Cole, what's your status?" Officer Anthony Thomas's voice crackled in Cole's in-ear piece.

"Titan and I are on the west side. We're taking the Midpoint Trail in." Cole clapped his hands and started walking, Titan right on his heel.

"I want Mackey caught yesterday. We've got two of the convicts back behind bars. The sooner Mackey's apprehended, the sooner everyone can get on with their Christmas plans."

Cole coughed to keep a laugh from escaping. Thomas's sarcastic tone reminded Cole he wasn't the only one who didn't exactly enjoy the holidays. Cole wanted Mackey found too, and if he had to work through Christmas or miss their staff Christmas party, he wouldn't complain. That would be a bonus miracle to the season. It would give Cole a legitimate reason not to attend any festive gatherings, instead of having to come up with another lame excuse.

Before Cole could respond, Ramble's voice cut in. "And I don't want to be sitting out on the action."

"You're doing one of the best jobs, manning the tip line at the station." Cole smirked and held back a chuckle.

"Says the one who's front and center with the action." Ramble huffed.

"What did the doctor say?" Thomas asked.

"More like Nurse Ainsley at this point. Said I need to take it easy, especially in this storm. But I only have another week left in the arm sling, and it's already much better."

Cole could picture Ramble pulling his arm out of the restraint to prove his point. "Ainsley's doing what any good girlfriend would do. Don't give her a heart attack and make her think you'll get hurt again."

"Someone's getting sentimental around the holidays." Ramble paused. "I'll let you know if any other tips come in."

Cole almost interjected with *I know what it's like to lose someone around the holidays*. Once again, he held back and didn't vocalize the thought. Now wasn't the time to walk down memory lane. If he wanted to keep people safe from a killer's snare and make sure they had a blissful Christmas season, he needed to do his job.

"I'll let you know if Titan and I find anything." Cole trekked down the narrow path. His shoes squished in the slush of leaves and dirt mingled with the freezing rain and snow. The canopy covering from the pine trees should have helped, but the wind worked against them and blew the pellets of icy rain every which way.

"Let's hope this tip pans out and Mackey hasn't gotten far," Thomas said. "Cole, I'll circle around and meet you at the overlook in fifty."

"Copy that. Mackey can only survive so long in the elements." Cole scanned the open expanse in front of him. The bare trees and overcast sky didn't help visibility. But Cole wouldn't let the forecast deter him. "If he's nearby, we'll find his footprints too. This weather is working against him."

Cole pulled out a bag with a piece of fabric in it. Thanks to a quick DNA test, forensics had confirmed the patch of clothing was Mackey's. And Titan's skills were top notch. His partner could find Mackey, even though the convict had changed outfits and was no longer wearing the easily identifiable orange jumpsuit. "Titan, sniff." Cole held the bag open, and the German shepherd stuck his nose toward the fabric. "Good boy. Titan, track." The dog veered to the left and cantered alongside the path.

"All right, Mackey, where are you?" Cole's voice was drowned out by the rain.

Other officers had spread out to cover more ground and cut Mackey off.

The latest tip had Mackey spotted near a makeshift cave, thanks to a few locals who had cabins up here in the woods. They didn't see many travelers on foot this time of year unless they were coming in for snowshoeing or ice fishing. Although the lake on the south side wasn't fully frozen over yet.

Cole forged ahead, following Titan. The dog let out a bark and picked up speed. Cole broke into a jog and grabbed his radio with one hand. "I think Titan's found something. When's the copter coming in?"

"What direction are you headed?" Thomas asked. "Copter should be airborne in five minutes."

"Northwest." Cole focused on Titan, whose black tail wagged behind him. "Good. We need as many eyes as possible."

The flight crew would be able to see a larger expanse than any of the officers on the ground. If Titan led them to Mackey, Cole wanted the copter to have eyes from above. Make sure Mackey knew there was no chance of escape.

The sleet fell harder now. Droplets flew off his waterproof jacket, and Cole wiped the precipitation off his brow. He followed Titan around a bend to a clearing among the trees. Titan let out a bark and barreled to a set of boulders. He sat on his haunches near a small opening and whimpered.

"I'm at a clearing, and it looks like there's a place to hide in the rocks." Cole pulled his Glock from the hip holster and kept it aimed at the ground in front of him. "Thomas, how far are you from my location?"

Each of the officers had a tracking device on their uniform. For search and rescue cases, or in this situation, search and arrest, it proved helpful in making sure no one got lost when they covered a large coordinate grid.

"Copy. I'm two minutes out," Thomas said.

Cole whistled. "Titan, go."

The dog barreled into the opening and disappeared.

Cole positioned himself to the right of the rocks and waited. The moment Mackey stepped out of hiding, Cole would be there to put an end to the man's plans. His pulse throbbed in his neck, and his cheeks warmed. The adrenaline rush warded off the frigid temperatures.

Seconds ticked by, and Cole held his breath. Where was the snarl from Titan? Or a human cry from the dog's quick response to latch onto the culprit? Cole exhaled, and his breath puffed in front of him.

He didn't have all day to wait around, and Mackey couldn't hide in there forever. Cole pulled out his flashlight with his free hand and flicked on the switch. With his weapon still in his left, he shone the light into the cave and ducked into the opening.

"It's time to give it up, Mackey." He moved the light around the space. A pair of footprints marked the territory and led to the back.

Titan turned around and whimpered.

Cole let out a grunt. The guy wasn't here. The space wasn't more than eight feet wide, and giant rocks closed off the back area. Only one entry and exit point.

"Titan, come." Cole crawled back out of the space and tucked his weapon and flashlight away. "You did good, boy." He rubbed the German shepherd's head, then handed him a treat.

"Negative on Mackey." Cole relayed on the radio. "But he's been here at some point."

"You're kidding." Thomas sighed.

"Hold on. It's not over yet, guys," Ramble said. "Another lead just came in."

"Where at?" Cole stopped walking and signaled for Titan to wait.

"Mountainview Ridge Overlook."

Cole pulled up his map of the area. "On foot, we're thirty

minutes away." Footsteps came from in front of him, and Cole lowered his phone to see Thomas approaching.

"We can make it ten by car." Thomas's breath came in pants.

At least Thomas had the same idea. Cole wanted to take the fast route. No way could they let Mackey gain extra ground.

More precipitation hit Cole's skin and stung his cheek. Hard pellets dropped faster to the ground. *Great.* His car might be equipped to handle the snow, but if the sleet kept up, it could delay their ETA.

"Be careful, you guys." Ramble's voice deepened. "The radar shows more precipitation in the forecast for the next hour."

"Work crews should be out treating the roads." Cole walked faster, his eyes focused on the trail so he wouldn't slip and fall. They just had to get out of this remote area first. Once they were on main roads, they shouldn't have a problem.

"They can only work so fast. A car careened into the guardrail and crashed at the overlook. The tip on Mackey's sighting came in from the driver. Kianna and Trace are en route too."

Kianna.

Cole's breath caught in his throat. It had only been a few days since he'd seen the Eastside Firehouse EMT. They had both witnessed the aftermath of the initial collision with the transport van carrying the convicts.

Kianna was gifted at what she did. Her calm demeanor and peaceful disposition were evidence she was in the right profession. Someone could be bleeding out, but she had a way of keeping them from panicking while she did her job. Not to mention she was gorgeous. Her face entered Cole's mind—the way she smiled at someone like they were the most important person in the room.

Cole's foot caught on a branch covered with leaves, and he jerked forward. Titan let out a bark. Cole compensated with his other foot and caught himself.

"It's okay, Tite." He smiled at his partner, even while his own pulse skittered.

"You good?" Thomas raised a brow.

Cole nodded and clamped down on his lips.

Now was not the time to think about Kianna. Not when she could be stripped from him in the blink of an eye. He'd seen it happen before. Which meant there was no use hoping for something that would only end in heartache.

Cole had to keep his head on straight. Focus on what lay ahead, not behind. And right now, that meant doing his job.

The tree line opened up into the parking lot, where his cruiser was the lone vehicle.

Thomas slid into the passenger seat while Cole opened the back for Titan to climb in. Once his K-9 was settled, Cole got into the driver's side and turned on the ignition, then put the heat on full blast.

"That feels good." Thomas leaned closer to the vents and took his gloves off.

Titan must have sensed the warm air too, because he turned around in his kennel and stuck his head between the bars, lifting his snout.

"Attaboy." Cole smiled, then put the car in reverse. "Time to go catch this killer."

He pulled out onto the road. Sleet pinged off the windshield. The car's wipers swished in a rapid motion to clear away the precipitation.

Five minutes later, Cole turned onto a main road. A plow truck drove past in the opposite direction, sprinkling salt behind it. Cole waved to the guy.

"They're making our job easier." Thomas leaned forward and saluted the driver.

"Thank the Lord." Cole followed the curve of the road, then hit the accelerator to climb the short hill. He eased up on the gas as the approaching stoplight turned yellow. "The roads still covered fast." He pressed down on the brakes, which kicked back from the slush.

He lifted off the pedal, then pushed down again. Except the tires didn't catch traction, and the front of the car veered to the left.

"Whoa, man. Watch the ditch." Thomas gripped the door handle.

Cole tightened his grasp on the steering wheel, fighting the urge to swing to the right and overcorrect. "I'm trying."

The car straightened but gave no sign of stopping as it continued to slide toward the intersection.

"We're going to run this light." Cole steeled his back against the seat. "Is there any oncoming traffic?" His voice rose a notch, and he glanced to the left.

"We've got another plow truck coming up on our right," Thomas shouted and tapped the window.

Please, Lord. Let the brakes do their job. Cole blew out a breath and flicked on his lights to alert the other truck.

Cole tapped the brakes once more. The cruiser lurched forward, then slid to a stop, halfway in the intersection.

The plow truck whizzed around them, spraying salt across their windshield.

Thomas whistled. "That was close. Good work, man."

Cole leaned his head against the seat. They were still a mile away from the Mountainview Ridge Overlook crash site. Every second created more distance between Mackey's arrest and his escape. No thanks to this weather, the manhunt for Mackey was becoming more treacherous than Cole had bargained for.

Only time would tell if they were too late.

TWO

"We're four minutes out," Kianna Russell radioed to the dispatcher from the passenger seat of the ambulance. Trace steered the truck down the street and made a left turn.

Kianna gripped the door handle and let out a breath. "The sleet doesn't look to be letting up anytime soon." The icy mixture collided with the windshield, and the gray sky grew darker.

"You're telling me. Whoever decided it would be a good idea to venture onto the roads didn't check the radar."

Kianna grimaced. *Please, Lord, don't let there be any fatalities.* No family deserved to lose loved ones, especially around the holidays. "Just get us there in one piece so we can get these people to safety." Even if her holiday wasn't going to be spectacular, she could make sure it ended well for someone else.

"I'll Be Home for Christmas" played over the radio station, and Kianna turned the volume down.

Trace gave her a side glance, his eyebrow raised.

"What?" She shrugged. "I'm not in the mood for festive holiday music."

"Bad memories?"

"Something like that." Kianna shifted her attention to the trees lining the road. She really didn't want to bare her heart right now. Not when the song already dredged up reminders of what she'd once hoped for. Except her reality had turned out exactly like the song predicted.

Only in her dreams.

"A lot of people hide behind the tinsel and lights to mask their grief this time of year." Trace sighed. "I get it. That used to be me."

"I'm sorry. I didn't mean to stir up reminders for you too."

Trace shook his head. "Don't be. God's brought me so far from that time. Reminded me of all the goodness He has shown me. It still hurts at times, but I have so much to be thankful for now. Like my beautiful wife and baby girl I get to see when this shift is over." He grinned.

Kianna stared out the window at the cloudy sky. Trace had lost love once to death. While her experience with love wasn't the same, it had the same effect. Grief. Confusion. Heartache. Longing. It all swirled around her like a winter storm, threatening to pummel her in an avalanche she couldn't escape.

"Everyone else might have the perfect Christmas with lights and mistletoe, but those good moments only come for other people." She let out a laugh, but it fell short. Somehow, God had prevented her from partaking in the celebrations of life.

"I hear you. But I can tell you from experience, it's not true." Trace gave her a sympathetic smile.

He turned the corner and pulled to the side of the road. A green four-door sedan sat by the guardrail.

Kianna let out a breath. Thanks to other pressing matters, their conversation ended.

The hood of the vehicle was pushed in, and green paint streaked along the metal guardrail, where the car must have hit before coming to rest.

The rescue squad truck pulled up behind them, and the crew hopped out.

"I'll grab the stretcher," Trace said, then exited from the driver's side.

Kianna pulled up her hood to keep the ice from searing her neck. Then she walked around to the back of the ambo and grabbed the medic bag. If the temperatures continued to drop, there'd be a nasty mix of slush and snow.

Eddie, from Rescue, followed her over to the car. Cracks lined the windows, and the side mirror lay a foot away on the ground.

Eddie rapped on the door. "Sir, I'm here with the rescue squad and medics. We're going to get you all out of there."

"How many?" Trace came up next to Kianna with the stretcher. He set the brakes on the wheels and wedged it into some rocks on the ground to keep it from sliding.

"Four. Two kids are in the back. Including one in a car seat." Kianna grimaced. None of them could be severely injured. Not at Christmas. This season was one for miracles. At least, she'd pray and believe in one for this family.

The driver rolled down the window and leaned forward. "My door is stuck. And my daughter." His voice caught. "She's bleeding on her face."

"We're going to help." Eddie smiled, then tugged on the passenger door. It opened, and he leaned in. Seconds later, he held a black-haired boy's hand and guided him out onto the pavement.

The kid sported a puffer jacket. Even so, Kianna grabbed a blanket from her bag and walked over to the child. He was tall and lanky, maybe ten years old, and his wide eyes scanned the area.

She bent to match his height. "What's your name?"

"Benjamin." He blinked.

"It's nice to meet you, Benjamin. I'm Miss Kianna, and I'm

going to make sure you're not hurt." She held out the blanket. "This will keep you extra warm, okay?"

Benjamin nodded.

She wrapped the aluminum thermal blanket around him. "Does anything hurt?"

"No. But my sister." He scrunched his forehead. "My sister has a bad cut."

"You're a good brother, looking out for her. We'll make sure it gets bandaged up."

"I'm her *big* brother. Of course I have to take care of her." His pupils expanded. "That's what my mom and dad tell me." Benjamin turned back to the car.

Eddie hoisted a toddler with curly brown hair onto his hip.

Trace hurried over and held out his arms to take the girl, and she began to cry.

"Posie!" Benjamin dashed off. He made it a few steps before his sneaker slipped on the slush and he fell backward.

Kianna raced forward and grabbed the boy's arm, putting her hand on his back before he could collide with the pavement.

"Thanks." Benjamin didn't even turn around. His focus stayed on his sister, and he reached out to take her hand. "It's okay, Posie. This is a nice guy. He's going to help us."

Posie whimpered but the tears had stopped.

Zack circled around to the front of the car. "The passenger side is snug against the guardrail. Can they climb out the back?" He nodded to Eddie.

Kianna tuned out the rescue crew and signaled to Trace. "Why don't we go sit on the back of the truck?" She pointed to the ambulance. "We can wait there for your mom and dad to come over."

Benjamin peered at Kianna, then Trace. "As long as I can hold Posie's hand the whole time."

Kianna smiled, and a warmth worked its way up her arms. The compassion and concern this child had toward his sister brought tears to her eyes. *Don't ever grow out of this innocence, kid. Keep protecting your sis. And any girl you meet when you get older.* This interaction threatened to whisk her away to memories of a time when her own hopes of being protected and treated with care had been squandered.

"You got it, dude." Trace's comment pulled her back to the present.

She blinked away the tears.

Trace gave Benjamin a thumbs-up with his free hand, then the four of them walked over to the back of the ambulance.

She helped Benjamin up into the truck bed, and the kid sat, swinging his legs off the ledge.

Trace worked on cleaning Posie's wound, and Kianna took Benjamin's vitals. The entire time, Benjamin kept his hand wrapped around his sister's fingers.

"There we go." Trace pressed a bandage on Posie's cheek. "You'll be all better soon."

"She's going to be okay?" Benjamin's mouth stayed open, almost like he was afraid to smile.

"I'd say so." Trace grinned. "She had a cut from some glass, but the Band-Aid will help it heal in no time."

"Benjamin! Posie!" Their parents called out and hurried over.

"Are they…?" The mom turned to Kianna, her lip quivering.

"They're fine." Kianna moved to the side to give them space for a minute. A few scratches lined the woman's forehead and cheek. Kianna would triage her in a moment. It was a good sign that both parents were out and moving.

Thank you, the woman mouthed before taking Posie from Trace's arms and enveloping Benjamin in a hug. The father moved into the embrace, and Kianna got Trace's attention and pointed to the man's wrist. It was black and blue and swollen.

Trace pulled supplies from one of the metal compartments in the vehicle and laid them out.

Tires crunched over the slushy roadway and came to a stop.

The police cruiser's lights flashed through the precipitation. The car door shut, and Cole Stuart and Anthony Thomas got out. They stopped for a second to talk with Ridge Foster, the rescue squad lieutenant, before making their way over to the ambulance.

"I'm going to stabilize your arm." Trace cut a piece of brown adhesive tape to bandage the father's wrist. "But it should be x-rayed to make sure nothing is broken, given how swollen it is."

"While you're doing that, I'd like to ask a few questions." Cole stepped up.

"Sure." The father nodded. "I'll tell you everything so you can catch the guy."

Cole exchanged a brief glance with Kianna, and her heart skittered. She turned her attention to the mom and wrapped the blood pressure cuff around her arm, even while her fingers quivered.

What was her body doing? There was no reason for the nerves around Cole. She'd only had a few brief interactions with the K-9 officer. And it certainly wasn't enough time to warrant feelings for the man. Even if they'd bonded briefly after witnessing the crash of the transport van just the other day. Kianna had only felt safe around Cole because he was doing his job of protecting people. If time had taught her anything, it was that in the end, it would be too good to be true. There was always some red flag that lurked under the surface, and sooner or later, it would break to the top.

Kianna squeezed the bulb and watched the pin on the gauge climb before releasing the air valve. "I'm going to clean the cuts on your face, but everything else looks good," she told the woman.

"I still can't believe it. One minute I was driving and this man was walking along the shoulder. He turned as we approached, and all of a sudden, he runs out, waving his hands." The father blew out a breath. "I jerked the wheel to the left to avoid hitting him, and I lost control. The tires spun out, and we hit the guardrail."

Kianna opened a rubbing alcohol wipe and continued attending to the woman.

"Can you describe the man?" Cole's brow furrowed.

"He had brown hair down to his shoulders and a beard. He wasn't wearing an orange jumpsuit, but I think it was—" The man shuddered.

"Mackey." Cole raised an eyebrow, and the other officer frowned. "Did you see which direction he went?"

Mackey. Kianna's stomach twisted. So they still hadn't found him. She didn't want to imagine what would happen if he wasn't caught. But the more time Mackey eluded the police, the easier it got for him to escape once and for all.

"Yeah. I lost consciousness, and when I came to, he was tapping on the window where my son was seated. At first, I thought he was going to try and get into our car, until my wife yelled that the police were on the way. Then he hopped the guardrail and took off that way." The man pointed across the road to the wooded area.

"That's helpful." Cole nodded, then turned to Thomas. "We need to widen our search. I'll call it in and start out with Titan."

"I'll take this family back into town, then meet you out there," Thomas said.

Kianna and Trace finished up with the patients, and Thomas escorted them to his cruiser.

Cole stepped to the side of the ambulance and radioed in.

Kianna turned to Trace. "Are you good to take the ambo back to the station?" She checked her watch. "Our shift is over, and I want to stay out here. Join the search."

Trace squinted against the snow flurries that had begun to fall in place of the sleet. "He's dangerous, Kianna. I'd let the police handle it."

"I know what Mackey is capable of, and I can't stand around

and let him go free. Not when he's responsible for killing someone I knew."

THREE

"I'm coming with you."

Cole froze at the statement and turned to Kianna, who had her arms crossed. "The police have it covered. Mackey's too dangerous."

Kianna's jaw flexed.

Cole frowned. Kianna wasn't an officer, and he didn't want a civilian slowing down the search. Plus, "I don't want you in danger. We've had one too many close calls." The father's statement was a prime example.

He admired her tenacity, but from what they knew of him, Mackey wasn't the kind of person you messed around with. He didn't care who got hurt. His only mission right now was to save his own skin—whatever the cost.

Cole understood the risks of his job.

But it wasn't fair for others to step in the line of fire as civilians. If something happened to Kianna, her family would be distraught. Life would never be the same.

"Then I'll search on my own." She pulled her hair up and took a ponytail holder from her wrist to secure the updo. "In my line of work, I've learned two are better than one." She shrugged.

Oh, she was good. Cole wasn't sure whether he should laugh or reprimand her for her persuasive tactic.

He could spend time arguing, but precious seconds were ticking by. "Don't you have a job to do? Trace shouldn't have to do everything by himself. After all, two are better than one." Cole winked.

"Touché." Kianna smirked. "My shift's over, so I'm on my own time now. And it looks like I no longer have a ride." She held out her hand to the ambulance pulling away from the shoulder.

"Daylight won't last forever." He nodded, then tugged on Titan's leash. "Let's get searching."

The dog let out a short bark and wagged his tail.

Kianna fell into step next to him, and they climbed over the guardrail and trudged through the wet, slush-covered grass.

Cole lifted his radio. "Titan, EMT Kianna Russell, and I are headed east, into the woods, past the Mountainview Ridge Overlook."

"Copy." Tazwell's voice sounded in his ear. "We've got the copter scouring the area too."

"Witnesses at the scene of the crash said Mackey headed this way." Cole rattled off the coordinates of the location and picked up his speed.

He burrowed his chin against his chest. The cold air began to seep into his face and penetrate his jacket.

"He couldn't have gotten far. Let's hope he's cornered soon."

Cole agreed with Tazwell. Their task force for this search was fifteen people. And with the rest of the town on the lookout as well, the guy couldn't hide forever. At least, Cole hoped not.

They stepped into the woods, and Kianna brushed pine branches away from their path. Their feet crunched on twigs under the slush. Thanks to the tree cover, there was less ice and snow in this area.

"How long have you and the dog been working together?" Kianna never took her focus off the path.

"Two years. I got to be part of his training process, and we bonded quickly. I'd say Titan is one of the best in the field. Isn't that right, boy?"

Titan's ears perked and he barked.

"I'd say he agrees." Kianna smiled. "Although, don't you think you're a little biased? What made you decide to join the force and work with this guy?"

Cole laughed. "And you don't beat around the bush. I help out at Tiny Paws, the local animal shelter, on occasion. Titan and I train some of the rougher strays to have better behavior so they find homes faster."

"That's noble of you." Her blue eyes met his gaze, and the look there made him shift his focus. The curiosity and warmth in her expression was dangerous. Like she was trying to get to know him.

He couldn't succumb to the pull. Not when getting to know someone came with added weight. If he let himself get invested, there was no telling what would happen.

Circumstances changed in the blink of an eye.

And a friendship now meant the grief of loss later.

He groaned.

"You okay?" Kianna raised her eyebrows.

"Yeah." He swallowed. What was he supposed to tell her? That he didn't want to answer her question because he was too afraid of vulnerability? Of being known, then losing someone?

He shook his head. Even in his own mind it sounded ridiculous, never mind spoken out loud.

"My dad was in law enforcement." Cole veered to the left and continued to follow the path, but he scanned the perimeter, squinting in search of any movement among the trees. "He let me tag along to the office every year on 'take your child to work' day, and I loved it. The adrenaline of hunting down the bad guys and keeping people safe was exhilarating. Even if I only heard about it from the office conversations. My dad garnered a lot of respect. The way he cared for the community and his own family each day made me want to do the same."

"I can't imagine how hard he worked. And the courage it took to protect people." Kianna smiled. "Is he still working?"

"He retired almost two years ago," he said matter-of-factly. Rather, he'd been forced to retire. Cole's throat tightened. No, he wouldn't dwell on what had happened. It wouldn't change the outcome.

He had a mission to focus on right now. By doing his job, Cole could honor his dad. Walk in his footsteps and leave a similar legacy.

He'd find Mackey no matter how long it took.

Kianna pulled up her hood and tugged the zipper of her jacket higher.

"Why were you so"—how did he say it nicely?—"adamant about searching for Mackey?" Especially when it was frigid out and she could be safe and warm at home.

"He killed someone I was close to." She pressed her lips together.

Cole froze in his tracks, and air whooshed from his lungs. "I'm so sorry." He wanted to ask who, but he already had an indirect answer.

Mackey targeted foster kids. Those who didn't have steady families looking out for them. Who were vulnerable and easy to prey on because the promise of love and acceptance was enticing, regardless of who was offering those basic human needs.

"What happened?" Cole stopped moving for a minute and pulled out two water bottles. "Here." He handed one to Kianna, then took a swig. He didn't want them to be lured into a false perception of being hydrated just because it wasn't hot.

"Thanks." She capped the bottle and gave it back to him to put in his backpack. "When I'm not on the clock as a medic, I tutor kids in math and science. Each semester, a few of the teachers at Last Chance Middle School give me a list of kids who are falling behind and need extra help."

Cole started walking again, and Kianna followed suit.

The whir of helicopter blades buzzed nearby. He lifted his head but couldn't make out the aircraft through the tree cover. Which meant the crew would be having a challenging time too. People were searching, but so far, no more reports had come through his headset on sightings of Mackey.

Cole focused back on the area around them. "What does that have to do with Mackey?"

"One of the kids referred to me was Jaxon. He was in foster care." She grimaced.

A knot formed in Cole's stomach.

"He had ambitions. Dreams of going to law school. But math wasn't his strong suit, and his foster parents didn't have time to help him."

"So you took it upon yourself to help him pass his class."

"I grew a soft spot for the kid. And when he mentioned having another guy in his life who'd started playing basketball with him at the park courts, I was thrilled. Everyone should have a mentor who can help them through life. Especially young men."

"It was Mackey. Grooming instead of investing." Bile rose in Cole's throat, and he coughed.

Kianna nodded. "Jaxon started running late for our tutoring sessions. When I asked him about his tardiness, he said he and his friend had been finding treasures around town and were selling them online. The profit they made was being set aside for a college fund for Jaxon. Until Jaxon discovered the truth that the money was really going to Mackey. He told me, then went to the police, but Mackey got to him first." Kianna sniffled. "His body was found a few days later."

Cole gripped Titan's leash harder. He recalled the last part of the story all too well. The endless hours of search and rescue that had turned into search and recovery. "The manipulation of that man. Lording his power over those kids." Preying on their innocence. "He looked to the least of these and stripped away their dignity."

"The exact opposite of what Jesus did." Kianna's voice quivered. "It breaks my heart to see anyone treated as such when we've all been made in *Imago Dei*."

A verse from Matthew 20 came to Cole's mind. "Christ came to serve and not to be served." The Lord cared for the outcasts. The lowly. The vulnerable.

"Indeed." Tears gathered in Kianna's eyes. "All I wanted to do was show those kids they mattered. And I missed the signs with Jaxon that could have kept him safe." She rubbed her hands together and blew on them.

"You had the right intentions, so don't beat yourself up over the outcome. It won't change anything. All we can do is move forward." Cole bit down on his tongue. He didn't have the right to tell her that. Not when he wasn't following his own advice. Sure, he spoke from experience, but he hadn't taken steps to move forward when the circumstances with his dad had rocked his world.

"I want to see Mackey caught and locked away for good. So he can't take advantage of one more child." Kianna shoved her hands in her pockets.

Leaves swayed on a branch in his peripheral vision, and Cole paused, waiting for any more movement that would signal another person in the area.

"What's that?" Kianna whispered.

Titan cocked his head. A low growl escaped through his bared teeth.

They all stood still.

Seconds later, a bird flew out of the tree.

Cole bit back a groan.

"He's got to be here somewhere." Kianna huffed. "It's freezing. Certainly that would slow down his pace."

Cole and Kianna started walking again.

"Any sightings?" Cole radioed in. "It's bleak down here." The sky itself was dark, and Cole had to remind himself not to give up.

"Negative. We're going to have to land the copter soon, given the wind and snow picking up again." This time, the voice of one of the helicopter pilots, Alexia, came through Cole's earpiece.

"This is Thomas. The family from the car accident has been dropped off. Cole, I'm headed your direction now."

"Copy," Cole said. "We're still searching the east side of the woods. I can't imagine Mackey would try to hunker down here." Not when the land stretched for several miles.

"There's a gas station we're keeping an eye on about five miles out on the south side," Tazwell radioed in. "So far, no activity."

The wind whipped around them, and leftover leaves from the fall foliage blew.

Cole focused on taking one step at a time. They couldn't stop moving. Not if they wanted to avoid the chance of hypothermia setting in.

Several minutes later, Kianna pointed straight ahead to pine trees that parted into a wide opening. "It looks like there's a clearing."

Cole powered up his map of the area on his phone.

Titan let out a bark and tugged on his leash.

Cole unhooked his partner's restraint, then pulled out the piece of fabric from Mackey's outfit. The dog sniffed. "Go." He gave the command.

Titan bounded in front of them.

"According to the map, the trail leads to an open area before winding down to an embankment and curving out again to a main road."

Could this be the section Mackey was hiking? If they caught him now before he got down to the road, Mackey wouldn't have the advantage.

Cole and Kianna jogged over to Titan, whose nose was snug to the ground.

"There's more footprints," Kianna shouted.

Titan let out another bark.

They were closing in.

"There are fresh prints on the east side at coordinates ninety-five and forty." Cole spoke to the team over the radio.

He closed the distance to Titan and moved to the right to get a better angle of the imprints to take a picture. He shifted weight to his left leg and bent down. His foot overturned on uneven ground, and he stumbled sideways.

"Cole, watch out!" Kianna screamed.

He tried to regain his footing, but his other shoe slid on the slush.

Kianna reached for his hand, except it was too late.

Cole tumbled down the embankment.

FOUR

Kianna raced to the edge, careful to avoid the same divot that had caught Cole by surprise.

Titan barked, then whined and continued to pace.

If Cole was hurt…

Kianna grimaced. She didn't have her medic bag with her, which meant she'd need to get creative on how to help him.

She crouched, and the wet snow and dirt seeped through her pant legs and sent shivers coursing through her.

She peered over.

Cole sat on the ground and was brushing snow off his pants. "Are you okay?" she yelled. The declining slope was more than twice his height. And with the slick conditions, Cole had slid down fast.

Bushes and a few small trees scattered the open field below. Who knew if there were any rocks masked under the snow?

Cole stood up and took a step toward the base of the drop-off. "I'm fine."

He gave her a thumbs-up, but she wasn't convinced. At least he was talking and moving. Those were good signs.

"I'm going to work my way back up."

He grabbed a handful of branches on a nearby bush and used them to pull himself up the steep incline.

Titan nuzzled up next to Kianna's side, and she rubbed his head. "It's okay, bud. Cole's coming back. He's not going to leave us."

Leave us.

Her own words pierced her heart, more painful than a pointed icicle falling and striking her.

Why did her mind have to go there now?

This situation was *very* different from the fallout from her previous friendship.

She and Cole weren't even friends.

Acquaintances and first responders. But that's where their connections ended.

The wind picked up again and nipped at her cheeks. Sitting here made the cold weather more noticeable.

Cole had climbed a quarter of the way back up the embankment. She wished there was something she could do to help. Just waiting here seemed useless.

He pulled himself up another few inches, but his foot slipped, and he slid down again.

"Cole!" Kianna shouted. Her voice echoed in the open expanse.

He clawed at the side of the hill for something to hold on to.

Instinct had her reaching over the edge with her arm. But it didn't matter. He was too far down.

Cole braced his foot against a bush to keep from falling all the way down again, then peered up at her.

Titan let out a low growl.

"I'm not going to fall down too, boy." Kianna smiled as if that would reassure both of them.

"I can't get good traction with my shoes," Cole called up.

He began ascending the hill again, but a few steps in and he backslid.

Kianna's breath hitched. They needed a rope or something to use.

She cupped her hands around her mouth. "Hang on. I'm going to try and find something to pull you up with."

She turned around and stood up, surveying the wooded area. Tree branches were too short and would just snap, and any of the longer ones would be nearly impossible to break off.

Titan walked at her heel, and Kianna leaned down to rub the dog. Her hand brushed over the German shepherd's collar.

"Your leash. Where's your leash, boy?" It was worth a shot. Kianna hurried back over to the edge. "Is Titan's leash with you?"

Cole slung his backpack off one shoulder and pulled out the restraint. He wrapped it into a tight ball, then tossed it up to her.

She latched on to the nylon strap. "I got it!" She unraveled it and tied the end snug around her gloved hand to ensure a secure grip. Then she let the rest of the strap fall over the edge of the hill.

It dangled two feet short of Cole's position.

He began to climb up the slope again, each step slow and methodical. Every few seconds, he'd stop and extend his hand.

"You're so close. Just a few more steps." Kianna blew out a breath, and the hot air puffed in front of her.

Cole thrust himself up, and a tug on the strap pulled her forward.

"I got it," he exclaimed.

Titan must have understood the victory, because he yelped and turned in a circle.

Kianna dug her feet into the ground and leaned back. She refused to lose her grip.

Cole held on to the strap and climbed the rest of the way. He pushed himself over the top of the hill and crawled a few paces away from the drop-off before standing.

His cheeks were red—whether from the cold or the exertion, Kianna couldn't tell.

Titan jumped up and put his paws on Cole's legs.

"I'm here, bud. Everything's okay." He scratched the dog's head, then turned to Kianna. "Thank you." The creases on his forehead disappeared.

She handed him the leash. "You sure you're not hurt?"

"I'll be fine." He took off his backpack and unzipped it. "But you look cold." He pulled out a scarf. "Here."

She could say the same about him. The temperature must have dropped a few degrees.

"Thanks." Kianna took the scarf, and her hand brushed against his. Even though she wore gloves, heat worked its way through her fingers and to her face. There was no way of hiding her rosy cheeks now.

Cole was just being chivalrous. A simple gesture that showed concern for another human.

Right?

Kianna wrapped the scarf around her neck. The wool fabric created a cocoon that thawed the edges of her cold skin.

She wasn't going to read into the situation. The last time she'd done that, her heart had been shattered into tinier fragments than a single snowflake.

How long had they been out here, anyway? It must be getting close to late afternoon.

A buzz came through Cole's radio, and he put his finger to his ear.

A figure to their left caught Kianna's attention. "Who's that?" She waved her hand to get Cole's attention.

Titan let out a bark and took off.

The person was still a ways off, but Kianna's heart beat

double-time. If it was Mackey, Cole could make the arrest and end this hunt.

"There's someone out here on the east side of the forest," Cole relayed in his radio. He paused, then said, "Copy."

"It's one of my buddies." He waved to the person who was making his way over to them with Titan on his heel.

Kianna's shoulders dropped. They were so close, yet so far away from finding Mackey.

The officer was decked out in a hat and a scarf that covered most of his face, but Kianna still recognized him from the scene of the car accident.

The name lettered on his jacket read *Thomas*.

"You couldn't have come a few minutes earlier, man?" Cole laughed and shook his head.

"This weather is slowing everyone down." Thomas squinted against the flurries. "Where are the footprints?"

Cole pointed. "Just watch out for the uneven ground. I already had one run-in with the embankment." Cole turned to Kianna and grinned.

She wasn't sure what to make of his response, so she smiled but didn't say anything.

Thomas bent down to inspect the shoe marks. "They appear to be pointing south and following the perimeter of the trail before winding down toward the main road."

"Shall we?" Cole waved in the direction of the trail.

"No sense losing any more daylight." Kianna followed Titan and the officers. The movement added warmth once again to her bones.

The German shepherd led the group and stopped every few minutes to sniff the air before returning his nose to the ground. The flurries had tapered off, and a few breaks in the clouds made visibility more favorable.

The gravel path was slick, and a few times, Kianna had to catch herself from falling.

"How close are we to the main road?" she asked. The pine trees continued to grow farther apart, but there was no telling the distance to town due to the minimal traffic. The air was still. Almost serene.

Except, instead of the peaceful hush that blanketed an area after a fresh snowfall, the quiet mocked them.

It whispered that they were trapped in a snow globe with no way out. And the only person who knew the escape route right now was Mackey.

"About five minutes out," Cole said. "Mackey's chances of circumventing us are growing." He grunted.

"This isn't over until it's over." Kianna would not let the convict gain the satisfaction of eluding officials in this town and making a clean break.

She focused on every detail of the area. From the clusters of bushes with red berries on them to the tall tree trunks—wide enough for someone to hide behind. There were even dry patches surrounded by areas of dirt mixed with slush.

Thanks to the precipitation that washed it away, or because someone had disturbed the area?

Titan sniffed the air and halted.

Kianna stopped walking and scanned the area. "Hang on." She moved to a pile of twigs poking out of the slush and leaned down. "This looks like someone's watch." The gold face and brown band stood in contrast to the white snow. Droplets of red tinged the area. Kianna gasped. "Is this blood?"

Cole pulled an evidence bag from his pocket and picked up the piece.

"Titan." Cole whistled and the dog trotted over. He held out the watch to the K-9, who sniffed it. "Search."

The dog bolted past the bushes.

Cole ran after Titan, his weapon drawn.

"I need backup near Greenleaf Road." Thomas spouted off the coordinates of their location, then jogged after Cole.

Kianna took off after them.

"Over here." Cole's voice carried through the air, breathless.

Kianna dashed past a few trees before coming to where Cole and Thomas crouched.

A woman lay on the ground, her jacket covered in snow. Blood seeped through and covered her arm. More red droplets lay on the ground.

Kianna unraveled her scarf. The fabric would work as a tourniquet and tide them over until the ambulance came and she had more supplies.

"She's unresponsive." Cole glanced up and frowned.

Kianna knelt on the woman's left side. Her face was pale, her brown hair matted and tangled.

She pressed her fingers to the woman's neck. "There's a pulse, but it's light. She's ice cold too—no doubt hypothermic."

"This has Mackey written all over it." Thomas grimaced. Then he pressed the button on his radio. "I need an ambulance, stat. Unresponsive female. Bullet wound and hypothermic."

"Can you help me lift her off the ground so I can wrap this around her shoulder?" Kianna asked Cole.

"On three. One, two, three." Cole held the woman's upper body while Kianna worked to secure the scarf and keep the bleeding at bay.

Now they needed to wait for the ambulance and pray the woman woke up. She was the best chance they had of learning Mackey's whereabouts and what he had planned next. For Jaxon's sake and the safety of the other children in Last Chance County, Kianna would do everything to keep this woman alive and not let justice fade away.

FIVE

Cole stood guard with Titan by his side while Kianna assessed the woman. He admired her willingness to serve others. Especially when it inconvenienced her. She must be freezing now that she'd used the scarf to secure the woman's wound. The wind picked up, and tree branches swayed.

Kianna pulled off her gloves and slid them onto the unconscious woman's hands. "Ma'am, help is on the way. We're going to get you warmed up and out of the cold soon." Kianna spoke as if the woman would be able to understand everything happening, then she checked for a pulse once more.

"How far out is the ambo?" She gazed up at him.

Cole checked the time. "Five minutes." He studied the woman's pale face, her lips tinged blue. Even with her eyes closed, the woman seemed familiar. How would he know her?

Thomas finished talking to someone on his radio and stepped back over to join Cole and Kianna.

"Do you recognize this woman?" Cole asked. Familiarity niggled at the back of his brain. Like he should know who she was.

Thomas frowned, then took his phone out. "Does this look like her?" He held up an image of a woman in a black button-down polo and khakis, with a set of keys and handcuffs secured to a belt loop. Her lips were pressed in a fine line, and her arms were crossed in front of her, her brown hair secured in a ponytail.

"That's her!" Cole pointed at the picture.

Kianna stood up. "Who?"

Thomas handed her the phone. "This is the female guard who was traveling with the convicts when they escaped."

Kianna's eyes widened.

Cole lifted his radio button to his mouth. "Victim is suspected to be Rainy Athers." Once they got her to the hospital, Cole would be ready to question her. If she regained consciousness. No, she had to wake up. She was their shot at getting answers about Mackey.

"It's believed she was in on the plan to help the convicts escape, right?" Kianna slipped her hands into her pockets.

Thomas nodded. "I want to know why she was left out here to die if that's the case."

Cole agreed. Had she turned on Mackey? Decided she didn't want to be a part of his schemes any longer? Or was there something else going on?

Titan leaned back on his haunches and let out a low growl.

Cole scanned the perimeter, not sure what had the dog on alert.

Seconds later, tires crunched against the ground and lights flashed.

Kianna waved the ambulance over, and Nathan, who was behind the wheel, steered the truck off the gravel path and parked next to the bushes. He and Trace hopped out, and Kianna grabbed the medic bag from Trace while Nathan went around back to pull out the gurney.

Titan stayed in his position and snarled. "Help's here, Tite.

You know these guys. They're the good ones." Cole's assurance did nothing to alleviate his partner's sense of danger.

Cole lowered his hand to his weapon and wrapped his fingers around the base. If he'd learned anything over the years with Titan, it was that he could trust the K-9's instincts.

What was it that—

Cole's thoughts were shattered by a spray of bullets that pelted the air.

Titan barked and jumped to all fours.

Nathan and Trace dropped behind the gurney, then ducked around the corner of the ambulance.

"Get down," Cole shouted. He drew his Glock and pointed it in the direction of the attacker.

Thomas had his gun drawn and took cover behind a tree, then returned fire.

Kianna let out a scream.

"We've got an active shooter. Backup needed west of Mountainview Ridge Overlook, stat." Cole relayed the information to his team on the other end. He wanted to go after the attacker, but what about Kianna?

More bullets kicked up snow on the ground around them, and bark flew off the tree trunk next to Kianna.

"I see where they're shooting from," Thomas shouted. "I'm going in." He took off, staying low to the ground and returning fire.

"Titan, attack." Cole ordered his partner, and the German shepherd raced off and dashed past Thomas.

Kianna had her arms locked under Rainy's shoulders and was pulling her behind the shrubs, toward the ambulance.

"What are you doing? You're going to get yourself hit." Cole hurried over to her but kept his Glock at his side.

"And leave her to take the brunt of the attack? When she can't defend herself? Not a chance." Lines etched Kianna's forehead, and she winced. She lifted her arm and brushed away the hair from her face. Blood dripped from her wrist. The back of her hand was bright red.

Cole clenched his jaw. Whoever had opened fire had hit a target. Cole needed to go cover for Thomas. Make sure the shooter didn't get away. But first, "On three." He shoved his weapon in his holster, then took hold of the woman's legs and hoisted her in the air.

"I've got the gurney," Nathan shouted. He pushed the makeshift cot toward them while Trace covered his back, and Cole and Kianna laid the woman on it. Nathan wrapped a blanket over the lower half of her body.

"You have it from here?" Cole retrieved his weapon from its holder and glanced over his shoulder to where Thomas and Titan had disappeared.

"Go find that person." Kianna followed Trace, who pushed the gurney, while Nathan guided it, then lifted it into the back of the ambo.

Cole didn't wait another second. He bolted toward the tree line, keeping his gun aimed and ready. No more shots had been fired.

"I'm coming your way, Thomas," he radioed. "What's your status?"

"Over by the edge of the trail," he replied.

Cole could make him and Titan out in the distance. But where was the attacker?

He approached the end of the trail that connected with the main road. A few pine trees dotted the area, and tire marks impressed the snow-covered street.

A frown filled Thomas's face. "He got away," the officer said.

Cole wanted to shout. Instead, he ground his teeth and blew out a breath. "A getaway car?" He pointed.

Thomas shook his head. "A nice Mercedes too. I already put a BOLO out on it. Hit a tire, so they won't be able to get far."

At least there was some good news.

"So that means someone else must be in on this heist. How else would Mackey keep eluding us?" Cole wished he could be in multiple places at once, but he could trust the other officers to follow the leads.

Two more cop cars pulled up, and Detective Savannah Wilcox stepped out. "Mackey's using this storm to his advantage." She let out a whistle.

The tables would turn soon. Once he was done here, he'd head over to the hospital to check on the status of Rainy. They needed leverage. Intel from the inside. Cole was ready to switch who was calling the shots.

"There's several bullet casings over here." Thomas showed Wilcox and the others to where the shooter had been staked out.

Wilcox pulled out evidence bags and took pictures before collecting the fragments. "I'll expedite the lab request for these. Find out what gun it came from and where."

"If we're assuming this was Mackey, I bet he got it from the female corrections officer, Rainy Athers. I didn't see any weapon on her person." Cole knelt to the ground and took note of the hollow point of the bullet. If he had to guess, the caliber was a .38 auto.

Wilcox jotted down some notes, and once they were finished securing the scene, Cole and Titan got a ride back to his car from the detective.

"It's been quite the day so far, huh, Tite?" Cole opened the back door of his K-9 vehicle for the German shepherd to climb in. Then he scooped a helping of dog food into a bowl and set it next to the dog's kennel.

His own stomach growled and reminded him it was well past lunchtime.

Thankfully, the sky had cleared, and the roads appeared drivable now that the trucks had plowed and set down salt.

Cole would take the reprieve from the weather, no matter

how short, given the time it provided for everyone to keep hunting for Mackey.

He pulled into a drive-thru and ordered two subs. One with ham and provolone, the other with turkey and avocado. The smell wafted through the interior of the car, but Cole refrained from opening the paper wrapper and chowing down.

He had a few things to take care of first.

Cole pulled into the police spot in the hospital parking garage and grabbed the bag of food. "I'll be back, Tite." He scratched behind the dog's ears, then checked that the car's heat system, adapted to keep the K-9 comfortable, was running.

There were no rules against bringing his K-9 partner into the hospital, but if Rainy was awake, Cole didn't want Titan's presence to intimidate her out of sharing any information. And Titan had been working hard out in the cold, so he deserved much-needed rest.

He headed to the ER check-in desk. The automatic doors whooshed open, and a blast of warmth enveloped him. A welcome reprieve from the icebox outside. A few patients sat in chairs, waiting to be seen. Some rested their heads against the wall. Others leaned over, their eyes glazed, while staring at the TV screen showing a rerun of some cooking show.

"A woman was brought in by Kianna Russell, Trace Bently, and Nathan Welch in the ambulance. Her name's Rainy Athers." Cole flashed his badge to the receptionist, whose nameplate read *Cheryl*.

The woman typed something into her computer. "She's currently in surgery."

Great. Hopefully she would be awake afterward, and he could talk with her. *Lord, we need answers. Please help her wake up and recover. Right now, Mackey is winning, and we need Your guidance to stop him in his tracks.*

In the meantime, it would give Cole the opportunity to check on Kianna. Make sure she was okay. "And Kianna Russell?" Cole tapped his foot against the tile.

"She's being triaged. Room seven." The woman waved him through the doors.

He walked past the nurses' station and a man who sat on a cot in the hall, being assessed by a doctor.

"The bandage should hold up, and your arm should heal in a few weeks."

Cole rapped on the wall.

"Come in," a woman's voice answered.

He pushed back the curtain. Kianna sat on the edge of the bed, and a nurse placed a piece of tape across the gauze on Kianna's hand, then turned to discard her blue gloves in the trash.

"Hey." Cole stepped into view.

Kianna's eyes widened, then her lips curved up. "You're here?" Her brow furrowed for a split second, and she tilted her head.

"You were hurt. I had to make sure you were okay." Suddenly the heat in the room seemed to intensify, and the back of his neck grew warm.

"I'll be right back in with your discharge papers." The nurse waved.

"Thanks, Charlotte." Kianna nodded, then the woman disappeared.

"How're you feeling?" Cole didn't dare move, unsure how she felt about him showing up.

"Just a couple of stitches. Should be all better soon." She swallowed. "Thanks for coming. You didn't have to do that."

Cole lifted his hand to dismiss her comment and realized he was still holding the bag of food. "I figured you might be hungry, so I got some sandwiches."

A slow grin spread across Kianna's face. "Now that you mention it, I'm starving." She laughed. "I'll never turn down food."

"Exactly." Cole set the bag on the counter. "I needed some fuel before stopping to talk with Rainy. She's still in surgery." Except his heart was telling him a different story than his lips had uttered.

A flash of something crossed Kianna's face, but it disappeared just as quickly.

Now that he'd seen for himself that Kianna was okay, he could relax.

Of course he'd come for the investigation.

But what he didn't want to admit to was the swirling emotions that were brewing in Kianna's presence. Ones that melted the icicles around his heart.

SIX

Kianna swung her legs over the side of the hospital bed. Her pulse skittered, and her head floated like she'd stood up too fast. It had nothing to do with the attack earlier, or even the minimal blood loss from the bullet graze on her hand.

It had everything to do with the man who stood mere feet away from her.

For a minute, she'd let her heart believe Cole had initiated the simple gesture of checking in on her and getting food because he enjoyed her company and cared for her. Dare she say she hoped he liked her?

Of course, that was a silly notion. Her fantasies had been put into perspective when he'd reminded her why he was in the hospital. To get information from Rainy. The closest lead they had on Mackey's whereabouts. And naturally, like any good person, he'd make sure she wasn't severely injured after the shooting in the woods.

He was a nice guy. But that didn't mean he was interested in her.

She'd been foolish to even entertain the idea. Hadn't she

learned from past experience? She'd been hurt once, and still her heart hadn't caught up with the reality.

Cole cleared his throat. "Earth to Kianna."

Kianna blinked and turned to Cole. "Sorry." She grimaced.

"You sure you're feeling okay?" He wore worry across his brow, and his brown eyes narrowed like he was trying to discern for himself the state of her condition.

"Absolutely." She offered him a smile she hoped didn't fall flat. What else could she say to him? That she was fine physically, but her heart was torn with conflicted feelings?

No. Better to put her thoughts behind her and move on. Wallowing in her emotions would only remind her of the fantasies that would never be reality.

Right now, they had more important matters to focus on.

A short rap sounded from behind Cole, then the curtain rolled back, and Charlotte walked in.

"Here are your discharge papers." She handed Kianna the forms. "I know you know, but if anything worsens or changes, make sure you get it checked out."

"Thanks, Char." Kianna tucked the papers in her pocket. "Let's find a time to hang out soon."

"A girls' night in would be wonderful. Make some hot chocolate and watch *The Holiday*." Charlotte grinned and let out a short squeal.

Kianna had connected with Charlotte after interacting with the nurse several times a week when she brought patients to the hospital. Then when Kianna had found out Charlotte went to the same church, they'd bonded over their shared beliefs and professions, and the rest was history.

Kianna swallowed, and her throat constricted at the thought of watching a rom-com. She didn't want to disappoint her friend. "Or have some girl time without the movies." She winked to pretend the idea of watching a sappy, romantic Christmas movie didn't bother her.

But her friend picked up on the unspoken words.

"We'll add our own touch of holiday cheer." Charlotte gave her a hug, then excused herself to go check on another patient.

"Why don't we go eat in the cafeteria?" Kianna stood up and tossed the sheet that had been draped over her legs onto the bed.

Cole grabbed the bag of food. "Sounds good."

"Then we can check on Rainy." She followed him out into the hall and down to the elevator.

"We?" He raised his eyebrows.

"I was at the scene too." Kianna pressed the button for the third floor. "Plus, she might be more inclined to speak if a woman is in the room."

"Fair point." Cole nodded.

They found a table in the cafeteria by the window.

Kianna was grateful they didn't have to wait in line for food. The line wrapped around the corner as other medical personnel grabbed a quick dinner before getting back to their shifts.

"I got turkey and avocado, and ham and provolone. Which one would you like?" Cole pulled out the subs.

"That's a hard choice." Kianna placed a napkin on the table. "Want to split both?"

Cole handed her two halves, and she took a bite of the turkey.

"For the record, I can't stand the cheesy holiday movies either." Cole opened a water bottle and took a swig.

Kianna choked back a laugh and swallowed. All the men she'd ever known rolled their eyes at the holiday rom-coms, including her dad and brother. So Cole's comment didn't take her by surprise.

But something told her there was more behind his confession. "Based on your tone, I'd say you aren't a fan of holidays in general." She raised her voice and leaned forward to be heard over the clanging of dishes and other people talking.

"That obvious?" He grimaced.

"Welcome to the club." She raised her water bottle and clinked it against his, then took a sip.

"Why not?" They both said in unison, and a glimmer shone in Cole's eyes.

Were they really going to bond over being Scrooges during the holiday season?

"There's a holiday party the PD puts on. And every year I have to come up with a lame excuse as to why I can't go." Cole leaned back in his chair and sighed.

"Eastside Firehouse is having one too." Kianna crossed her arms. "Just say you have a family gathering. Everyone's always having some party or another."

"That would be far from the truth." Cole cleared his throat. "I haven't seen my parents in over a year."

Kianna closed her mouth to keep her shock from showing. Despite her disdain for the festive season, she couldn't fathom not spending time with her mom and dad. "Even if it means putting on a smile, singing Christmas carols, and baking cookies with my parents and my brother's family, I can't imagine not visiting them."

Did that mean…

Chairs screeched along the floor, and a group of doctors walked past their table, chatting. Kianna studied Cole's lips to understand what he was saying.

"They're still alive," he said, like he'd read her mind and answered her internal question. "I know it's wrong. It's just"—he shrugged—"seeing them is a reminder of how things used to be. And how things will never be the same again."

"What happened?" Kianna asked, her voice barely above a whisper.

Cole ran his fingers through his hair, then propped his arms on the table, pushing his half-eaten sandwich to the side.

"My dad suffered a stroke a year and a half ago. Last Christmas was the first time he was in a nursing home."

Kianna sucked in a breath. "Cole." She shook her head. "I'm so sorry."

"Me too." Tears welled in his eyes, and he fisted his hand over his mouth.

She took the moment to eat more of her food, giving him time to compose himself. She didn't want to rush him with sharing details or make him feel uncomfortable for showing emotion in front of her.

"It's a miracle he's alive at all. That's what doctors say. And I'm grateful God spared his life." He sat up in the chair like he was trying to convince himself that what he'd said was true.

She could empathize with his wrestling.

"God is writing a beautiful story, even when it includes sorrow." Kianna sighed and put her hands on the table. "I get it. You know the truth about what God is doing, but often you need to keep reminding yourself of it because your heart has a harder time catching up."

"Exactly." Cole gave her a sad smile. "I want to cherish the moments I still have with him, but I don't know how. He's confined to a wheelchair, and his speech is slurred, so it takes him longer to form thoughts and sentences."

"So you stopped visiting. Because it's easier to hold on to what was instead of what is."

"My mom keeps asking me to consider joining them this year for Christmas. I haven't responded yet."

"One thing I've learned with the few patients I've encountered who have to adapt to a new way of life is the more you show up and spend time with them, the more normal life feels." Kianna smiled. She didn't want the advice to come across as insensitive. Rather, she wanted to give him hope. "You'll never know unless you try. God can work in any circumstance, even the impossible ones."

"You sound so sure." Cole twisted the cap off his water bottle and chugged half of it.

Her words came out so confidently, like a simple act of faith could change everything. Even when the situation appeared bleak. Kianna stared at her hands for a moment. Did she really believe the truth she was preaching to him? That God could do anything? Especially when her heart desired something God hadn't given her yet. A husband and family of her own.

"What is it that keeps you from enjoying the season?"

She lifted her gaze to his. "There's always an overromanticized view of the holidays. If you just have the right mood, with the right music and decor, the right people by your side, and the Christmas cheer, everything will be magical." Kianna swept her hand through the air like a series of gold sparkles would follow her movement.

A nurse squeezed behind Cole to sit at the next table.

Cole scooted his chair in and clasped his hands on the table. "We're told the perfect set of circumstances will create the perfect holiday, when that's never the case." He chuckled. "Even Christ's birth was messy. Being born in a cattle stall." He wrinkled his nose. "Still, the sinless Son of God entered into our bleak circumstances to bring hope."

Silence descended between them even while the noise around them carried on.

Did Cole realize what he'd said?

No matter how bleak the situation with his dad, he could have hope.

And if it was true for him, it had to be true for her.

"Unfathomable, right?" She cocked her head. "I want to focus on the True Hope of the season. But sometimes it's hard with so many other voices clamoring for my attention. Especially when this time of year takes me back to my own hopeless situation."

"What do you mean?" Cole furrowed his brow.

"Someone I *thought* was a good friend strung me along." Kianna finished off her water, then fiddled with the plastic cap. "Two years ago, Derek came home for Christmas and wanted to catch up." Kianna's stomach twisted, and she pulled in a breath, then continued. "I was excited. I had assumed we were just in the best-friends zone. But he told me we were basically long-distance dating, given how many times we'd hop on a phone or video call, and he wanted to talk about our relationship. A few hours before we were supposed to meet up, he said he needed to reschedule. I went to grab coffee at Bridgewater Café and found him with another girl. And they certainly weren't shy about showing their interest in each other either."

Cole's eyes widened. "You're joking."

"I wish." Kianna finished off her sandwich, then balled up the paper wrapping. "We stepped outside to talk for a minute, and I asked what was happening between us. He looked me in the eye and said he'd been leading me on and had no intention of dating me."

Cole's jaw dropped, but he didn't speak.

"That was my reaction." Kianna gave a short laugh. The whole situation seemed unbelievable. "I left the café that day and haven't talked to him since."

Cole shook his head. "First, a real friend would communicate with you, not keep you guessing. Second, I'm so sorry you were treated that flippantly." Cole's brown eyes stared into hers, and he leaned closer. "You deserve better. To be cherished. Protected." His Adam's apple bobbed.

Kianna couldn't break eye contact with Cole. Not while his eyes searched hers. Her heart fluttered, and the nerves tingled in the tips of her fingers. She waited in case he was going to say more. Like maybe *he* would cherish her. That *he* could be someone who'd prove godly and respectful men still existed.

Kianna blinked, and the moment was lost.

Cole cleared his throat and leaned back in his seat.

"Thank you," she mustered. While her heart longed for a glimmer of possibility, she couldn't entertain the idea further.

Not when deep down she'd be advocating for the exact thing she despised about this season. Finding the perfect person in the perfect set of circumstances to make the perfect holiday.

She could trust the Lord with her heart's desire and rest in the hope He brought—no matter what circumstances followed her.

"Thanks for sharing that with me." Cole broke the silence. He took her trash and put it in the bag that had held the sandwiches.

"Thanks for trusting me with your dad's story." She smiled. "It means a lot."

Cole pulled in a breath. "While neither of us can change the reality that Christmas is coming whether we like it or not, with everything that's going on right now, we can at least focus on something else for a little while." He stood up and pushed in his chair, and Kianna did the same. "Ready to go see if Rainy is awake?"

"It would be a Christmas miracle if she is."

They headed to the nurses' station, and Cole approached the desk. "Is Rainy Athers out of surgery?"

Charlotte glanced at the computer. "Indeed. And she's awake."

Kianna and Cole followed the directions Charlotte gave them to Rainy's room.

Kianna just hoped the woman remembered everything from before she'd blacked out and would be willing to share information that could lead to Mackey's arrest.

SEVEN

Kianna's presence next to Cole kept him from barging in and demanding answers. Instead, he rapped on the door. The situation that had brought them here was sobering. The woman had almost lost her life. If he wanted Rainy's cooperation, he needed to be tactful in his questions, not put her under duress.

No response came.

He jiggled the doorknob, then pushed the door open. The smell of alcohol and commercial-grade cleaner wafted to his nostrils. The bland beige walls added to the sterile feeling in the space.

In a moment, Cole was no longer here as a detective on a case. Instead, he was here as a son, unsure what to say to his dad, who lay in the bed. His father. His role model, unable to move his left side or speak complete thoughts.

Lights flashed in his vision, and Cole turned his focus to a TV on in the room, playing a home remodeling show. Rainy Athers muted the show and turned her attention to the two of them.

She sat up in the bed, an IV attached to her left arm and a

blanket covering up to her torso. Her appearance now, in her hospital gown, was a far cry from how she'd looked bundled up in a jacket in the snow. She was thin, but her arm muscles were toned. Her upper right arm was wrapped in a bandage. Her face was pale, but at least there was more red in her lips now.

"Ms. Athers?" Cole stepped forward and pulled out his badge. "I'm Cole Stuart, K-9 officer, and this is paramedic Kianna Russell." He extended his hand, and Kianna moved next to him and nodded.

Rainy's brow furrowed, and she blinked several times.

"We're the ones who found you on the mountain." Kianna smiled at the woman.

Cole opened his mouth to ask his first question, but Kianna beat him to it. "How're you feeling?" Her gaze turned to the monitor that tracked Rainy's vitals.

Leave it to Kianna to make the woman feel seen and comfortable.

Right. He didn't need to jump into the interrogation. Compassion would go a long way.

Rainy was probably still groggy from the surgery and pain meds. Which meant they couldn't take too long to talk.

Lord, please guide this conversation. Give us direction on Mackey's whereabouts so no more people get hurt. And bring healing to Rainy. Help her see how You spared her life.

"Doctor said I should make a full recovery." Rainy yawned, then blinked again. "The bullet didn't hit any arteries in my arm. I'll need some PT, then I'll be back to work." She shifted to sit up higher in the bed and winced.

Kianna rushed over to the woman's side and untangled the IV cord from the bedsheet. "Can we get you anything?"

"Water would be great." The woman licked her lips. "Thank you." Moisture built in her eyes. "For saving my life."

Cole handed Rainy the Styrofoam cup on the bedside table. "My partner, Titan, did the work of finding you, ma'am. And

God helped us save you." Cole would give credit where it was due. Who knew how God could use this situation to work in her life?

"It was so cold. I figured I would die out there, and no one would find my body until the temperatures thawed."

"What were you doing out there?" Cole pulled a pad of paper from his shirt pocket.

Kianna took a seat at the table next to the bed.

"It was a foolish move on my part." Rainy frowned. "I did it to save my own skin. Thought maybe Mackey would really let me go and not kill me."

"So you were with Mackey?" Cole raised a brow.

"With him, yeah. But not in cahoots with him."

"Why should we be confident about that answer?" Cole crossed his arms. After the transport truck had crashed, officers had speculated whether Rainy had been in on the escape. "After all, you were the only officer who got away unharmed, while Brighten was left for dead at the scene and died at the hospital. With your disappearance, it sure looks like you were involved."

Rainy hung her head. A sign of guilt?

Kianna pinched her lips, her brow raised.

If Rainy had been in on the plan, a confession would be good, but it wouldn't lessen her sentence. Not as an officer who'd sworn to uphold the law.

Rainy lifted her chin and made direct eye contact with him. "The only motive I had was saving my life so I could see my family on Christmas." She sighed. "That was my last shift before the holiday. Transporting the convicts. And my first holiday ever off the clock. I was planning to go see my family in Montana. My brother's been deployed, and he's coming home Christmas Eve. He clued me in on the surprise he has planned for my parents and his wife."

Cole's lungs burned as if he'd been running out in the cold for an hour.

He made the mistake of shifting his focus to Kianna, whose eyes welled with tears.

That was *not* the answer he'd been expecting Rainy to give. His shoulders relaxed now that he knew she hadn't helped stage an escape for the convicts. Sure, she'd been a patsy. Easily persuaded to do Mackey's bidding. While he didn't agree with her actions, he'd argue her case held validity.

This woman was more noble than he. She'd been willing to think about her family. She'd run toward them.

All he had ever shown was cowardice. He'd taken every opportunity to flee and hide from the reminders of his family. The circumstances too difficult to entertain. Who was he to hide when his dad was still living?

Kianna had been right. He still had a chance to show up and make the moments count. Still had a chance at helping his dad. All the years his dad had invested in their family, and Cole had thrown it all away.

"How long were you with Mackey before he left you?" Kianna's question broke through Cole's train of thought.

He could worry about how to make amends with his family later. Hopefully in time for Christmas. *If* they caught Mackey.

"After the truck crashed, Jason attacked Officer Brighten, and there was nothing I could do to help. It was terrible." She pinched her eyes shut. "I tried to pin Mackey, but he got to my gun, and I knew I was outnumbered." The beep on the hospital monitor by Rainy's bedside quickened.

Kianna shifted in her chair to study the numbers. Cole didn't want to send Rainy into a critical state because of the added stress of remembering the events of the last few days, but he also needed answers.

Rainy took a deep breath, and after a few seconds, Kianna leaned back in her seat.

Rainy opened her eyes and stared at the wall, then continued. "I told Mackey he could turn his life around. That he didn't have to add another killing to his rap sheet. So he gave me an ultimatum." The woman rubbed her forehead, then took another sip of water. "It was either die now or help him navigate the woods."

Cole scribbled the information on his paper. Surely the woman had to know that Mackey was going to dispose of her either way. The convict had made it clear—no one double-crossed him and lived. When Jaxon had tried to go to the police with information, Mackey had gotten to him first. Captured the kid and left him in the woods to die. Did Rainy think she would have been any different?

"I've been a hiker for years. I know those woods like the back of my hand and figured I could use that to my advantage. Find help, or lure him to you guys." She waved her hand in Cole's direction.

"So what happened?" Cole leaned against the wall.

"We started out for the tree line and spent a decent amount of time walking. We got to the overlook, past the embankment. He started fidgeting with the gun more. I told him we were coming up to a cave soon, when actually we were nearing the road again. But a car decided to drive by at that time, and it freaked him out." Rainy shivered. "He rounded on me and slammed me in the head with the gun. Next thing I know, I wake up, and he's dragging me through the snow."

Rainy pulled in a shaky breath and clutched the white sheet in her fingers. "That's when I knew he was done with me. I tried to take him by surprise and kick him, but he was too fast. Dropped me like dead weight, then pulled the trig-ger." She took another sip of water. "I was in and out of consciousness from the pain, but he was talking on the phone."

"Someone's helping him." Kianna shot out of her chair, and the legs screeched against the floor. "Sorry." She winced.

Cole pushed away from the wall and paced the short width

of the room. Moving always helped him think better. "Do you know who he was talking with?"

Rainy shook her head. "No clue. I didn't dare move a muscle. If he knew I wasn't dead…" Her breath hitched.

Cole grimaced. He had studied Mackey's case for years and even helped put him in jail the first time, but thinking about the man's complete disregard for life never got easier. It was grotesque and left him repulsed by the state of humans in their depraved, sinful ways.

And yet, was Cole any better? Abandoning his father just to save his own skin. So he wouldn't have to watch his dad live out the rest of his life confined to a chair in a nursing home. A shiver trailed down Cole's spine.

"A few minutes passed, then he disappeared. But the cold had set in, and I was too weak to get up." Rainy braced her hand over her bandaged arm.

"Did Mackey give any indication of where he was headed?" Cole rubbed his right temple to alleviate the tension building. He wanted concrete answers. Information that would nail the guy. He was tired of running in circles.

"He mentioned canine currency. Although what he meant by it beats me."

Someone knocked on the door, and Cole turned around. His fingers closed around his weapon.

A nurse stepped in, and Cole dropped his hand to his side. "I'm here to check your vitals and give you a dose of medicine." The woman walked over to the computer in the corner and logged in.

Cole closed his pad and tucked it back in his pocket. He had enough information to inform the other officers and start investigating this canine currency thread. "Thanks for answering my questions, Ms. Athers. We'll be in touch. For your safety, I'll get an officer stationed at your door."

"Thank you both." Rainy smiled.

Cole and Kianna stepped out into the hall and headed for the elevator. Suddenly, Kianna's eyes widened, and her mouth formed an O. "Check this out." Kianna handed him her phone while they rode to the ground floor. "I got an email reminder from Tiny Paws Animal Shelter. About their adopt-a-pet event. What if canine currency has something to do with the shelter?"

"You're thinking like a cop." Cole winked. The speculation was brilliant. It gave him a lead.

Kianna shrugged, but he didn't miss the added tint that warmed her cheeks at his compliment.

He'd fill the team in on what he and Kianna had discovered, and no doubt Sergeant Donaldson would get people to investigate.

They stepped off the elevator and headed to the parking garage. The cold air bombarded Cole's face as they made their way to his car, thanks to the parking area not being enclosed.

He used his key fob to unlock the vehicle, and Titan barked.

Kianna slid into the passenger seat, and Cole pressed the ignition. "You were living the good life, soaking in the warmth here, Tite." Cole turned down the climate control feature.

Titan barked in agreement, and Kianna laughed.

Cole pulled out onto the road and followed the on-ramp before merging. Flurries swirled around the windshield. Cole had just turned on the wipers when his phone vibrated. Seconds later, Kianna's elicited a chorus of beeps.

She sucked in a breath. "Snow squall warning," Kianna read.

Cole tightened his grip on the steering wheel. They had three-quarters of a mile before the next exit. He hoped those few minutes were enough time to get to safety.

EIGHT

"Watch out. There's a truck up ahead on your right." Kianna's fingers cramped, and she loosened her grip on the door handle. Her chest tightened. *Just breathe. Keep us safe, Lord.* The seconds ticked by like hours without any sign of the squall letting up.

The snow had come with fury. Kianna squinted, but her effort was in vain. Visibility was minimal.

Cole eased up on the gas and turned on the four-way flashers. "I don't want to pull off and be a sitting duck."

"Just keep moving, I suppose." Kianna offered a smile, but she was pretty sure it came out strained.

"Just keep moving," Cole said in a singsong voice.

A genuine smile formed on her lips. He had a way of easing her nerves. And the image of the famous animated fish repeating her mantra almost took her focus off the situation at hand.

Titan whined from the back seat.

"It's okay, Tite." Cole glanced in the rearview.

The windshield wipers whizzed back and forth, but they did

nothing to clear away the haze of snow that continued to swirl straight toward them.

Red lights appeared in front of them, and Cole hit the brakes to keep a bigger distance between the two cars.

While there were a few reasons she wasn't a fan of the holidays, winter storms certainly topped the list. "And this is why I prefer sun and sand." She rubbed her fingers along the glass, as if that would clear the hazy window.

"You and me both." A muscle in Cole's jaw twitched, his back straight, eyes continually shifting between the mirror and the front windshield. "I can barely see someone until I'm on their tail."

Kianna leaned forward. The heat from the vents blew against her cheeks. "Those lights behind us are getting close." She wanted to slide into the driver's seat and take the wheel. At least then she would feel like she was being productive. She blinked, and the blur of red in front of them approached quicker.

"Hang on." Cole twisted his body to check the oncoming traffic as he prepared to veer into the left lane.

Except it was too late.

The impact jerked Kianna forward before her seat belt locked, forcing her body back against the seat. Metal screeched. "Cole!"

The car careened forward.

A horn blared next to them. Titan barked.

Everything blurred around them, and Kianna's head swam, her eyes unable to focus.

Cole hit the brakes, and the tires slid over the wet snow. "I can't see who's in front of me." He grunted. The vehicle bounced, trying to gain traction. Kianna still couldn't make anything out against the gray-and-white swirling snow.

The front bumper collided with something, then the car came to a halt. But the vehicle's antitheft alarm blared.

Each beat of the alarm pulsed through her head, and Kianna

plugged her ears with her shaking fingers. Smoke rose in front of her. Or was it snow? Her eyes had a hard time focusing. She needed to undo her seatbelt and get out of the car.

Titan's barking added to the deafening noise.

Cole turned to her. His mouth moved, but she couldn't make out what he said.

"What?" She took her finger away from her left ear.

"Are you okay?" he shouted. His face glowed from the interior overhead light.

"I think so." She swallowed, trying to still the quiver in her voice.

Cole's eyes scanned her from head to toe.

"You?"

He pinched his lips but nodded. Titan whimpered from his place in the back seat kennel.

Cole turned and locked eyes with Titan. "It's okay, bud. We're fine." He practically shouted over the alarm that still hadn't ceased. The impact must have triggered something under the hood of the car. "Can you get out?" Cole turned to her.

Kianna gave him a thumbs-up, then pushed open the door. A blast of cold air and snow pelted her face, and she lowered her head. The motion sent a wave of pain down her neck, and she winced. She swung her legs out, but her upper body wouldn't move.

Right. The seat belt. She leaned back in and unlatched the mechanism, then slid out.

Glass crunched under her shoes.

Cole and Titan were already out and along the shoulder. The dog still barked, attempting to raise his voice over the incessant alarm.

The hood of the car was bent up and in, and a spiderweb of cracks lined the windshield.

Kianna cupped her hands around her mouth. "That was a close call."

"I don't even want to think about it." Cole shook his head and peered over the dented guardrail.

"We should go make sure the other people are okay." Kianna pointed behind her, then lifted her hand to shield her face.

A rush of wind greeted them while another car drove past and, in a second, disappeared into the vortex of snowflakes.

Cole had Titan on his leash, and they backtracked to the car that had rear-ended them.

A middle-aged man with black hair stood by the driver's side of his sedan along the shoulder, his phone held in the air.

"Are you okay, sir?" Kianna stepped over, Cole right beside her. "I'm a paramedic."

"I'm fine." The man's tone remained neutral.

Was he okay, or was that how his body was coping with the shock of the accident? Kianna stared at him. There were no visible signs of injury, but it was hard to tell when everything except his head was covered in winter apparel.

Cole stepped forward and inspected the dents on the car. The hood was sunken on the right side, but that was the extent of the damage. "My name's Cole Stuart. This is my K-9 dog, Titan."

"I'm Kianna Russell." She extended her hand, and the man reciprocated with a firm shake.

"I'm Jack. I'd say it's nice to meet you, but given the circumstances, not so much. And to think I hit an officer." He grimaced. "This storm is nasty. Didn't even see you until I was right on top of ya." Jack shuffled his feet and gulped. "Is your car okay, sir? I'll give you my insurance. Anything. Whatever you need."

"I'll get it towed," Cole said. "Let's worry about paperwork when we get somewhere warm."

"I'll call the station. See if Bryce or Trace can come get us." Kianna pulled out her phone.

"Won't do much good. Doesn't seem to be any service." The man scoffed.

Kianna frowned. "Must be a downed power line."

"I can give you a ride into town. Where were you headed?"

"You can drop us off at the police department." Cole frowned. "I need to get in touch with my supervisors."

Jack nodded. "Sure thing."

Kianna slid to the far right side of the car, then Titan bounded in. "Hey there." Kianna chuckled. The dog nuzzled her leg and sat on his haunches on the floor.

"He sure likes you." Cole squeezed in next to them and shut the door, his arm brushing against hers.

Kianna smiled, even as heat crept into her cheeks. It was already ten degrees warmer in the cramped space. What was that saying? *The way to a man's heart was through his stomach.*

Titan's tail wagged.

In this case, it would be through his dog.

Jack started his car, then eased onto the road.

Kianna stared out the window. The snow was still falling, but she could make out the road now.

She might dream of being swept off her feet in the midst of snowflakes swirling and sparkling around her. But today reminded her that those breathless moments only happened in the movies.

Ten minutes later, they arrived at the police department.

Kianna sat in the waiting vestibule by herself while Cole talked with Jack and got paperwork filed for the accident.

She held a steaming cup of coffee in her hands that the receptionist, Jules, had been nice enough to get her. Even Titan had been attended to and was lapping up food and water near Allen Frees and Victoria Drake, the town liaisons, who stood next to one of the cubicles, talking with Ramble.

Kianna blew on her drink and took a sip.

Picture frames lined the wall in front of her, giving accolades to different officers who'd helped save the day over the years.

Phones and pagers rang every few minutes while officers popped in and out of different rooms.

She'd pulled out her phone to check the weather forecast when footsteps and panting stole her attention.

Cole and Titan made their way over. Cole sat down in the chair next to her, a frown on his face, while Titan remained on guard in front of him.

"You okay?" Kianna scrunched her brow. Through the window, the snow seemed to be letting up a bit, and Kianna could make out the brick building and the faux green shrubbery of the Italian restaurant across the street.

"It's been a long day. I think you should go home and get some rest. I'll get the officers up to speed and take care of things."

Kianna bit down on her lip. Just like that, he was going to dismiss her? After all they'd already been through—her literally saving him after his fall down the embankment, then surviving a car crash. "I thought we were working together on this." She stared at him. Her mouth hung open, but she didn't care.

"It's too dangerous. You could have been hurt. Even killed. I can't put your life in jeopardy again." Cole's jaw twitched.

"It wasn't your fault." Kianna rubbed the base of her neck. The knot there sent more pain radiating through her head. She had been injured thanks to whiplash, but she wouldn't tell him that. It would only prove his point. "You could have gotten hurt too."

"That's different." Cole crossed his arms. "I won't be responsible for something happening to *you.*"

"You aren't. I am." Kianna folded her arms too. "I can help you." She didn't want to lose her chance at helping put Mackey away. Never mind she wasn't an officer. This case was personal to her, and she wanted to see it through. "You said it yourself. I think like an officer. I thought we made a good team."

A flash of regret filled Cole's eyes. He dropped his right arm and pointed to Titan. "You were wrong. I already have a partner."

A pit grew in her abdomen. She blinked a few times. Tears threatened to brim along her lash line, but she refused to welcome them.

She wanted justice as much as he did. For Jaxon and every other person Mackey had victimized.

"I thought you had my back." She narrowed her gaze. At least she'd had his.

"I do." He propped his arms on his knees and leaned forward. His biceps protruded, and Kianna shifted her focus. His eyes softened, the creases disappearing. The way he tilted his head drew Kianna in. All that remained was…compassion? Pity?

How had she been so naive? She'd started this search with Cole to stop Mackey. And along the way, she'd let her heart do the one thing that was off-limits.

Any feelings she'd let herself grow for this man began to melt faster than the snow squall letting up outside.

"Your determination makes you good at your job. That's what you need to focus on. Leave Mackey to me and my team." Cole stood and tugged on Titan's leash.

Kianna refused to let him look down on her. She stretched to her full height. "So I'm just a civilian. Whose life also happens to be at stake with a convict on the loose."

Cole opened his mouth, then clamped it shut. A muscle in his neck bulged. "The more time I spend here, the less time *I* have to make sure Mackey doesn't stay out there for good."

Kianna sighed. The inflection in his tone said it all. The way he'd enunciated *I*. She and Cole were merely two individuals whose paths had crossed because of their fields of work. And she'd built up false expectations for what that meant—both professionally and personally.

"What about the Tiny Paws shelter?" she asked, knowing it was a vain attempt. Still, she had to try. Like she didn't want to believe he'd been completely honest the first time he'd said no.

"The adopt-a-pet event is canceled." A woman's voice came from behind Kianna, and she jumped. "They just announced the change."

Kianna turned.

Victoria. She wore a dark-blue sweater dress with a white scarf draped around her neck. Her brown hair was curled, and her red lipstick sealed the outfit.

Warmth snaked its way up Kianna's neck. How long had the woman been standing there? Had she heard their whole conversation?

"Good call," Cole said. "The roads are terrible."

Titan whimpered next to him.

"Titan." Victoria scrunched her nose. "I need to get going." She waved her phone. "Duty calls."

Allen Frees wheeled his way over to them.

"Hey, Frees," Cole waved.

"Stuart." Frees stilled his hand on the wheelchair. "Any new leads on Mackey?"

"I hope so. Planning to catch up with Basuto and Donaldson right after I drop Kianna off."

"Ah. Well, don't let me hold you. Mackey isn't going to wait around either." He rolled around to the front desk.

Titan whined like he knew who they were talking about.

Kianna sucked in a breath. Nothing like adding salt to her already exposed wound.

Cole put on his jacket, so Kianna followed suit. He ushered her outside, then they climbed into his Blazer.

"What's your address?" Cole shifted the car into Drive and pulled onto the road. The weather had changed to a slight snowfall, and light peeked ever so slightly through the afternoon clouds.

"128 Hillview Circle." Nausea swirled in her stomach with each passing minute that hastened their arrival at her house. Her time helping on the case was coming to a close, and there was nothing she could do to stop it.

When he pulled up to her house, she grabbed her purse and reached for the handle.

Cole shifted the vehicle into Park. "Thanks for everything."

She shut her eyes for a moment, her back to him. She needed to gain composure, or she'd make a snide remark. After a few seconds, she shifted to face him. "Stay safe. You too, Titan."

The dog sat up on the seat and wagged his tail.

At least one of them still wanted her around.

She got out of the car and headed inside.

She needed to get some rest. Cole was right about that.

But he'd been wrong about pushing away her help.

She pulled back the curtain and peered out the window.

Except it was too late.

The car turned past the corner.

Her chance to rectify the injustice of Jaxon's killer walking free disappeared. Along with any hope of a possible romance with Cole.

He'd just driven out of her life.

NINE

Cole had braced himself for the pushback, except it didn't come. Kianna had gone into her house and let him drive away. And for that, he was thankful. He'd meant what he'd said. Cole didn't want her to get hurt or die on his watch. He never should have let her tag along on the hunt for Mackey in the first place.

He turned out of her development and headed toward the police station.

He knew the reason for dismissing her help, but he wasn't about to admit it to her.

Cole had begun to enjoy her presence. Being around her pushed him to work hard and to think outside the box. Like when she'd mentioned the animal shelter being a possible lead where Mackey might go before escaping with his partner.

Partner.

Cole hadn't missed the hurt on Kianna's face when he'd commented about already having one.

He glanced in the rearview mirror to where Titan lay curled up, sleeping.

For Kianna's safety and his, he couldn't let her stick around. He'd pushed the importance of her physical safety. Which was imperative. But it ran deeper. If he let himself get too invested with Kianna, sooner or later, it would all be stripped away. And the sweet moments they'd shared would only be memories of what had once been.

Like the one over dinner, at the hospital. Opening up and sharing about his family with her had reminded him what it was like to have a confidant. A companion in life who witnessed beautiful moments and hard ones.

Another car approached him in the opposite lane. What would he have done if Kianna had died earlier today? He might not blame himself for his father's health decline, but he would have held himself accountable for Kianna.

Regardless, the glimmer of good moments could be taken away without warning. Like the snow squall snatching the light of the sun and shrouding everything in its path. He couldn't let himself get emotionally invested when time was fleeting.

Right, Lord? You say that the grass withers and the flowers fade. Only Your Word remains forever. So why put my hope in anything that will disappear?

Not only had it happened in his family, but he also experienced it with his job every day. Life as someone knew it could be gone in a flash.

If he could, Cole would keep everyone he cared about safe and happy. But he couldn't. So instead, he'd do what he could to preserve goodness and keep evil from winning.

It was time to come up with a plan to catch Mackey before he could collect his money and bail.

Several minutes later, Cole walked into the station and unzipped his jacket.

"Eyyy, Stuart is back." Officer Anthony Thomas greeted Cole when he walked in, stepping around the front desk, where he'd been talking with Jules, the receptionist, to give Cole a slap on the back.

"It's good to be where it's warm." Cole unhooked Titan's leash, and the dog trotted over to the food bowl by the seating area.

"This storm is going to break the winter record for Last Chance." Thomas's blue eyes widened, and he whistled.

"Let's hope it throws Mackey off and he slips up." Cole went over to the water cooler and grabbed a Styrofoam cup, filling it with warm water before opening a packet of hot chocolate.

"Everyone's in the conference room," Thomas said.

"Good." Cole snapped the lid on the cup, then followed Thomas down the hall.

Thomas, Ramble, Tazwell, Wilcox, and Basuto were already seated at the table, laptops out.

Cole greeted everyone, then took a seat.

"Let's get this meeting started." Basuto glanced at his watch.

A chorus of agreements followed.

"Did you get to talk with Athers, Cole?" Wilcox asked. "By the time I got there, she was asleep again."

"I did." Cole filled them in on the details of his conversation with Rainy. "So we know there's someone local in cahoots with Mackey. And he wants to take care of his 'canine currency,' whatever that means."

"Who were the visitors or callers Mackey had while in prison?" Basuto tapped his pen on the table.

Ramble clicked away at his computer. "Not many. In the two years he was there, it was mostly people from outside organizations and city officials. And a Benjamin Raider." The inmate database appeared on the conference TV.

"Who's that?" Tazwell swiveled in her chair to face the screen.

Cole tapped his pen against the table. "He caught Mackey in

the act of selling off a diamond cat collar that one of the foster boys stole before he killed him." A sour taste filled Cole's mouth, and he took a sip of the hot chocolate. Even when Cole had been investigating the case on Mackey to put him away the first time, he couldn't fathom how this guy's mind worked. Using people for his own advantage and peddling the goods to make a buck. All while discarding a human life. It was sick.

"Benjamin is also the manager of Tiny Paws Animal Shelter." Ramble glanced up from his computer.

Interesting. "There was supposed to be an adopt-a-pet event tomorrow at the shelter, but it was canceled," Cole added. "Maybe that's where we start."

"Why?" Basuto crossed his leg and steepled his fingers.

"Gives us a chance to talk to Benjamin without throngs of people. Find out more about this 'canine currency.'"

"I'm with Cole." Tazwell leaned forward in her chair. "Benjamin knows Mackey; he might be able to shed light on how the guy's mind works."

"What if Mackey needs to collect something at the shelter? Could money be hidden there?" Wilcox added.

Cole drummed his knuckles on the wood table. "If there is a payout for him there, with the event canceled, Mackey will show up at the shelter."

"Let's get two officers at the shelter, pronto. Thomas, Stuart, you good?" Basuto stood up. "I don't want to take any more chances of missing this guy."

Cole agreed. It might not be a solid lead, but it was time to explore every option for the sake of nabbing Mackey. Unfortunately, that meant Cole wasn't going to get any shut-eye tonight. Good thing he was used to night shifts. Another jolt of caffeine would help. He downed the rest of the hot chocolate. "Lieutenant." He nodded, then headed out to get Titan and fill up a thermos of coffee.

The German shepherd lay on the floor, his eyes closed, still near the food bowl. At least one of them had gotten a few moments of sleep.

"Tite." Cole clapped his hands. "We've got work to do."

His partner opened his eyes but didn't make an effort to move just yet.

Cole put a cup in the Keurig and let it brew.

"C'mon, boy. Time to work." Cole whistled.

Titan stood up and stretched.

Odd.

Cole bent over and rubbed the dog's ears. When he straightened, he caught sight of a pool of vomit near the food bowl.

"What happened, Tite? Not feeling well."

As if in response, the K-9 projectiled more.

"Aw, man, that's nasty." Thomas came over and held his fingers to his nose. "Titan, you can't be sick. We've got a criminal to catch."

The dog paid no attention to them. He whimpered and curled up on the floor.

Cole poured his coffee, then headed to the bathroom and grabbed a roll of paper towels.

He had to get Titan to the vet. He wasn't about to take a risk with his partner's life. No matter how badly Cole wanted to be staking out the animal shelter, his partner's welfare came first.

"I can't go with you, man," Cole said to Thomas while he wiped up Titan's vomit.

"I'll go," Tazwell piped up, sliding her arms into her coat. The overhead system crackled, and the alarm beeped. "Break-in at Tiny Paws." The dispatcher spouted off the address.

Cole raised a brow.

"Looks like we're onto something." Thomas grabbed his jacket from the coat rack.

"Lieutenant, permission to go with Thomas?" Tazwell was

fully expecting a positive response, because she already had her coat zipped up.

"Go catch the thief," Basuto ordered.

Cole grabbed his phone and dialed Brett Filks's number. The vet picked up on the third ring. "What's up?" Grogginess filled the man's voice.

"I know it's late, but I've got an emergency with Titan. He's throwing up and doesn't want to move."

"Bring him in." The sleepiness in the man's voice disappeared. "I'll be there in five."

Cole carried Titan out to the borrowed car and laid him on the back seat. The German shepherd opened his eyes a sliver, then closed them again. "We're going to get you fixed up soon, Tite."

Cole hopped into the driver's seat and headed to the clinic. If it weren't for the freezing temperatures and dark night, Cole would have sped down the roads. But he couldn't risk another accident. Not only because he didn't want to total a vehicle that belonged to the city, but for Titan's sake.

"Just don't puke all over the back seats, boy." Cole frowned when he glanced in the mirror and Titan didn't respond.

Cole pressed down a little harder on the gas. He couldn't lose his K-9. They'd bonded as working partners, and Titan had become Cole's best friend too. As Titan's handler, Cole did everything with the German shepherd. They'd built trust. And at the end of the day, Cole always had someone to come home to.

I thought we made a good team.

Kianna's comment rang in his mind.

He'd pushed her away. All because he was scared of what could happen if he got too close.

But it didn't matter now. She was gone, and the reality that he could lose his other partner was like a patch of black ice that threatened to send him careening over the edge.

He tried to control the outcomes to make life favorable. After one loss with his dad, he didn't want to risk the same disappointments with others. He couldn't seem to alter circumstances, no matter how much he tried.

Rejoice in all circumstances, for this is God's will for you.

The memory verse flooded his heart.

Forgive me, Lord. I've lacked gratitude for what You have given me. I need to praise You for what You do give me and trust You to walk with me no matter what comes next.

Kianna had been right.

In an effort to hold on to the good, he'd pushed away any chance of making more memories. All the wasted time he couldn't get back now.

And what did Cole have to show for it?

Nothing.

No memories were created while he stayed holed up in his little corner, trying to preserve the life he'd once known.

Before he realized how much time had passed, Cole pulled into the vet's parking lot. He'd driven on autopilot. All the roads a blur. Thank the Lord he'd gotten here safely.

Brett met them at the door and took Titan from his arms.

The dog stirred, then vomited again on the entryway mat of the building.

"Sorry, man." Cole scanned the foyer. "Let me grab some paper towels to clean it up."

Brett shook his head. "I'll take care of it. I want to collect it to send in for testing."

Cole paced in the waiting room while Brett checked out his partner. He wished he could be in two places at once and find out what was going on at the animal shelter.

Thirty minutes later, Brett walked back out, his lips thin.

Cole stopped moving and his calf muscles tightened. "How is he?"

"He's alive. But he has bradycardia and some wheezing in his lungs. I have him on fluids."

The air whooshed from Cole's lungs, a breath he didn't realize he'd been holding.

"I also pumped his stomach. What has he consumed within the last twenty-four hours?"

"Food and water." Cole frowned.

"Well, based on his symptoms, I suspect he ingested something poisonous. But a toxicology report will confirm. I'm going to get his GI contents delivered stat."

Cole ran his hand down his jaw, then lifted his radio off his shoulder. "Basuto, can we get the food left in Titan's dog bowl sent to the lab? Titan's possibly been poisoned."

"On it," his boss replied.

"I want to keep him the rest of the night to monitor his vitals, but I'm confident he'll make a quick recovery." Brett swung his stethoscope around his neck. "You brought him in right away, and with his stomach pumped, he will heal much faster and have minimal organ damage."

"Thanks for making us a priority." Cole shook the man's hand.

"You got it. I'll give you an update in the morning."

Cole pushed open the front door, and an icy blast greeted his face, waking him up faster than the caffeine. Someone had poisoned Titan and almost gotten away with killing him.

He unlocked the car and slid into the seat, resting his head back for a second before he grabbed the radio. "Any update on the burglary?"

"Thief escaped, but we just got done looking at the security camera." Tazwell's voice came through. "Whoever it was had their face well hidden."

Cole blew out a breath.

Of course they had.

"Basuto, can I have a copy of the footage sent to review? I'm heading back to the station now."

"Ten-four," Basuto said.

Cole was reaching for the engine start button when cool metal touched his temple.

"I suggest you listen to what I say, or I pull this trigger."

Cole lifted his gaze to the rearview mirror, and in the glow from the parking lot lights, he stared into Victoria's eyes.

TEN

The morning light streamed through Kianna's bathroom window, and birds chirped, but it did nothing to soothe her nerves. She dug her toothbrush harder against her gums and rubbed back and forth. She stared at her reflection in the mirror. The bags under her eyes were proof of the restless night she'd had, unable to shut her mind off after the events of the previous twenty-four hours.

She put her toothbrush back in its holder, then splashed cold water on her face before massaging serum into her pores. Mackey was still AWOL, and Cole had made sure she understood that he was going to finish this case without her. Which was exactly what he was supposed to do as a police officer. As an EMT, catching criminals wasn't her job.

But she couldn't just sit around and do nothing. Not after she'd invested so much time tracking down this guy. How would Jaxon's parents handle the news if Mackey was never caught?

They needed hope.

She needed hope. Not just with Mackey being caught, but with Cole.

Hope.

In his name the nations will put their hope.

Kianna sighed. *Forgive me, Lord. I was putting a lot of weight on a fleeting hope. I just thought You might be leading me to Cole. To a guy who would show me there was reason to enjoy the holidays again.*

But he'd made it clear she was just another civilian to him. The only reason their paths had collided for a brief moment was because of their careers. Never mind that she'd sensed a bond growing between them. Why had he shared about his family, then?

Kianna worked through the knots in her hair with a comb.

She needed to reorient her mindset.

Christ was her hope. A lasting love that wouldn't change with time. Even while she still longed to be married.

It's a good gift from You, Lord. I don't want to throw that dream away either. Yet not my will but Yours.

She changed into her work uniform, then grabbed her phone and headed to the kitchen.

"Hey, Google, play my daily song mix."

Kianna took out a bowl from the cupboard, then measured out oatmeal.

"O Holy Night" rang through the space, and Kianna stopped pouring the almond milk into the dish and smiled.

Yes, Lord. I hear You.

She set the timer on the microwave to heat up her breakfast, then leaned against the counter.

The chorus broke out, and the woman's voice built in anticipation. *A thrill of hope, the weary world rejoices.*

That was where her true hope lay. In Christ.

She could rejoice today, and even this holiday season, because of Jesus.

Is it possible to delight in the hope of You alongside someone else, Lord? Maybe even with Cole?

The timer beeped, and Kianna cupped her hands around the warm bowl, steam rising off the top.

She didn't know whether things would ever work with Cole. But she was certain of one thing: With God, nothing was impossible. He would give her hope and contentment no matter what the future brought.

After adding cinnamon and a drizzle of honey, she sat down and took a bite.

She could always text Cole and see how the case was going, whether they'd gotten any closer to Mackey's whereabouts. There was also time before her shift to stop over at Tiny Paws and drop off a few goodies for the extra pets that would be boarded there for the holiday until the adopt-a-pet event was rescheduled. It would give her a chance to poke around the place for a bit, maybe even talk to the manager.

Her instincts told her that what Rainy had overheard about the canine currency had something to do with the animals.

A knock sounded on her door.

Kianna rinsed out her bowl, then put it in the dishwasher.

The knock sounded again, this time faster, harder. "Coming!" she yelled.

Kianna opened the door. "Victoria, what's wrong?" The woman lived in Kianna's neighborhood, and they occasionally saw each other taking walks, but they weren't close.

The woman's face was pinched, and tears dried on her cheeks. "Hurry, please." She reached out her hand and took hold of Kianna's wrist. "The car. I..." The woman hiccupped. "I was leaving the development on my way to work, and I saw Mackey. Cole tried to stop him, but he—" She pointed behind her.

Kianna squinted against the sun that shone off the snow-covered grass. A Blazer, like the one she and Cole had used yesterday, was parked by the curb.

Was that Cole's car? Had he found a lead in this area? "Is Cole hurt? Or Mackey? Hang on." Kianna closed the front door a crack so she could open the hall closet and pull out a spare first aid kit.

She put on her jacket, grabbed her purse and the medical supplies, then closed the front door. "Where are they?" Kianna's pulse sped up.

"It's not Mack..." Victoria shook her head. "It's Cole. He hit Cole."

Kianna stilled. "No." *Please, God, don't let it be critical.*

"Mackey hurt him. I can't tell how bad it is." Victoria's brow furrowed.

Kianna broke off into a jog, Victoria at her heel.

Her lungs burned from the cold air.

Kianna sidestepped a patch of ice on the sidewalk and almost barreled into the side of the car.

Victoria's shoes crunched through the snow behind her, but Kianna blocked out the other woman.

She opened the car door and swallowed. Blood trailed down the side of Cole's face, his skin pale, eyes closed. "Cole. It's Kianna. Can you hear me?" She set the first aid kit on the dashboard, then took Cole's hand to check for a pulse.

Her shoulders relaxed. Steady. Strong.

A hand gripped her upper arm.

"Victoria, call 911." Kianna peered over her shoulder.

"There's no need." Victoria smirked, and in an instant, the woman had her other arm wrapped around Kianna's neck and her hand clamped down on Kianna's face with a cloth.

What in the world?

Kianna tried to elbow the woman, but a potent smell filled her nostrils. Her head began to throb until her eyes lost focus and the world spun into a web of darkness.

Kianna. Someone shook her shoulders. *Kianna, wake up.* The person's breath tickled her ear, and she let out a groan. A pine scent wafted toward her nose, making her want to curl up and sleep more.

Had she been dreaming?

She went to turn over and wrap herself tighter in her sheets, except she couldn't move.

Where was she?

A dull ache clung to her temples. Kianna blinked a few times.

"That's good. Wake up, Kianna." Cole's voice registered next to her.

Finally, her eyes worked with her brain and opened.

Lines etched Cole's brow, his eyes assessing her.

She pushed herself up on the leather seat. Sunlight shone through the car windows. Trees and snow lined the landscape outside with no houses in sight. They weren't in her neighborhood anymore.

Victoria. Cole. The attack.

Kianna gasped. "Cole?" she whispered, twisting her upper body. She went to move her hand to the caked blood on his cheek, but a rope tied around her wrists held her back. "Thank God you're alive." She bit down on her lip, and tears spilled onto her face. "What happened?"

"Hey. It's gonna be okay." Cole lifted his bound hands and used his knuckles to wipe away a tear from her cheek. "I'm so sorry. I never meant to drag you into this." He leaned his head back against the seat.

"We've already been over this. I volunteered on my own accord." Kianna stared at the bruise on his forehead. The discolored skin had formed a goose egg. "You're hurt. You need some ice for that."

"After we get out of here." He peered out the window. "Victoria is working with Mackey."

"She's the one who lured me to you." Kianna grimaced.

"I need you to follow my lead, okay?" Cole placed his hands on top of hers. "I'm not going to let anything happen to you."

Kianna nodded, or else her voice would betray her. Determination stared back at her in his eyes, and something else. Admiration?

"I thought we had a plan. And now you show up?" Victoria's shrill voice pierced the air.

Kianna jumped in her seat.

The woman stood a hundred or so feet away outside, near a mound of snow on the other side of the paved two-way road. She flung one arm in the air. Her other hand gripped a red canister with a slim spout. A man with a long beard stood next to Victoria, a frown on his face.

"Cole, she has gasoline." Kianna's voice tremored. "And that's—"

"Mackey," he finished. "They're having quite the argument, which should buy us some time."

"Where's Titan?" Kianna did a quick scan of the car but didn't see the K-9 anywhere.

"At the vet." Cole's nostrils flared. "Victoria poisoned him."

"Is he—"

"He's fine." They spoke at the same time.

"Poor guy." Kianna frowned, then glanced out the window again, where Mackey and Victoria continued their fight. "She showed up on my doorstep. Said Mackey hurt you."

"She attacked me. Not Mackey." Cole grunted. "She was hiding in my car. I tried to thwart her plan, but when I went to snatch the gun out of her grip, she slammed the base into my head, and I blacked out. I don't know how she knew where you live though."

"She's one of my neighbors."

"Isn't that convenient." He shook his head. "Well, she messed with the wrong people."

Kianna bit back a grin.

Cole's hands were clenched in front of him. He was ready to fight.

Courage worked its way through her veins. With him by her side, she could face Mackey and Victoria head-on.

"Does the police force know Victoria is behind it?" Kianna mirrored Cole's stance and raised her head, back straight.

"We're on our own at the moment. But my boss knew I was coming back to the station. So when I don't show up or radio in, he'll have all hands on deck."

Cole lifted his hands. "Let me see your wrists."

Kianna held out her arms. The thick twine was wrapped around several times. He used the tips of his forefinger and thumb to work at the knot securing the bonds, but it didn't loosen.

"If I create a distraction, can you run and go get help?"

Kianna swallowed. "I can't leave you to fend them off yourself."

"I can't let you die here either. We're the ones standing between Mackey and his freedom. And Victoria isn't going to let us stop him." Cole wiggled on the car door. "It's locked."

Kianna tried her side but couldn't get it open. "They probably have the childproof setting on." Thanks to the fancy new technology, there wasn't even a lock switch to lift up, since it was computer programmed.

Cole unbuckled his seatbelt, then climbed into the front seat. "If the keys are in here, I can drive us to the station."

Kianna pulled back the leather pockets in front of her on the back of the passenger and driver seats. "Nothing back here."

Cole opened the glove box. "Don't see anything either."

Victoria wasn't making it easy for them.

"Plan B. Cut these ropes."

"There's scissors in my first aid kit." Kianna leaned forward just as Cole turned around with the bag. Their noses almost collided, and Kianna sucked in a breath. Cole's proximity and his evergreen cologne threatened to unravel her. From this angle, his brown eyes searched hers, beckoning her to find safety here with him.

Cole opened his mouth, then cleared his throat. "Whatever you do, don't look out your side of the window."

Kianna swallowed, then leaned back, the moment lost. Cole had the right mindset. They were trapped in a car, a murderer and his accomplice outside. She turned to her left, where Victoria and Mackey stood. If they took note of the movement in the car and realized their victims were awake, who knew how they'd respond?

Cole slid back into the seat next to her and unzipped the first aid bag.

"Give me your hands." Cole held the scissors.

She followed his second order but did exactly what he said not to do for his first. She peered over her shoulder and out the closest right window. The car was parked up against the edge of a drop-off. The snow-covered area did nothing to hide the steepness of the descent. Boulders and trees littered the steep drop. One slip and they'd be dead before they knew what they'd hit.

Kianna whipped her head around and jerked her hands. "There's no way out."

"Whoa. Watch it." Cole pulled the scissors back.

"Sorry." She grimaced.

"Here." Cole had severed her ropes and now handed them to her to do the same on his.

"I'm going to see if I can unlock the doors from the driver's side. I'll hop out from the front, and you escape through the back. Keep running and don't look back. If my assessment of the area is correct, we're on the south side of the Mountain Ridgeview Overlook. There are a few houses tucked in the woods north of here, about a mile away. Go to the closest house and call 911. Tell them Victoria is working with Mackey and that they have my car. As long as Victoria didn't disable the GPS tracker on this vehicle, they can pull it up for a precise location. They'll send out the crew."

The plan could work, except it wouldn't. Kianna might get away, but what about Cole? She wouldn't think that way. He could hold his own. He would make it out alive. Backup would be right around the corner. She would hope for the best outcome. No matter the odds stacked against them.

"Cole."

"Kianna."

They said each other's names simultaneously, and if it weren't for the dire circumstances, it would have been funny.

Before Kianna could speak again, Cole said, "Whatever happens, I need you to know I'm sorry." Cole put his hand on top of hers, his thumb rubbing back and forth.

Kianna parted her lips to speak but decided to let him finish first. She'd been in the wrong too. Not respecting that he had a job to do and that he was just looking out for her. Still, the apology soothed over the cracked edges of her heart, restoring the gaps left by hurt.

"It wasn't fair of me to push you away. You were right about so many things. I've kept people at arm's length to avoid pain. You helped me see that. And you've been a great partner on this case." His Adam's apple bobbed. "I just wanted you to know."

Kianna smiled, even while her lip trembled. "Quit talking like we're going to die, okay? We're going to get out of this together. Partner." She squeezed his hand.

He climbed into the front seat. With a brief nod of his head, he hit the unlock switch and opened the door.

Right as the car alarm screamed.

She'd told him they were partners. And now, thanks to his apology, she couldn't imagine leaving his side to fight this battle alone. Never mind their plan. They were going to do this together.

ELEVEN

Cole jumped out of the car, his head and heart thrumming in time to the beep of the antitheft alarm. There was no way to make a surprise ambush now.

Kianna raced past him. The sooner she got help, the quicker they could put an end to things.

Mackey and Victoria whirled and pointed their weapons.

"No!" Kianna screamed. She pivoted and made a beeline for Victoria.

What was she doing? He was supposed to handle Victoria and Mackey so Kianna could make it out alive.

Cole sprinted toward her.

A bang resounded, then a second.

He dropped to all fours and rolled to the side.

Another round of bullets sprayed the area around him, kicking up ice and snow. A cold sensation seared his neck, then trailed down his back.

"Let go of me," Kianna cried.

The bullets had failed to take Cole out, but her plea stabbed his chest, hitting the mark on his heart.

Cole jumped up and came face-to-face with the criminal he'd

put away once. This time, though, Mackey was the one with leverage, and the smug look on his face told Cole he knew it.

Cole took a step toward the man who had Kianna in his grasp. He used her as a shield, and his weapon was flush against her neck.

"Don't even think about it." Victoria dropped the gasoline tank and trained her weapon—or rather, his Glock, still in her possession—on Cole, center mass. Where had she learned tactical skills? This woman worked for the city in an office. Not a special ops force.

Cole kept his hands in front of him but could feel the scissors in his back pocket. It wasn't his ideal weapon, but if he could get close enough without Victoria pulling the trigger, he'd have a shot at turning the advantage around.

"Another move and she dies." Victoria tilted her head.

Cole shifted his gaze to the left, and bile rose in his throat.

"Officer Stuart. So we meet again," Mackey sneered. "This time you brought a little lady to join in the fun. I prefer my victims to be teens, but it's not like I haven't killed another woman."

"No one gets away with murder, Mackey." Cole dug his heels into the snow. He would not let the man escape and snuff out any more lives. Not when it would mean another family was destroyed, along with the chance to make memories together. "There are witnesses to your schemes, Mackey. You can't hide forever."

Mackey laughed. "Such a shame. That female corrections officer thought she knew better too. You're both wrong. Soon, you'll join her in the grave."

Kianna smirked. "You left her for dead, but you failed at your job." Her voice was strong, despite the loss of color in her cheeks.

"Be quiet," Mackey shouted. "No one eludes my grasp. That woman is dead."

"You're bluffing." Cole stood his ground. "You've been too busy hiding to make another kill."

"Not when I have an accomplice." Mackey narrowed his gaze.

Cole turned to Victoria, who still had her gun trained on him. Her finger hovered too close to the trigger. "It was an unfortunate tragedy, really. Her body couldn't muster the strength to recover after surgery, and her heart gave out. She never even made it home from the hospital." Victoria pouted.

"No!" Kianna struggled, still in his hold.

The smile that lit up Mackey's face made Cole want to hurl. "She barely felt a thing. I promise you won't notice what hit you either." He stroked Kianna's hair, and she flinched.

Cole resisted the urge to rush Mackey and take him to the ground. "Don't touch her like that." If it weren't for the two guns trained on them, he'd have the man in a wrist lock. Instead, he ground his teeth.

Mackey laughed.

Cole flexed his hand. "How'd you bypass the officer stationed at her door?"

"When you work for the city, you make lots of friends. Who trust you." Victoria smiled.

"Give it up. The police have been scouring the area for you." Cole stepped forward.

"Don't move," Victoria shouted.

"It's time to put an end to this." Mackey yanked Kianna and pulled her toward the car they'd just escaped from. "And soon we'll be on our way to paradise."

Victoria flicked her weapon at Cole. "Move it." She pointed to the car.

Cole didn't budge. There had to be a way to catch Victoria by surprise and then incapacitate her and Mackey without Kianna in the crosshairs.

As if she knew, Kianna peered over her shoulder. Fear and determination filled her expression.

The moment they were back in the car, it would be too late.

Victoria closed the gap and gripped Cole's arm. She moved to his side, and cool metal kissed his neck. "The waiting is over." Victoria's breath raised the hair on his back.

"When you add two more murders to your count, you'll have the whole FBI on your tail." Cole wasn't going to give Mackey and Victoria the satisfaction of thinking they'd won. "If you kill us, you'll have signed up for war against the police force."

"Not if it's a tragic accident and all the evidence disappears," Victoria interjected.

"They're never going to fall for that." Cole dug his shoes into the snow.

"Your boss has already received an email informing him you're taking a long weekend to attend to a family emergency. Certainly, he won't question a grieving son who needs to be with family after his dad dies."

The blood drained from Cole's face, and he clenched his fists. There was no way she'd know anything about his dad. And Basuto wouldn't buy it either. Would he?

It didn't matter. Whether his boss caught on or not, it would be too late.

"Let her go and take me." Cole might have squandered his chances to make things right with his family. And if his life ended up being buried and forgotten, so be it. But he couldn't let his choices affect Kianna. Not when she still had a family who she wanted to spend the holidays with. "She has nothing to do with this case. She's not even an officer."

"Oh, but she wants to support you in your grief and attend your father's funeral." Victoria pouted. "She's hoping for her own Christmas miracle with you. Such a tragedy she dies with you while traveling."

The cold air slapped Cole in the face. He wouldn't let Kianna take the hit.

"Enough chitchat," Mackey bellowed. "I want my crypto and outta here. We don't have long. The countdown is already set."

"It's right here, Mack." Victoria released her grip on Cole's arm and held up a flash drive, but the gun never wavered from his skin. "I got it from that mutt at the shelter. Put the girl in the car, and I'll take care of him."

So their intuition had been right. They'd hidden the money with a canine.

With Victoria's attention momentarily on the flash drive, this was Cole's shot to take her out and pray he subdued her before she could pull the trigger.

He swung his arm and snagged Victoria's wrist, yanking it up and behind her back. A screech tore past her lips. She whirled and rammed her elbow into his nose.

A sickening crack sent him stumbling back, and warm liquid flowed to his lips.

"The clock's ticking," Mackey huffed. "We gotta get out of here. In the car, now."

Cole straightened in time to see Mackey punch Kianna in the gut.

She keeled over and heaved.

Cole raced toward the man just as he shoved Kianna into the back seat.

The door shut with a thud, the click of the lock snapped, and Kianna's hands trailed down the window, yanking the handle.

"Cole, look out!" Kianna's muffled scream sent him spinning around.

Victoria squeezed the trigger, and a bullet whizzed past his arm.

He spun to the side but kept his balance, prepared to turn and make a lunge for Victoria.

In Cole's peripheral vision, Mackey held up the car key and flung it toward the steep drop-off.

Cole pivoted, ready to dive for the key. But it was too late. The fob disappeared over the edge.

Another shot rang, and a bullet whacked him in the chest. Air whooshed from his lungs, and pain spread across his pectoral muscles as he dropped to the ground.

His chest burned, and dots danced in his vision.

Victoria might have hit his Kevlar vest, but the force still sucked the air from him.

Cole went to stand, but he faltered, and his knees hit the ground. He pinched the bridge of his nose to stop the pool of blood tainting the snow.

Cole closed his eyes and focused on breathing. He wouldn't be any good to Kianna if he passed out. And he couldn't focus on the blood right now. It would only sap the strength he needed to muster to get himself and Kianna out of here.

Cole opened his eyes and lifted his gaze.

Mackey and Victoria had sprinted down the road, except they weren't moving fast thanks to the still-slick roads and mounds of snow along the shoulder.

Kianna pounded on the car door.

Cole met her wide-eyed gaze.

He glanced back over at the fleeing convicts. There was no way he could catch up to and detain them. Not when they still had weapons and he was fighting to maintain consciousness.

Mackey had said something about the countdown already being set. He pushed himself off the ground and groaned.

Who knew what that meant? But he wasn't going to wait to find out.

Help me save Kianna, Lord. Keep me conscious long enough to help her.

Something clanked behind him, and Cole turned to where the scissors had fallen out of his pocket.

He grabbed them, then hurried to the car, his breaths coming in labored pants. "Stand back." Cole held up the scissors and pointed to the window.

Kianna's brow tightened. Her eyes scanned his face, and he could only imagine what he looked like. But she followed his order and scooted to the other side of the car.

He raised his arm and plunged the tip of the scissors into the window. A crack split the glass and sent a spiderweb of lines through the pane. Cole drove the scissors through the weakened spot once more, and glass shattered, raining down around them.

Sirens pierced the air, and Cole spared a glance over his shoulder at the approaching police car and ambulance. His backup was here. Somehow they'd located them.

Thank You, God.

His head throbbed. Perspiration beaded on his forehead, but he refused to succumb to the darkness that the pain beckoned him toward.

He needed to help Kianna out of the car.

Another car door slammed, and a low growl followed by a bark carried across the wind.

There was no need to turn around. Cole would recognize that sound anywhere.

How had Titan gotten here?

His German shepherd barreled past him, kicking up snow with his hind legs. The spray caught Cole in the face, but he didn't care.

A smile lifted the corners of his lips.

Cole wasn't fighting this battle alone. That reality and knowing Titan was alive and well gave Cole the boost of energy he needed. He extended his arms to Kianna, who stood on the car seat in a hunched position. "Let me help."

She braced her hand on his arm, then swung one leg through the window. "You're the one who needs help." A pained look furrowed her brow.

"As long as it's you who's helping." He winked.

Shock filled her face, then she clamped her lips shut, but Cole still noticed the laugh she'd tried to suppress.

Cole grabbed under her arms and lifted her out through the window, then set her on the ground with a grunt.

He stumbled to the side, and Kianna wrapped her arm around his bicep. "You need to sit down."

"Get away from me, you mutt," Victoria shouted. Titan was quickly gaining ground. "Get away!" She raised her weapon.

Titan bared his teeth and pounced.

Victoria screamed and fell to the ground. The flash drive tumbled from her grasp.

The dog's teeth sank into her arm, his feet on top of her.

Thomas raced to Titan's side and trained his weapon on Victoria.

Mackey dove for the flash drive in a desperate attempt to regain his money.

"He's not going to get away." Cole broke away from Kianna's grip.

"Cole," she shouted, but he forged ahead.

His feet pounded against the snow, and Cole focused on taking the next step, trying to ward off the pain pulsing through his body. The cold air made his nose drip. He used his sleeve to wipe, and it came away clean. At least his nose had stopped bleeding.

Mackey turned to Cole, who was closing in. He shoved the flash drive in his pocket and scrambled to his feet.

Cole tackled Mackey to the ground and gripped the man's arms, twisting them behind his back.

Mackey thrust his body, but Cole used his knee to pin the man, refusing to let him get away again.

"It's over, Mack. You're headed back to prison."

"You little—"

"Nice save." Thomas stepped up next to him, then bent

down and clasped the handcuffs around Mackey's wrists, ignoring the expletives the guy spewed.

Cole stood up, but the sudden change made his head spin. He blew out a breath and unzipped his jacket. Titan ran over to Cole and barked, his tail wagging.

"How did you get here, Tite? I thought Brett was still keeping his eye on you." Cole rubbed the spot behind the dog's ear. "Nice work out there."

Titan snarled and bared his teeth at Mackey, who was being led away by Ramble.

"He needs to get to the hospital stat." Kianna's voice came from behind.

She hurried over to Cole with Nathan, who pushed the gurney. She set the medic bag on the ground and stared at Cole. Her eyes searched his, then took inventory of his whole body.

"Sit down." She pointed to the gurney and took hold of his arm.

"K, I'm fine." His breath came out in short pants.

"Nuh-uh. That's the shock talking." Her chin trembled ever so slightly. "Your nose is already black and blue. And Victoria hit you point blank." Cole sat down on the cot while Nathan pulled a BP cuff out.

"I'm really okay." He squeezed her hand, then guided it and placed it over his chest. "She hit my vest."

Kianna pulled her hand away and frowned. "You're sure?" She peered up at him. "I don't believe it. Take off your jacket." Creases etched into her forehead.

Cole smirked and raised his eyebrows. "That's quite the request."

Kianna's cheeks turned bright red, but he liked seeing her nervous around him. Liked the idea that just maybe there was a reciprocated interest.

"That's not funny," she whispered.

"Hey." Cole shrugged out of his coat and clasped Kianna's hand in his.

"You're really okay." Tears pooled in Kianna's eyes.

Cole went to brush a tear that trailed down her cheek, but before he could, she leaned up on her tiptoes and sealed her lips to his.

He stilled for a moment before returning the gesture. He'd wasted too much time afraid of what might happen. He'd almost lost Kianna. And Cole was tired of missing out on life. No, he wasn't going to let another moment slip out of his grasp.

Kianna's nose pressed into his face, but the tenderness of her touch overrode any pain from his injury.

For so long, everything seemed to have been lost in Cole's life. All the moments of joy whisked away.

Until now.

Kianna reminded him why he should fight.

He wrapped his arm around her neck and wove his fingers through her hair.

They were alive—creating a new moment, one that electrified Cole with excitement and curiosity at what was to come.

Kianna eased away, her breath hot on his cheek.

"Thank God you're okay," she whispered close to his ear, her finger gliding across his jaw.

Kianna buried her face in the crevice of his shoulder, and Cole held her in his embrace.

Nathan had put his supplies away and grinned. He pointed behind him, then headed back toward the ambulance.

Kianna's heart beat against Cole's chest, and he stayed there, unmoving. This moment was a Christmas miracle.

Cole propped his chin on top of Kianna's head and lifted his gaze to the sky. *Thank You, Lord.*

How many times had the Lord protected him? Come to his rescue and guarded his life. The Lord continued to watch over his coming and going.

He'd spared Cole's life.

Again.

Who was he to sit around and waste it anymore? Not when there were people to make amends with. Not when there was an opportunity to invest in the future. Could it really be with Kianna?

He was ready to give it his all.

But first, he needed to make sure everything was wrapped up with this case.

Cole leaned back and put his hands on Kianna's shoulders.

"Stuart." Basuto called his name and jogged over.

Cole squeezed Kianna's arm and smiled before pushing off the gurney and walking over to his boss.

"This was in Mackey's possession. Cryptocurrency." Cole pulled out the flash drive and handed it to him.

Basuto said, "I'll get this entered into evidence."

Before Cole could respond, Titan ran over to Cole's side and whimpered. Then he raced to the car, still by the edge of the cliff.

"What is it, boy?"

Titan doubled back before racing off to the car again.

Cole jogged over to where the dog sat on his haunches, whining.

"What does he see?" Kianna asked.

Cole followed the dog to the car and crouched to Titan's level.

Titan barked.

Cole scanned the trim near the front tire, and his eyes landed on a flashing red light.

Cole shot up and cupped his hands around his mouth. "There's a bomb. Everyone away now," he shouted.

TWELVE

Cole grabbed Kianna's hand and dashed for the tree line across the street.

People near Kianna yelled and ran every which way. Her head spun from the commotion, and in a split second, a boom resounded, drowning out everything around her. She pitched forward from the force of the explosion.

Cole caught her at the waist, then dropped to the ground with her, rolling to the side. Shrubs scratched against her jacket while snow dusted her clothing, but Cole tucked her close to himself.

His chest heaved against her, and the warmth of his breath flooded her face.

Tremors worked their way down her body. Kianna focused on counting her own breaths. Letting Cole's heartbeat in her ear steady her own racing pulse.

One, in. Two, out.

The smell of smoke and the distinct pine scent that clung to Cole's coat flooded her senses.

She turned her head, nuzzling her cheek into the crook of

Cole's arm, and peered past his shoulder, where flames fizzled against the snow.

She squinted against the ball of fire engulfing the hood of the car and sending heat waves rippling through the air.

Unchecked tears streamed down her cheeks.

If she had still been in the car and Cole hadn't rescued her... If they hadn't stopped Mackey...If they...

Kianna's breath hitched.

Cole eased back, bracing one arm next to her head. "Shhh. It's okay." His fingers brushed against her forehead and worked their way to the edge of her hair, pulling out a few leaves. "You're safe."

His only concern was her. The reality of his words shook her body once more. He'd taken the brunt of the force, for her. "And you?"

His brow knit together; creases etched the bridge of his nose. "Fine." He leaned back on his heels and offered his hand.

Kianna gripped his sturdy hold and let him pull her up. She dusted snow off her pant leg, the cold, wet substance seeping into her hands, turning her exposed fingertips red.

Officers shouted into their radios. Some of them hefted snow on top of the car's hood, working to douse the flames.

More sirens screamed as the fire truck pulled up. Within seconds, rushing water pumped from the fire hose.

"I need to find Titan." Cole did a one-eighty. He hesitated for a second, almost like he was going to ask her permission. "I'll be back." Then he took off.

Of course he needed to check on his partner. Still, Kianna was very aware of her current position.

Everyone around her worked together, shouting orders.

Standing there by herself, Kianna felt exposed.

Unnoticed.

Her own thoughts worked to drown out the chaos encircling her.

She shook her head.

Cole said he'd be back. Did he truly mean it? Although, their kiss had to mean something. After all, he'd reciprocated her invitation. She sighed. She'd worry about that later.

For now, Kianna scanned the area, taking note of who she could go help.

Nathan stopped next to an officer who was clutching his arm.

Tires squealed against the slushy mixture on the road, then the police cruiser sped off—no doubt the one with Mackey and Victoria in it.

These people had come to their rescue, risking their own lives. Kianna had always been grateful for her team and the people she worked alongside. But today, the realization held more weight.

She followed Nathan back to the ambo, where a bag of first aid supplies was unzipped.

She grabbed a handful of wipes, then hurried over to Tazwell, who was wiping blood off her cheek. "Here." Kianna handed her an alcohol prep pad and bandage. "Thank you. For helping with this case." Kianna smiled.

"Doing my job as much as you are doing yours now." Tazwell grinned.

"How did you know where to find us?" Kianna turned to Nathan and Trace.

"When you were late for your shift and didn't pick up your phone, I asked the chief what was up." Nathan wrapped gauze around his patient's arm. "He said he got an email from you that you were heading out of town to help Cole with a family emergency."

"I thought it was odd you were helping with such a personal matter when you've just gotten to know each other. So I asked to see the email." Trace chimed in. "You said you were hoping to find your Christmas miracle with Cole." Trace scrunched his brow. "I told him you're a curmudgeon when it comes to the holidays."

"Hey now." Kianna crossed her arms. "I wouldn't say I'm a curmudgeon." She laughed. "I simply have a dislike for all the romanticized hype around the season."

"Exactly." A contemplative look filled Trace's face. "I knew something wasn't right. So Macon touched base with Basuto to see if you were still with Cole. When he said they couldn't get ahold of Cole and his car's GPS tracker was down, I knew you were in trouble."

"How did you know where to look for us?" Kianna moved to the side of the ambulance so Nathan could grab tape from the supply drawer.

"Basuto was able to pull up the satellite in the car, which gave an approximate location, and we followed the cruisers over."

"Thanks for speaking up." Kianna gave Trace a hug. "And for covering for me." Kianna winced.

"It's not every day I get to work with this guy." Trace slapped Nathan on the shoulder.

"Looking to swap me out?" Kianna's mouth gaped with a feigned look of hurt.

"No way." Trace winked.

"I'm glad." She sighed. So many emotions. So many realizations that things could have ended very differently. "Thank you for everything."

Trace shrugged. "The Lord was watching over you, that's for sure."

Warmth worked its way up her arms, and she breathed in deeply, letting the cold air fill her lungs. The Lord had never left her side. And there were people who cared for her. "Of course. But you still had my back." There were no words that would rightly express her thankfulness.

"That's what partners do," Trace said.

Kianna caught sight of Cole, still talking with Basuto, Titan now next to him.

Should she go over and tell him thanks too? What else would they say to each other? From the looks of it, everything was wrapped up. Packaged with a bow on top. Everyone safe and the convicts apprehended.

The only thing tying them together after this case was their kiss.

She should leave well enough alone and focus on her life. Go spend time with her family and celebrate what God had given her. It would do no good to hope for something that was far from being a reality. No matter what had happened between them earlier. They'd been in the heat of a moment, thinking they were both going to die. Except she'd stand by her choice to kiss Cole if he asked. She'd grown an attraction for the man that went deeper than his good looks—to his heart.

Was she willing to risk her heart getting broken again if he said he wasn't thinking when he kissed her back? That he didn't like her in that way?

Cole leaned down and rubbed Titan's head. He'd made it clear what he believed about partners.

He must have sensed her looking his way, because he lifted his gaze and connected with hers.

Kianna pushed off the edge of the truck and turned to help Trace put away supplies, then close the back doors of the ambulance.

His actions spoke for themselves. She wouldn't try to read between the lines and expect a different outcome.

"Rainy's gone."

Kianna turned around at the voice and found Cole standing there, Titan by his side.

Kianna closed her eyes for a brief second, then opened them. She didn't want it to be true. "What about her family?" Kianna's voice cracked. "She was supposed to see her brother."

"I know." Cole swallowed, and his Adam's apple bobbed. "I want to reach out to them. Offer my condolences and find out when the service will be held."

"I'd like to go too." Kianna bit her lip. Would he read into her request wrongly? It had nothing to do with going together. She just wanted to grieve with the family too. Kianna didn't have to explain her reasoning to Cole. "Could you let me know the details when you find out?"

"Of course." He shifted his stance but didn't make an effort to leave. "Thank you for everything."

Kianna dismissed his comment with a hand wave. "It's no big deal. I'm just glad Mackey and Victoria were stopped."

"No." Cole shook his head. "It is a big deal." He dropped his hands to his side. "I meant what I said earlier. You risked your life as much as me to find Mackey. And if I hadn't had your help, who knows how things could have turned out? You've taught me a lot in the last two days."

Was this goodbye? Kianna tucked her hands in her jacket pockets. She couldn't leave without knowing if the kiss had meant anything to him. Before she could speak, he said, "I never want you to feel undervalued. Or think you shouldn't speak up or help out. You're good at your job, Kianna. You care about people. I hurt you when I pushed you away." He leaned back on his heels and sighed.

"Thank you. That means a lot. I'm glad I could help you." She smiled even as a slight tremor coursed through her body. His comment hadn't addressed the fire that roared in her heart. But he'd told her to speak up.

There was no more time to waste. "About earlier." She shuffled her feet, tempted to avert her gaze. Except she was a big girl, and she needed to take in his expression. Know how he really felt about it. "The kiss. I—"

"Don't apologize." He reached out and took hold of her

hand. "I don't play around. In that moment, I was serious. All in. And I still am." He searched her eyes.

Kianna gulped, working to hold back her shock. "I feel the same way, Cole." She placed her other hand on top of his. "I don't want this to be the last we see of each other now that the case is closed." Although, maybe next time there could be a little less running to stay alive.

"I'm going to visit my dad this week." He grinned. "The life we once had might be gone, but a wise person once told me it doesn't mean new memories can't be created." He winked. "And I'd like you to come."

Kianna's eyes widened. Somehow, in that moment, everything changed. If there was hope for Cole forging new memories when it came to his family, who was she to think it couldn't be the same for her? "I would be honored." Kianna squeezed Cole's hand. Deep in her heart, the fire continued to blaze, melting away the fear of being hurt again. And she knew, this was just the beginning of the most wonderful time of the year.

"Rainy Athers was a woman who loved well and made sure you knew it."

Kianna took the crumpled tissue in her hand and dabbed once more at the tears brimming on her lash line. She spared a glance at Cole, who sat next to her in the church pew while they listened to the pastor give the eulogy.

His pinched face held back his own emotions.

It had been four days since Mackey and Victoria had been taken down. Four days since the toxicology report came back and the security cameras showed Victoria poisoning Titan's water. Thanks to the police working overtime, they'd confirmed the hardware wallet, which resembled a flash drive, in Victoria's possession had nine hundred thousand dollars of cryptocurrency on it that she'd embezzled from the city with a plan to help Mackey escape from prison and hightail it off to a secluded island. The two lovebirds had been dating before Mackey had been incarcerated the first time. They'd met when Victoria was a social worker who'd worked with the kids Mackey was grooming, before she switched jobs.

The whole situation was inconceivable. Still, Kianna could relax knowing the two felons would be locked away for good and no one else's life would be in jeopardy.

Although, her nerves still worked overtime in another area. After the memorial service ended, Kianna would meet Cole's family. What would be her first impression of Cole's parents? Would they like her?

"I'd like to close out the service with this reminder," the pastor continued, breaking Kianna's train of thought. "While we grieve today at the loss of a precious and beloved friend, daughter, and sister, we do not grieve without hope. This is the season of hope. Where we can rejoice, because a baby was born, who brought hope for the whole world. That little baby grew up and secured an eternal hope for all who believe in Him. And because of that, this is a 'See you later, Rainy.'"

They ended the service singing "O Holy Night," and there was not a dry eye in the room. After Cole and Kianna offered their condolences one last time, they headed outside.

"You sure you want me meeting your parents today?" Kianna's fingers tingled, and she let out a short laugh. "I really should have brought along that poinsettia." She slid into the passenger seat of Cole's car.

Cole closed her door after she was settled and walked around to the driver's side. "I told you a present isn't necessary." He started the engine, then grasped her fingers in his and gave them a gentle squeeze. "They're a fan of anyone I care about. Gifts or no gifts." He leaned in and, with a feather-light touch, brushed his mouth against hers. She returned the gesture, bracing her hand on his forearm. He trailed his finger across her jaw, and she let the warmth of his touch flood her body, erasing the chill from the car.

Kianna eased back and whispered in his ear, "You make it easy for me to open up my heart again."

Cole hooked his thumb under her chin and sobered. "I intend to keep it that way." He pressed a kiss to her forehead. "One day at a time. So you never have to second-guess."

"Mmm." She cocked her head. "I don't deserve you."

"That makes two of us." He winked.

Just when she thought he was going to wrap her in his embrace once more, he pulled in a breath and put the car in reverse. "If we stay here any longer, we'll be late."

"That would be a terrible first impression." Kianna laughed.

Cole turned up the radio, and "I'll Be Home for Christmas" played through the speakers.

Kianna glanced at Cole, and they exchanged a smile, his right hand still intertwined in hers.

It was a fitting song for this drive. And this time, she had no desire to shut off the Christmas tune. Now was the time to hold on to the hope of the season and make a few new memories in the process.

EPILOGUE

Chief Macon James leaned back in his chair. He could hear the department Christmas party in full swing in the engine bay, music pumping down the hall. "It's over?"

The PD chief, Conroy Barnes, sat across from him in his usual suit, a red tie today. Conroy nodded. "It's over. Everyone accounted for, or at the morgue. The situation is contained."

"Good." Macon's gaze drifted to the framed photo on his desk. Him and his wife at the department barbecue over the summer, their son on her hip. His brother Houston and his wife Sophie beside them. Their first baby was due in the new year.

Life moved on.

Chapters closed, and the world kept turning. Next week they'd face a new situation, and the crew would be knocked back a step. For a second, until they rallied and remembered that in anything, working together meant they would be stronger.

"You really good?"

Macon shrugged. "It's Christmas. What's not to be good about?"

Conroy shook his head, a smile on his face. "Whatever you say, bro." He got up and held his hand out. "Tell the crews thank you for everything they did. This could have been a whole lot worse without your people and what they did the past few days. Lot more people would've been hurt."

Macon stood, shaking his friend's hand. "I'll tell them."

"Have a good one."

Conroy headed to the door and stepped into the hall. Macon shut down his computer and followed his friend, but while Conroy went out the front door of the firehouse, he went the other direction. Past the kitchen, where Ridge's twin sisters were making yet another batch of cookies.

Macon stopped at the door. "Smells great, ladies."

The teens beamed at him, then looked at each other. He didn't have a prayer of deciphering the expression that passed between Maddie and Ella, so he left them to it and continued through the double doors at the end. Into the engine bay, which had been completely transformed.

The fire trucks and the ambulance had been moved onto the drive and lights strung up all over the bay. Decorations everywhere, with a huge tree in one corner.

Macon stood at the doors and tried to pick out his firefighters in the ocean of kids in baseball uniforms, other children racing around playing some kind of elaborate game of tag, and people from town. Groups of counselors from the Ridgeman Center. Natalie's entire ladies' Bible study group. Half the police department seemed to be in here, as well as more firefighters than he'd seen even at the barbecue. Faces Macon knew, or people he'd seen in photos and heard stories about.

Heros.

Ordinary folks who just tried to do the right thing. Make the next right choice in front of them. Which was all any of them could do. Loving God and honoring one another above themselves until it was a way of life to stand in the gap.

To work every day to make the world a better place.

"Hey." His wife, Natalie, made her way over, looking exceptional in that black dress. The telltale bump of another baby on the way giving her that glow she never seemed to lose.

At least, not to him.

"Hey yourself."

"The babysitter isn't expecting us till late." Her eyebrows rose.

"Is that right?" He slid his arms around her waist and drew her close. "Merry Christmas to me."

She tipped her head back and laughed. "If this one is a girl, we should call her Noel."

"What about MJ?"

"As in 'Macon Junior'?"

He shrugged, pretending he hadn't thought of it. "Or Mary Jane."

"I'll think about it." She kissed him, smiling.

"Speech!" Captain Bryce Crawford called out from the far side of the room.

When Macon looked over, he saw Penny tucked against Bryce's side. Beside them were Logan and Jamie, visiting from Alaska for the holidays. Beside them were Andi and Jude and the rest of their family.

So many lives he'd watched change since he'd come home.

Macon was handed a plastic cup of something fizzy. He offered his hand to Natalie, and they walked to the sound system in the corner. With the music shut off, he grabbed the microphone.

"Is this on?" He didn't have a free hand to tap the mic.

Someone called out, "Yeah, Chief!"

Macon smiled, and Natalie leaned against his arm. He lifted the mic to his lips. "I haven't been the chief of this house for long. And yet, some days it feels like forever."

Izan yelled, "That's because of Amelia!"

A chuckle rippled across the room, followed a second later by the projectile from a kid's dart gun. It bounced off Izan's forehead and he yelped. On the far side of the room, Amelia handed the gun back to a grinning little girl.

"It's been my honor to lead this house through all of it. And to stand here with you now, knowing this is a place where love binds us together. Where people reach out a hand when someone needs it. Where truth is spoken, and the grace of Jesus Christ teaches us every day to be the people He has called us to be.

"As we celebrate the Christmas season this year, and every year we have on this earth, let's remember the best gift we can receive. The good news, the gospel of Jesus. That God sent His son to this earth to save even sinners like us."

Macon lifted his cup. "Merry Christmas!"

Cheers and answering shouts of celebration erupted across the room. Natalie tugged on the back of his neck until he leaned down and kissed her. "Good job."

"They make it easy."

She grinned. "No, they don't. But we love them anyway."

He laughed. "It's true."

ABOUT LISA PHILLIPS

 **Lisa Phillips** is a USA Today and top ten Publishers Weekly best-selling author of over 80 books that span Harlequin's Love Inspired Suspense line, independently published series romantic suspense, and thriller novels. She's discovered a penchant for high-stakes stories of mayhem and disaster where you can find made-for-each-other love that always ends in happily ever after.

Lisa is a British ex-pat who grew up an hour outside of London and attended Calvary Chapel Bible College, where she met her husband. He's from California, but nobody's perfect. It wasn't until her Bible College graduation that she figured out she was a writer (someone told her). As a worship leader for Calvary Chapel churches in her local area, Lisa has discovered a love for mentoring new ministry members and youth worship musicians.

Find out more at www.authorlisaphillips.com.

facebook.com/authorlisaphillips

instagram.com/lisaphillipsbks

bookbub.com/authors/lisa-phillips

goodreads.com/lisaphillipsbks

amazon.com/stores/Lisa-Phillips/author/B00HZSOSOO

ABOUT MICHELLE SASS ALECKSON

After growing up on both the east and west coasts, **Michelle Sass Aleckson** now lives the country life in central Minnesota with her own hero and their four kids. She loves rocking out to 80's music on a Saturday night, playing Balderdash with the fam, and getting lost in good stories. Especially stories that shine grace. And if you're wondering, yes, Sass is her maiden name. Visit her at www.michellealeckson.com.

facebook.com/AuthorMichelleAleckson

instagram.com/michelle_aleckson

x.com/MchelleAleckson

goodreads.com/michellealeckson

bookbub.com/authors/michelle-sass-aleckson

amazon.com/stores/Michelle-Sass-Aleckson/author/B08M8P51B7

ABOUT LAURA CONAWAY

Laura Conaway is a Publishers Weekly bestselling and award-winning author who resides in Pennsylvania. She creates stories with a healthy dose of suspense and happily ever afters while her characters discover triumph through trials. As a former librarian, she's always searching for the next best read and loves solving mysteries like Nancy Drew. When she's not inhaling sweet potato fries to motivate writing, Laura spends her time playing guitar and sharing about the Greatest Story ever written. Connect with Laura at www.lauraconawayauthor.com

facebook.com/lauraconawayauthor

instagram.com/conaway_laura

bookbub.com/authors/laura-conaway

goodreads.com/lauraconaway

amazon.com/stores/Laura-Conaway/author/B0BK235BZN

CONNECT WITH SUNRISE

Thank you so much for reading *Last Chance Christmas*. We hope you enjoyed the story. If you did, would you be willing to do us a favor and leave a review? It doesn't have to be long- just a few words to help other readers know what they're getting. (But no spoilers! We don't want to wreck the fun!) Thank you again for reading!

We'd love to hear from you- not only about this story, but about any characters or stories you'd like to read in the future. Contact us at www.sunrisepublishing.com/contact.

We also have a regular updates that contains sneak peeks, reviews, upcoming releases, and fun stuff for our reader friends. Sign up at www.sunrisepublishing.com or scan our QR code.

LAST CHANCE
FIRE AND RESCUE

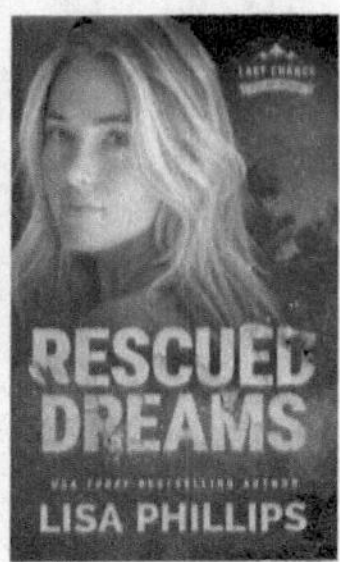

USA Today Bestselling Author
LISA PHILLIPS

with **LAURA CONAWAY, MEGAN BESING** and **MICHELLE SASS ALECKSON**

The men and women of the Last Chance County Fire Department struggle to put a legacy of corruption behind them. They face danger every day on the job as first responders, but the fight to become a family will be their biggest battle yet. When hearts are on the line it's up to each one to trust their skill and lean on their faith to protect the ones they love. Before it all goes down in flames.

We solve the problem of what to read next.

Available on Amazon

SUMMER RANGERS

Where heart-stopping adventure meets breathtaking romance in America's most dangerous playground.

FROM USA TODAY BESTSELLING AUTHOR

SUSAN MAY WARREN
AND TARI FARIS

We solve the problem of what to read next.

Available on Amazon

DISCARDED HEROES:
SCIONS

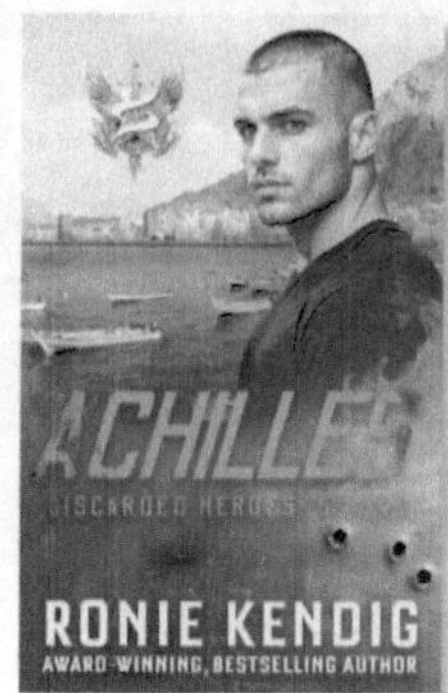

PARAMILITARY ROMANTIC SUSPENSE FROM
AWARD-WINNING, BESTSELLING AUTHOR

RONIE KENDIG

LEGACY CASTS A LONG SHADOW.

Meet the next generation of elite warriors carrying names that command respect—and paint targets on their backs. When international conspiracy collides with unexpected romance, these skilled warriors discover their toughest battles aren't fought with weapons. In a game where trust is a luxury and love a liability, they'll need more than tactical training to survive.

Step into a world where legacy meets destiny, and heroes forge their own paths out of the shadows.

We solve the problem of what to read next.

Available on Amazon

WE THINK YOU'LL ALSO LOVE...

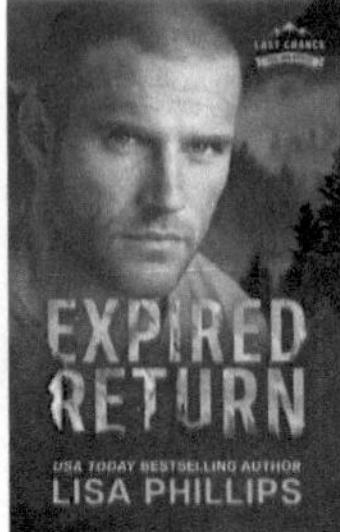

Fire Department liaison Allen Frees may have put his life back together, but getting the truck crew and engine squad to succeed might be his toughest job yet. When a child is nearly kidnapped, Allen steps in to help Pepper Miller keep her niece safe. The one thing he couldn't fix was the love he lost, but he isn't going to let Pepper walk away this time.

***Expired Return* by Lisa Phillips**

Stunt double Vienna Foxcroft's stunt team are the only ones she trusts. Then in walks Sergeant Crew Gatlin and his tough-as-nails military dog, Havoc. When an attack on a film set sends them fleeing into the streets of Turkey, Vienna must face the demons of her past or be devoured by them. And Crew and Havoc will be tested like never before.

***Havoc* by Ronie Kendig**

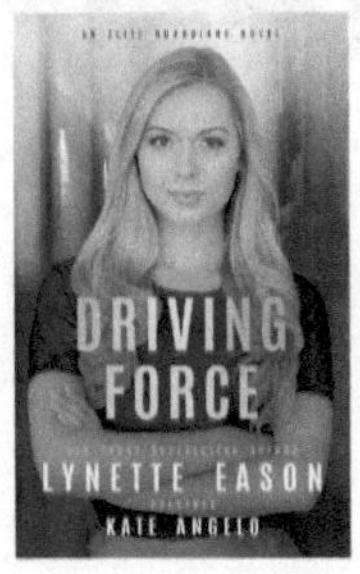

When an attempt is made on Grey Parker's life and dead bodies begin piling up, suddenly bodyguard Christina Sherman is tasked with keeping both a soldier and his dog safe... and with them, the secrets that could stop a terrorist attack.

***Driving Force* by Lynette Eason
and Kate Angelo**

We solve the problem of what to read next.   Available on Amazon

LAST CHANCE COUNTY NOVELS

Last Chance Fire and Rescue Collection

Expired Return

Expired Hope

Expired Promise

Expired Vows

Rescued Duty

Rescued Faith

Rescued Heart

Rescued Dreams

Last Chance Christmas

Last Chance County Series

Expired Refuge

Expired Secrets

Expired Cache

Expired Hero

Expired Game

Expired Plot

Expired Getaway

Expired Betrayal

Expired Flight

Expired End